REJECTION

ALSO BY TONY TULATHIMUTTE

Private Citizens

REJECTION

Fiction

TONY TULATHIMUTTE

wm

WILLIAM MORROW

An Imprint of HarperCollins*Publishers*

REJECTION. Copyright © 2024 by Tony Tulathimutte. All rights reserved. Printed in the United States of America. No part of this book may be used or reproduced in any manner whatsoever without written permission except in the case of brief quotations embodied in critical articles and reviews. For information, address HarperCollins Publishers, 195 Broadway, New York, NY 10007.

HarperCollins books may be purchased for educational, business, or sales promotional use. For information, please email the Special Markets Department at SPsales@harpercollins.com.

FIRST EDITION

Designed by Leah Carlson-Stanisic

Library of Congress Cataloging-in-Publication Data has been applied for.

ISBN 978-0-06-333787-9

24 25 26 27 28 LBC 9 8 7 6 5

To Jenny, Alice, and Anthony

REJECTION

—but dearer are those who reject us as unworthy, for they add another life: they build a heaven before us, whereof we had not dreamed, and thereby supply to us new powers out of the recesses of the spirit, and urge us to new and unattempted performances.

—RALPH WALDO EMERSON

THE FEMINIST

If you ask him where he went to high school, he likes to boast that, actually, he went to an all-girls school. Which is sort of true—he was one of five males at a progressive private school that had gone co-ed just before he'd enrolled. People always reply: *Ooh la la, lucky guy! You must've had your pick.* Which irritates him, because it implies that women would only date him if they had few other options, and also because he hadn't dated anyone in high school. (In junior year a freshman girl had a crush on him, but he wasn't attracted to her curvaceous body type, so he felt justified in rejecting her, as he'd been rejected many times himself.)

Still, the school ingrained in him, if not feminist values per se, the *value* of feminist values. It had been cool, or at least normal, to identify as asexual. And though he didn't, he figured it was a better label than "virgin." His friends, mostly female, told him he was refreshingly attentive and trustworthy for a boy. Meanwhile he was grateful to learn that *female* is best used as an adjective, that sexism harms men too—though obviously nowhere near the extent it harms women—and that certain men pretend to be feminists just to get laid. When he graduated, he felt slightly sheepish about never having even kissed anyone. Everyone knew, though, that real dating started in college, where nobody would be aware of his track record.

But in college, he encounters the alien system of codes and manners that govern flirting, conveyed in subtextual cues no more perceptible to him than ultraviolet radiation. Learning in high school about body positivity and gender norms and the cultural construction of beauty had led him to believe that adults aren't obsessed with looks. This turns out to be untrue, even among his new female friends, who complain about how shallow men are. Now that he's self-conscious, he realizes he can't compete along conventional standards of height, weight, grip strength, whatever. How can he hope to attract anyone with his narrow shoulders?

The women he tries to date offer him friendship instead, so once again, most of his friends are women. This is fine: it's their prerogative, and anyway, lots of relationships begin platonically—especially for guys with narrow shoulders. But soon a pattern emerges. The first time, as he is leaving his friend's dorm room, he surprises himself by saying: Hey, this might be super random, and she can totally say no, but he's attracted to her, so did she want to go on a "date" date, sometime? In a casual and normal voice. And she says, "Oh," and filibusters—she had *no idea* he felt that way, and she doesn't want to risk spoiling the good thing they have by making it a *thing*, she thinks it'll be best if they just stay . . . and he rushes to assure her that it's valid, no, totally valid, he knows friendship isn't a downgrade, sorry for being weird. Ugh!

Right? she replies, dating's so overrated and meaningless in college anyway, and she knows that *he* knows he'll find someone who deserves him, because he's great, really great, so thoughtful, *so* smart, not like these SAE sideways-hat-wearing dudebros, of course he must already know that, and she really appreciates it. Then she thanks her for being honest, because it proves she respects him, and don't worry about him, he gets it.

He does get it. It sort of kills him, but he knows his rejector was only trying to spare his feelings, since men often react badly to "hard rejection." So he validates her condolences and communicates them back until she's convinced he'll be fine. "Grrr, friend-zoned again!" he says, shaking his fists toward the ceiling, and they laugh together, and hug, and he walks back to his dorm at sunrise.

He gets into bed and sighs. While he's confident he handled everything respectfully, the girl's praise only reminds him that none of his ostensibly good qualities are attractive enough to even warrant him a chance, which makes them seem worthless. He also suspects her flattery was . . . exaggerated, and a bit . . . patronizing? Like, if she didn't think friendship was a downgrade, she wouldn't have said she "just" wanted to stay friends. By persuading him to reject himself, was she simply offloading her guilt? He stews at the one-sided familiarity of the situation: once again, *he's* got to be the one who accepts, forgives, tolerates, pretends not to be wounded, pretends he has stopped hoping—all this sapping emotional labor to preserve his dignity and assuage her guilt, and also because he doesn't want to spoil his chances of dating her in the future, since it's her prerogative, after all, to change her mind.

Still, he respects her decision. He gets out of bed, feeling compelled to check in and let her know where he stands, so he composes a long postmortem email, reconstructing everything that happened from the beginning, assuring her that he knew nobody was to blame for a lack of attraction, and that if it isn't clear, yes, he *is* interested in her, but he's not one of those fake-feminist guys who snubs any woman he can't fuck, so, sorry if this is com*plete*ly graceless and exhausting, by no means is he making his embarrassment her problem, he just wants to get everything out in the open. He hits send.

An hour later he sends a second email: Just out of curiosity, could she say a little about *why* she rejected him? It'd be really helpful for him. Is it because he's narrow-shouldered? Is that a dealbreaker for her? Because he can't help that, as she knows. Or is it a specific thing he did or said, because if so, they could discuss that, clear up any miscommunication. Anyway, he'll be fine, hopes everything's cool—and if she ever changes her mind, he'll be around!

Considering his tremendous effort to be vulnerable, it seems unfair, *rude* even, when a day passes with no reply. Fearing that he might not receive one at all, he writes a third email clarifying that she's by no means obliged to reply, though if she wants to, he'd love hearing her thoughts. He is somewhat annoyed when she again doesn't reply, though he's glad to have given her that option. At least nothing's been left unsaid.

This exact scenario happens four or five more times, with different women. Later, when he relates these incidents, lightheartedly, to his other female friends, they assure him he's interesting, smart, thoughtful, good-looking (though they never say *hot*). They say nothing's wrong with him. "It's so bizarre that you're single," they say, trying to mollify him with optimism, as if their romantic experience has made them experts in his lack of it. But they have no experience of *having no experience.* He figures that even bad relationships are better than none, since they prepare you for future relationships, and heartbreak is romantic and dignified, whereas rejection only makes you a loser. Short of abuse, their worst case would be to be in *his* position.

Anyway, he doesn't want pity; he wants not to need it. All of his female friends have rejected him before, though not always explicitly: more often, when he's out with them in public, someone will mistake him for a boyfriend, which gives him a sky-blue moment of joy before his female friend laughs, blows a raspberry, and says, "Oh my god, ha, no way, that'd be like *incest*!" But he takes these insults nobly, and later consoles himself by masturbating to the idea of having incestuous sex with them. Sometimes he drops hints to his friends to set him up with their friends, but for some reason they never follow through.

He decides there must be other ways to stand out and be attractive. He cultivates academic achievement in his Gender Studies major, surmising that status and intellect will enhance his appeal. But, just like in high school, he finds himself overlooked even with the paucity of men in his major, and outside of it, the rich, handsome, and broad-shouldered guys still get all the attention.

Then again, so do the terrible and ugly ones! His female friends keep dating these guys with cratered skin, awkward manners, poor hygiene; talentless schlubs identified by their hobbies and tastes; philandering worms; controlling, abusive dirtbags. Even his gay first-year roommate had a girlfriend back in high school, before he'd come out. And yeah, maybe these guys all deserved love—but surely no more than him? At a house party, one friend talks about going home with a guy the night before who said all he wanted was to sleep beside her, then around 1 a.m. she awoke to him grunting as he ejaculated on her leg. When she cussed him out, he claimed he was "overcome by raw animal passion" and "couldn't help it," and she still let him stay. "Whatever, we'll probably be married in three years," she says, rolling her eyes.

He's about to insist she shouldn't devalue herself by deploying sarcasm to suppress trauma, that she's been violated and shouldn't be out tonight—and is astounded when everyone, including her, starts laughing. He joins in, figuring that this is some cathartic part of the healing process, even though it sounds to him like a clear case of sexual assault. Even more confusing, he'd asked her out once before; so, a literal *rapist* is more appealing than him? He keeps silent as another female friend says, "Men are dogshit." And sure, fair, he understands they mean the patriarchy and not him specifically—but why'd she say that with him standing *right there*, unless he didn't count as a man to them? Not wanting to seem fragile or impugn their judgment or center the conversation on himself, he says, "Ugh, yeah, we're *total* dogshit," and files this incident away in a thickening dossier of unfairness, a piece of insurance he will be able to use as evidence of their own imperfect principles if they ever try to call him out in the future. Privately, too, he reasons that if they're going to keep dating assholes, what do they expect.

Later, gut-checking himself to make sure his concern for his traumatized friend is legitimate, he texts her: hey, I'm around if you need to talk about what happened. or even just watch trashy TV :) whenever wherever!

She doesn't reply.

Dragging his virginity like a body bag into his mid-twenties, he watches a certain amount of domination-oriented porn, probably due to internalized sexism, though he's read that porn is a safe, healthy venue to explore kink, that sexuality is neither a choice nor shameful, especially if the studios follow good labor and aftercare practices. His female friends agree. He does not mention that he seeks out actresses that resemble them, which he deems victimless and acceptable as long as he consumes it critically, demarcating fantasy from reality, and maintaining his sensitivity for the performers.

He's more worried about *physical* desensitization: he doesn't use lubrication, since his roommates would overhear it. He comes to prefer the intensity of this "dry" method, but feels the friction is somehow eroding his psyche, and possibly dulling the nerves in his penis. Resolving to wean himself by using a condom while masturbating, he wonders in what other ways touch, or the lack of it, has warped him. He's read about that study of baby monkeys who were denied soft physical contact and grew up disturbed and sickly. It's hard to believe chastity was ever associated with purity, when it feels like putrescence, his blood browning, saliva clouding with pus, each passing day rendering him more leprously foul. What about those venerable virgins like Newton, Dickinson, Kant? No, their virginity was a matter of will. They believed God loved them for it.

At lunch one day, two of his male coworkers offer unsolicited dating advice, relishing the chance to showboat their sexual proficiencies. He's too honest and available, not aggressive enough— friend-zone shit, they say unironically. Don't be a fucking pussy is all! You gotta challenge them, be a puzzle for them to work out, that's how girls' brains work, it's evolution. They offer grotesquely specific advice about eye contact and hair touching. Learn palmistry, they say, bitches love getting their palms read.

Then they ask him how he makes a move; he says he asks first. "Wait, you *ask* if you can kiss them? My man," one says, laughing and slapping his back, "you don't *ask*." With jagged touchiness, he calls them out, insisting that consent is nonnegotiable, that even if they're joking, or *especially* if they're joking, it's textbook rape culture.

"Well, what makes you think you can speak for all women," one says, smirking. "You're a guy too. Why do you know better than us what women prefer? Especially considering they're dating us."

He's *not* speaking for all women, he says—unsure of how he'll answer, but certain he has something to say—he's . . . speaking, as a man, *against* men who're speaking against women.

"Go ahead then," his coworker laughs, "ask your *female friends* what they think."

He composes a long email reporting them both to HR, and later that night, bristling, he calls his QPOC agender friend from his college co-op, whom he's always gotten along with, in part because he's never been attracted to them. He repeats what his coworkers said, performing their dialogue with a "dumb guy" voice. His friend says, "Well, that's gross," and makes him swear never to become a mind-gamey asshole, going on to say that the so-called friend zone is a sexist canard that lets losers (like who, he wonders) blame their own unattractiveness on women.

He agrees, then asks if it isn't true that some guys simply lack charisma or attractiveness, and are thus more prone to getting befriended?

"Maybe," they say.

He asks his friend if mind games work.

"Sure, sometimes," they say, "that's why they're so common. But they never lead to anything good."

Never? he asks.

"Okay, yeah, shit's complicated. Some people are old-fashioned, or mistake abuse for affection. Doesn't mean we should *encourage* it."

He asks if it's wrong to ask permission to kiss someone.

"Depends more on how you ask."

He asks if they personally would prefer it.

"No, but I'm not all women. I'm not even *a* woman."

He asks if they believe most women would prefer it.

"Who knows! Every woman's different and things are always changing. Listen, I'm not sure what you're trying to get out of me here. Again: I'm *not* a woman."

Sure, he's aware of that, he replies, but it's important to him, especially as a cisgender heterosexual white man, to avoid placing the burden of educating him about women's experiences on a woman, which is why it's so great to have friends of other genders.

His friend says, "Yeah, I guess."

He thanks them for taking his call so late at night.

In spite of his QPOC friend's ambiguous advice, he decides that more experience will improve his odds. So he resorts to on-line dating, cropping out his narrow shoulders from his photos and carefully wording his bio:

He/him/his (or whatever pronouns you are most comfortable with). Unshakably serious about consent. Abortion's #1 fan. Loves books, Thai food, a glass of vinho verde on my balcony, endless conversation . . . and did I mention books? ☺ I can usually be found haunting the bookstores and bake-shops of our fair burgh, when I'm not dismantling the imperialist male supremacist hetero patriarchy. But I'd also be fine saying "To hell with it!" and staying at home for an Agnes Varda marathon sesh followed by discussion . . . and perhaps a wee snogfest? ☺ I *always* do my own cooking (thanks Mom!) so I'll make a killer brunch for you! Trans women are women, duh. All races, ethnicities, and body types—but NOT all ages—very welcome! Mutual GGG.

He suspects some of it risks sounding tryhard, but he prefers sincerity and clarity over fake mystique, and what reasonable woman wouldn't be attracted to a vocal ally? He sends thoughtful, grammatical messages, like a link to a *Psychology Today* article about limerence, followed by: Fascinating topic. I'm a total sucker for the intersections of psychology and romance. Would love to talk it over at the public venue of your choosing! The few dates this brings only yield more rejection: three postpone indefinitely, then ghost; three more are no-shows. One leaves while he's in the bathroom.

Dating online, he realizes, one has to choose between fraudulence, or the sort of honesty that can't compete with fraudulence. But then he thinks: Isn't the idea that women don't know what's best for them sexist, informed by his own petty resentment? Troubled by this paradox and unable to sleep, he texts his QPOC friend and asks them, Be honest: Has he actually been a creep this whole time? Is he . . . is he a *dudebro*, and has he, therefore, *deserved* to be single for the last thirty years?

His friend texts back, ok but can you really count the first 16 years, then adds that he *should* feel weird about his concerns, but he hasn't done anything, and a real creep probably wouldn't agonize so much over whether he was a creep, goodnight.

Then he replies: But if agonizing about being a creep is what proves he's not a creep, and he stops worrying about being a creep, wouldn't *that* make him a creep?

His QPOC friend doesn't respond. He's still unnerved, though relieved someone who was once female-identified has given him a pass.

He withdraws into work. Whereas before he only went out in hopes of meeting someone, now he stays in so he won't have to see anyone: the allopreening couples, the untouchable women, the broad-shouldered men; even a passing whiff of aloe lotion on a woman's skin makes him feel structurally unsound and shivery in his linings. When he does go out in public, he avoids looking at any woman's face, convincing himself it's respectfully uncreepy, but aware in the gloomy sub-basement of his mind that the real reason is because if she is beautiful, then the image of her face, and the question of how he might have introduced himself, and the beautiful life they might have had together, will torment him for days.

At age thirty-one he has sex. One day on social media he happens across the girl, the woman, he rejected in high school. She's cleaned up; her body type is no longer curvaceous, and he likes how in all her photos she wears a skirt and leggings, a thin dark cardigan over a blouse—a personal uniform suggesting fidelity to figured-out principles—but dislikes how her dyed red hair pinches off in a tiny bun that reminds him of the meaty tail-nubs on docked pit bulls. Though that's fixable. Seeing that they live in the same city, he messages her and suggests they meet.

She shows up forty minutes late, which he forgivingly tolerates, knowing that women's time is taxed by the pressures of female grooming. For about fifteen minutes their catch-up chat is small even if promisingly pleasant. He insists on paying for drinks, joking that it's not chivalry, it's reparations for sexism. He soon regrets it, however, because on her third whiskey ginger (and his first), she starts rambling about some guy who dumped her ages ago, then jokes about her eating disorder. Every few minutes her face scrunches like she's about to cry, then reverts weirdly to normal. Her blouse untucks, and when a guy playing pool nearby positions his cue close to her face, she slaps it to the floor.

Lonely as he is, does he deserve someone unstable? He'll have to reject her again, like in high school. What will he say? That he doesn't want to waste her time, that he thinks she's super great, but he doesn't feel a spark? Having seldom been in the position to reject anyone else, he feels terrible for having to inflict on her the same pain he's always felt himself.

Hours later, he still has not figured out a compassionate enough way to phrase it, and at this point, as they're leaving the bar, he decides he might as well kiss her goodnight for the sake of casual experience and then let her down nicely over text message. He asks if he can kiss her.

She says, "Uh, no."

He asks why not.

"What do you mean *why not*?" she says. "Because I don't *want* to. Who the fuck asks 'why not'? Fucking asshole."

He wonders if she is testing him. He asks if she is testing him. This time she gives him a two-armed shove, sending him to the ground, and instead of yelling, she smiles like a sock puppet and says, "Oh my god, are you wearing *shoulder pads*?"

Getting up, he briefly considers shoving her back, though not as hard as she shoved him, since that would not be fair. But before he can do anything, she is doubled over and clutching her calves in laughter, and when she recovers she says, with unbelievable nonchalance, "Okay, wait, I'm sorry, dude, I didn't mean to push you that hard. Come on, is this happening or what?"

The sex disappoints; her moans and arches feel contrived and uncomfortably "dirty," and when he tries to maintain eye contact in missionary position to establish a bond, she closes her eyes. Something—maybe his dulled penis nerves?—keeps deferring his orgasm, until she gets impatient and pushes him away. He acquiesces, not having finished, his embarrassing frustration mitigated only by the unburdening of his virginity, and the prospect of telling everyone about it. To reassure her that his sexual awkwardness was not her fault, he tells her she's beautiful. She waits nearly ten seconds and replies, "Uh, you have an interesting mind."

After this incident, he develops thoughts of self-harm, which are sharpened by his awareness that rejection, loneliness, and sexual frustration are nothing compared with institutional and historical oppression. His sadness, he knows, is a symptom of his entitlement, so he is not even entitled to his sadness.

As a thirtysomething, he feels too young to give up but too old to adapt. His self-reliance has ossified into a lifestyle of craved, defended solitude. He can't imagine having to share a bed every night, not being able to read or wake up or leave parties whenever he wants. No, this is not mere solitude. Solitude is fine, inescapable aloneness is not. Taking trips and seeing movies and attending events all seem pointless without anyone to experience them with, so it feels like his life cannot progress or even truly begin until he has found someone who will return his love.

And as he's aged, has his intimacy with his female friends deepened? Did these friends, who always maintained that romantic love was overrated, who said friendships were what mattered in the end, provide him an alternative to romantic love? No. After all his years of talking them through each and every breakup and gendered work dispute, sending them thoughtful gifts and memes, loaning them money for rental deposits, taking their dating app photos, reassuring them of their beauty when they hated how the photos came out, and supporting them when they were fighting with their boyfriends, after all that, these female friends of his have all moved on to cohabit, marry, and breed. Even if they're miserable, at least they're living real lives, with partners who prioritize them above all others. Lately he sees them once a month tops, even though he's known them far longer than their partners have. They've all stopped inviting him to dinner parties because *It was a couples thing and you would've hated it*, which, while true, was still exclusionary, backed by the hegemonic and regressive institution of monogamy. He realizes that these female friends have, at last, completed their long-term rejections of him; that, without ever having had a girlfriend, his life is strewn with exes, friends without benefits. But he can't complain about his friends to his friends. His male coworkers would roast him or pretend to sympathize yet secretly think he's a pussy. And his female friends might think that he's passive-aggressively implicating them, and also that he's a pussy.

Since any rejection now paralyzes him with rage for weeks, he stops dating. He resents his married friends, his contently single friends, his unhappily single friends who nonetheless have casual sex, and his parents when they gently question his sexuality. He also resents the grotesque fixations that have cropped up lately, like: If he's only ever used condoms and *the epidermis of his penis* has never made contact with *the mucous membrane of a vagina*, if he's never *ejaculated into a birth canal*, does that technically mean he's still a virgin? Have his possibly dulled penis nerves entrained a vicious cycle of "death grip syndrome," adding yet another obstacle to love? Was masturbation lowering his testosterone levels, contributing to his narrow shoulders? And does that give women the impression that he has a small penis, which he *statistically doesn't*?

All he's doing is sharing some of these valid gripes at a picnic one afternoon when his QPOC agender friend asks him, why doesn't he call that girl from high school who took his virginity? He replies that just because he wants to be in a relationship doesn't mean he has to settle for a sociopath.

"See, you're moving the goalposts, like always," his QPOC friend replies. "It's easy to feel sorry for yourself when you keep redefining rejection. You refuse pity but crave it so much that you won't admit how strongly you invite it."

He says they're being facile, though he knows their point is rather nuanced and specific and he hasn't even considered it before, but he can't walk it back now.

"I'm *facile*?" his friend says. "Nah, I'm tired. That's what it is, I'm tired," they say from behind their sunglasses, waving their mimosa. "I know you identify as a reject, I know that's like your 'brand,' like it's some unprecedented form of suffering that gives you secret saintly wisdom. All this nonstop high-frequency whining, that's what's *facile*."

He presses his lips shut while his brain feels like a swirling case of lottery balls, as his friend, pausing to hit a spliff, continues: "I mean, what the fuck do you want? Somehow you got a shit deal. Nobody knows why. Maybe you never really grappled with this because you thought you were exempt. But you refuse to change and are *shocked* when nothing changes. You keep doing all these unsolicited favors, putting in all this effort, and because the only forms of repayment you'll accept are love or sex, you always feel cheated. And it's not like you enjoy this, but you *do* enjoy pushing other people's faces in it, that's your main consolation. Wild how you're always right and nobody's ever had it worse, nobody's as pure and as wronged as you. Yo everyone! Check out the Woman Respecter! Last principled man right here! And that's why you need it, because you get to convince yourself you're being rejected for your virtue, not cause you're a bummer. You've turned your loneliness into this, like, fetish necklace of martyrdom. And all of us"—they glance around at the other picnickers—"have to sit here and rubber-stamp your feminism. If we don't indulge your wallowing, we're being callous and, like, complicit with some diabolical global conspiracy that's keeping you from getting pussy. But if we do, then we're 'disingenuous' because none of us will fuck you ourselves. Right? Am I right, ladies? Hands up, who agrees?"

Three women's hands shoot up, followed more slowly by the rest.

His QPOC friend gestures at them like, *Behold*. "I dunno what to say, man, except, motherfucking cishets! I for one am bored of your scab collection. I'm sorry your dick is sad or whatever. Suck it up, you bitter little boy, and move on."

Fantastic. That's fucking great. The clearest example yet of how even his friends dismiss him with straw-man arguments out of sheer intellectual laziness. Because he refuses the easy consolation of playing along with the oppressive patriarchal paradigm, they'd rather call him self-sabotaging, instead of thinking critically for *one second* about the bullshit social biases narrow-shouldered men suffer under, which originate in the same toxic masculinity they supposedly abhor. He doesn't have the luxury of having fun fresh relationship drama like theirs, so they got bored of him, even though listening to his problems is far easier than living through them. He listens to *their* problems *all the time*.

Vitrified with outrage, he replies to his QPOC friend that they are minimizing his problems just because having narrow shoulders isn't on the Official Registry of Politicized Traumas. They're saying he can't express his feelings because worse things happen? By that logic, he could say that their stupid anxieties about dating bi women aren't important because they're not being rounded up and thrown off rooftops like queer people in, for example, Syria. But *he* wouldn't say that to his QPOC friend! He would listen!

"Wooooow-ow-ow. You really don't want to press this," his friend warns, removing their sunglasses. "And B-T-dubs, I'm not your *QPOC friend*."

Are you fucking kidding me, he shouts, unsure if his exasperation is mock or real, you took it there, *you* made it about identity, all I'm doing is reflecting *literally the same exact* sentiment as you, so don't evade the point, and don't get the idea that framing it as a callout puts you in the right! And *I* brought those mimosas, by the way!

He grabs at his friend's drink. Everyone scrambles. His QPOC friend's friend, a much larger, broad-shouldered man, gets up and tells him, "Okay, my guy, time to move along." It defies all reason that he's getting ejected from a picnic for the sin of airing opinions in good faith, by this alpha dickhead flaunting his swollen deltoids. This was the male ally they preferred: not the intellectual who challenged them as equals in an open dialogue, but this muscle-confused *sasquatch*. They're all happy to hide behind patriarchy when it suits them. He snatches up his READ MORE WOMEN tote bag and leaves.

On his way home, with jittering fingers, he pulls out his phone to block his drunk QPOC friend on social media and sees they've posted:

> **Lena Gundam** @madonnaharaway
> smh @ men who squawk abt their feminism but rly hang out with women for the gendered power advantage foooooooh

He sees that the post already has over a hundred likes and counting. One of the women who was at the picnic replied omg deadassssss, and even that got thirty-six likes. The thought of a hundred strangers reading this petty, unsubstantiated accusation and reflexively siding with the QPOC without knowing anything about what happened leads him to mass-block everyone who failed to support him at the picnic.

He counterposts,

> ⬤ STOP ⬣ oppression NOW!!! @ListenAndEvolve
> smh @ performative "woke" "queer" folx who pretend to care abt equality but rly just get off on humiliating strong male allies who are trying to help and consequently punishing and alienating them for fervently upholding the basic tenets of contemporary feminism foooooooh

but deletes it because he can't figure out how to make it sound good, which is unfair, because the point is valid.

It would be pathetic now to keep seeing those friends. Maintaining friendships cost his female friends nothing, but it cost him a daily toll of endless triggering, which they'd never once acknowledged. They're fine with freeloading off his insight and generosity, but the moment he dares to question their opinions or have genuine feelings for them, it's like his attraction is some morsel of filth he's tried to trick them into swallowing.

Yet, free-falling into his thirties, it's harder to make new friends. If he stays in, he feels anxious about not meeting people; if he goes out, he spends the whole night at whatever depressing bar/poetry reading/art opening, scanning the room for women standing by themselves, whom he never has the will to approach, then goes home alone, weary and dark-minded, to face the sight of his empty bed, which is even emptier after he gets in it, lying awake with pangs of loneliness that feel like getting stabbed through a very soft pillow. He lost his virginity so long ago it feels like it's grown back.

On one of these long nights, an ugly curtain lifts in his head: He's old enough to know that relationships don't guarantee happiness, that the source of his pain is a patriarchal fantasy, agonizingly elaborated over decades, about love and sex as the basis of fulfillment. But he still feels he cannot be happy until this pain stops, and it will not stop until he has an experience of love that will at last disillusion him. When he uses dating apps, he finds himself decreasingly attracted to women of a suitable age range, which at first concerns him, since he used to mock age-gap relationships when he was younger. However this concern is quickly shunted aside by indignation: Why should everyone else have had the opportunity to date twentysomethings, and not him? Perhaps, he thinks, he could *temporarily* date a few younger women, who would greatly benefit from his wealth and life experience, then eventually "catch up" and "move on" to age-appropriate women without regret. To attract these younger women, he goes keto, takes improv classes, and consolidates his reputation at work, though he'd long since lost his relish for it when he realized it didn't magically improve his dating odds. None of it does.

Around this time, he starts to feel breathless, like he's wearing a compression garment around his lungs. His stomach is tense and swollen as a basketball, he urinates frequently, his heart skitters and rushes, he has trouble swallowing. He can seldom achieve full erection: his customary "dry" method has lost its efficacy, and male masturbation toys prove ineffective. When he manages to ejaculate it falls out of him like a touchless soap dispenser. So he's finally managed to sexually bore even himself. One day at work, while he's waiting for the microwave to finish heating up a cheese-and-mushroom tart, a quantity of urine dribbles out unbidden.

His primary care doctor refers him to a blood lab and a urologist, who conducts an ultrasound and diagnoses him with a levator spasm, probably stress-related. In researching its causes, he learns that loneliness can manifest psychosomatically as anxiety, even shorten your lifespan. He also reads, in blog posts about chromosomal perpetuation, that children bear trace amounts of the DNA of all their mother's sex partners in their own DNA—so it is true, confirming suspicions he didn't even know he had, that sex partners matter *biologically*, that they leave a mark.

These findings send him into action. He hits the gym, where he targets his deltoids with set after set of shrugs and lateral raises, and afterward takes zinc sulfate, lysine, and arginine to increase seminal volume, horny goat weed and pumpkin-seed extract for libido, cabergoline to lessen the refractory period by lowering prolactin. He gets a prescription for Depo-Testosterone and Deca-Durabolin to manage hypogonadism and improve pelvic muscle tone. Then somatotropin. Then trenbolone. The goal is to get his ejaculate to "arc" again. When after three months he sees few changes except for unaccountable surges of anger and a longer post-masturbation cleanup, he begins regularly donating sperm, to give them a nonzero chance of propagating, and also starts using a penis pump to the point of vascular damage, giving his penis the look of a dead manatee. If it's going to be numb and useless it may as well be big.

He knows he is sick and must find relief. He wants so badly to believe that his life isn't broken and can still bring satisfaction. In each second is the slow fizz of cell death, telomeres shedding their base pairs two by two like an ignited fuse. He contemplates all the organisms in the natural world having sex constantly, effortlessly. Stray dogs. Mosquitoes. Dandelions. Yeast. At work, when he isn't thinking *This is all I'm good for*, he thinks *I should kill myself*. But then he imagines his former female friends hearing of his death and not caring, or even laughing. To them it wouldn't be tragic; they did not need him as much as he needed them, or at all. This maddening thought keeps him dismally alive.

For a while he tries paying for sex, hoping more experience will give him confidence, and while he is strongly pro–sex workers' rights, he still resents having to pay for something that someone, somewhere, ought to offer enthusiastically, for free. Even while having sex, it comes freighted with so many expectations, such intense anticipation of disappointment, that he doesn't enjoy it. To finish he silently imagines the woman is pregnant and that his more potent semen is killing off the other man's embryo, displacing it with his own. He tips well.

Sometime after turning forty, he makes a rare excursion from his apartment to visit his old favorite restaurant in a hip neighborhood he lived in a decade ago, the kind of upscale Italian bistro where they serve meatballs but not spaghetti. The foyer is crammed and it's a fifty-minute wait. This place never used to be crowded, it had been a quiet place to read without feeling lonely; now it is massed with couples and their offspring colonizing yet another space, basking in the triumphalism of love, instead of confronting the real harm of their prejudice and superiority and, yes, the *privileges* they enjoy.

He waits out on the muggy sidewalk until his name is called, and at the entrance, a fleet of strollers exits the restaurant through the narrow vestibule. He flattens against the plastic wall to let two, three, four strollers pass, then tries to enter the restaurant when a fifth woman approaches, pushing an enormous three-wheeler with BMX tires and a crusty-eyed newborn scrunched inside it. He expects her to let him through, but instead she pushes the vestibule door open and he feels and hears a crack, looks down at his leather sandals and sees his big toenail folded up at an astonishing angle, says, Ow ow ow. Rather than apologize, she trades an eyeroll with her husband, who says, "Buddy, she can't get *through* if you don't *move back*."

Your convenience doesn't outweigh mine, he asserts to the father, I have an equal right to be here, plus you damaged my foot. Instead of replying, the father pushes him by the shoulder out onto the sidewalk, again violating his bodily autonomy.

Being civil and slow to anger, he says nothing, even as fury chain-reacts down through his chest. The strollers recede to the end of the block, spanning the sidewalk's whole width, and now, first limping then sprinting, he catches up to them and (carelessly, with his injured foot) delivers a solid righteous side-stomp to one of the strollers' chassis. The mother catches it before it tips over, and he serves another wild kick before shooting off through traffic across the street. Their shouts degrade into noise as he rounds the corner at a hobbled gallop, and he makes sure they hear him laugh.

At home, legs trembling full of acid, grimacing, he peels off his bloody broken half toenail. The wound looks like a cut pomegranate and he dabs it with alcohol, adding injury to injury, the pain piercing an opening inside him through which more tearful laughter escapes. He does feel somewhat guilty about what he did, yet he will not deny that it felt so, so *good* to ruin the evenings of the tyrannical assholes who loved to dehumanize innocent single narrow-shouldered men. Just a quick startle, no harm done. Actually, *he's* the one who was harmed. The only thing that bothers him is that he knows no one would condone what he did.

More years pass, all alike. Something goes wrong in the bathroom: it was not a levator spasm after all. His doctor repeatedly assures him it is not a death sentence but will require significant immediate changes to his lifestyle. The diagnosis clears his head like a window continuously opening. Finally, it's happened: they've killed him. He might as well be dead already. It is now certain he'll never get the one thing he's ever wanted. All because he internalized and accepted his unwantedness, languished too long in mealymouthed consolations, let himself be deceived into pitying those who would never pity him. Nothing can be done.

He's never wanted to consider it, but with his hard-won lived experience and the stark authority of his disprivilege, he can declare that women, in aggregate, are just—wrong. That either they have failed feminism, or feminism has failed them. Yes, it's complicated; and no, no woman in particular is to blame; but it's irrefutable that in general, a *preponderance* of women harbor the very sorts of double standards feminism sought to eliminate, and indulge a narcissistic victim complex by which they tolerate and even seek out aggro misogyny in their romantic partners, while relying on men of conscience to handle the emotional scutwork. In his newfound communities of narrow-shouldered men he finds lived experiences that align near unanimously with his, in the comments of blogs like *The Empirical Agnate* and *Rationally Rude*, on forums like *Seneca's Revenge* and *NSOM* (Narrow Shoulders/Open Minds), where he finds provocative opinions of undeniable salience, heroically uncowed by any anticipated backlash. At last, he's found men willing to declare unapologetically that narrow-shouldered feminist men are in truth the *most* oppressed subaltern group, excluded from both male privilege and female solidarity, a marginalization far worse than those based in race or gender, which were mere constructs, as opposed to the *material* fact of narrow shoulders. He can trust these other men in a way he cannot trust anyone else, as they are the only people on earth to take seriously his suffering and recognize that he isn't to blame for it. While he disagrees with many of their heterodox positions on jaw morphology and age of consent, it is precisely the plurality of perspectives here that confirms the problem isn't his alone: it is systemic.

Now that he is mostly confined to his bed, in one late-night tour of the *NSOM* forums, which he moderates, he's busy drawing red circles around the telltale shoulder pad divots in photos of male celebrities, when he notices one thread attracting dozens of replies. Some normie interloper has been trolling the *NSOM* boards with inflammatory posts. This has happened before, but never at such length:

coldshoulder02
Unregistered User
Location: BC
Age: 23
Posts: 1
Rep Power: 0

just found this board and I'm fucking obsessed yall. not even just by the misogyny or the term-paper talk yall use to hide it. no, what's mesmerizing is, no lie, I'm *one of you*. I'm 23 and a virgin, never had a gf or even a date, mostly solo queue League and work at Staples. I stumbled across this place because I have real NS, hell I'm built like a closed umbrella, and I always wondered if other guys felt insecure about it too. I work out sometimes but I'm not crazy fit or anything and wish I were bigger. I think racist/sexist jokes are funny but I feel bad about it. so, probably like you.

then I come here and WOW. what happened, boys? I can't lie and say it isn't nice to find other NS guys, but this place is like staring into a cursed mirror where the longer you stare at it the uglier you get, but it's so fascinating you keep staring. go head and call me white knight/betafag/lib or whatever weak shit you got called in gym class in sixth grade. I'd rather die a sane virgin than fall for this mess.

idk maybe it's more about what happened to me. maybe it's bc I figured out some meds that work for me, or bc I have women in my life (grew up with four sisters). I'm not saying I'm better than any of yall, if I did I'd be the same as yall. so women either reject you or they don't act 100% the way you want them to (the term for that is "slavery"). bottom line is nobody's hurting or stealing anything from you. yall just hitched your psychosexual angst to your self-worth and it's women's fault somehow. however unfair you think it is, you're MAKING IT WORSE. hope yall logoff and find peace.

He scrolls down through the ensuing dogpile, watches see hawk1488 post memes of skinny guys labeled betafag OP lifting two-pound weights, reads michaelJ_fux's post femoid psy op piss off. By the end of the thread, his scalp is sodden and prickling. He feels that same flushed, hangdog supervisibility, that cleansing shame he used to feel when being scolded by his QPOC friend or reading feminist literature that diagnosed his unseen advantages and corrected his gaffes. He remembers thinking: if a stranger can so accurately describe what I've thought without even knowing me, they must be right, and I should listen to them. Now he wants to do likewise for this online stranger, whose familiar and bracing conviction, uncompromised by experience, floods him with nostalgia. It's painful seeing this poor sap misled, as he himself was, like a sprinting dog about to hit the limit of its leash. The other users taunt the newcomer because it hurts less than admitting familiarity. Even if it's too late for himself, he feels a responsibility to awaken this younger man to reality.

You may think you understand us, he posts, but I've been you far longer than you have. I want to tell you about the reality of having lived four decades of silent virtuous pain and never having your humanity and desirability recognized, he posts. It's not that I haven't done the intellectual labor to empathize with the broadest possible spectrum of female perspectives, I've read Sanger and Friedan and MacKinnon and Dworkin and Firestone and Faludi and Winterson and Butler and Solanas and Schulman and hooks and Greer. I understand them, and they perhaps understand the viewpoint of the patriarchy and its beneficiaries—but what have any of them read to understand *us*? Where in the archive do we even exist? My entire life I've been nothing but useful to women, selfless to the point that when I die my entire being will evaporate without residue, with no one left to know what I've had to endure absolutely by myself. Think of all the times you've been ill, with no one to bring you soup. Those nights you wake in the dark full of fear with no one to talk to. Every unshared bed. Every expired condom. Those couples you see everywhere, laughing and going home and fucking in every conceivable position: it will never be you. *It will never be you.* This is why you are wrong that they haven't stolen anything from us: They've stolen our lives, our happiness. Our future and the people in it. You will never have a woman, and you will never have a son. Women's fucked-up preferences may have been ingrained there by the patriarchy, but women, as moral agents fully equal to men, are no less responsible for them, and I will not infantilize them by claiming otherwise. Me, I've done more than my part: I've actively combated

misogyny both in the world and within myself, tithed monthly
to Planned Parenthood, marched and canvassed and fundraised
and posted for women's rights. I'm commitment-friendly, prosperous, successful, not ugly, in fact a solid eight from the neck up
and nipples down, six-inch penis from base of shaft, high sperm
count and seminal motility, +7° canthal tilt and 14.6 inch bi-
acromial breadth, veritably a straight flush of stable-pair-bonding
qualities, AND I have never ONCE catcalled, gaslit, interrupted,
or mansplained, taking every single rejection in stride without
any social support, no shared costs, inside jokes, pet names, in-
timate confessions, indeed any fond romantic memories whatsoever, none of the bliss of puppy love unspoiled by bitterness, the
naïve love that knows no betrayal, nor trusting companionship
that weathers hate and temptation, nobody waking up nestled in
your elbow, no one to try new restaurants or take selfies or travel
with, to say nothing of the conveniences, stability, and tax breaks
enjoyed by the conjugal, on top of enduring the only real stigma
that exists anymore, the only one that makes you *less* dignified
for being honest about it: BACHELORHOOD, he posts. I've
never complained, objected, or harassed anyone all these years
no matter how cruel or senseless the rejection, if anything I enabled their rejections, and even took it as my duty. Which is all
the more insidious, actually, that they convinced us to normal-
ize and accept this, become complicit in our own oppression by
pretending it's not happening or doesn't matter, or even if it is
happening and does matter, you deserve it: that's right, *THEY* are
gaslighting *YOU*, all to absolve themselves of guilt, at the meager
cost of our lives. We are made to eternally repent for the sins of
the worst men, while those very same men reap the benefits of our
care and counsel. And we are not even humored to speak on the

matter. For they have built a cunning trap, a rhetorical kill switch, where if you try to speak up for them, they say *Stay in your lane!*, and if you say nothing, they say *Silence is violence!* Indicted from birth, lashed forever to the rack of apology, never forgiven much less rewarded, regardless of action or intent—do you see how they have made our existence impossible? This, after all we've sacrificed for them; I would have died for them if they'd asked, I would have thrown my bleeding body on the barricades of the patriarchy, and they would have let me do it, indifferently accepting my death as their due, with not a punctum of guilt as they go off to bed and wed my murderers. That is the long con, their big lie. By now my bachelorhood, and yours, cannot be ascribed to circumstance or bad luck, only injustice. We must reject it. Like my many, many female friends themselves always used to say, nothing's wrong with me, any woman would have been lucky to have me, I've only asked for the same modest redamancy that everyone else—including chauvinists, liars, addicts, narcissists, abusers, rapists, and low-IQ men—enjoys everywhere. I'd be the last to demand any special treatment for my actual, unselfish, principled feminism, and to be sure, no *specific* woman is *required* to be attracted to us . . . but the fact that not *one* has been, out of *billions*, is proof of a categorical failure, a *mass abrogation of the social contract* by the legions of treacherous, evasive, giggling yeastbuckets, he posts. I have always, always been there for women. When have they ever been there for us? How, after decades of relentless refusal, can they ever repair this silent androcide, the calamity of our aborted futures?

He receives no reply. The stranger probably didn't even see his post. Examining what he'd written, scouring it with an unsparing eye toward logic and tone, he finds no error. He closes his laptop, surveys his dimmed room: humidifier, prescription bottles, weights he can no longer lift, bedside wastebasket full of tissues wadded with phlegm and cum. With his mouth in a grim hyphen, he inspects his penis, which is not only flaccid and cadaverously livid from overpumping but has developed some sort of irritating sun rash that isn't sun rash, ever since he resorted to masturbating with a textured plumber's glove in order to feel anything at all. This can't happen again: all this not-happening. The nothing that is made of words, the reading and processing and discussing and journaling and posting with which he'd attempted to understand the hundreds of women's voices he'd then gone on to uplift and amplify, only to hear that those voices were mocking him, all the *listening*—wasted effort constituting a wasted life. Words by themselves have no substance, he realizes, they are only ever meant to underscore acts. Being correct has been its own reward and no reward at all. Now with whatever miserable span of life remains to him he must commit himself to action, pull out the serrated knife of virtue that's been stuck in his chest for so long he thought it was a part of him. Before he dies he must stop nothing from happening.

Weeks later, after some false starts, he is standing in the vestibule of his former favorite restaurant when a woman enters behind him, a short young twentysomething in a yellow smock with little pin-tucked ruffles, her collarbones lightly pied by sunburn. He stands aside to hold the door for her, and she thanks him. In spite of his resolve, he smiles back and nods courteously at this small final vindication, before pulling on his ski mask, shrugging the backpack from his narrow shoulders, and following her in.

PICS

Love is mutual: which means Alison's never been in love. Her high school boyfriend of three years had turned out to be gay, and she'd made him admit, after much needling, that he'd never been attracted to her. In college she'd dated a more popular guy who turned their shared friend group against her in the breakup, leaving her with a distrust of both lovers and friends, not to mention herself. Nothing but isolated hookups since, though she gets hit on in the usual degrading ways: being commanded on the street by random men to smile, getting called a bitch when she doesn't. Her dating app inboxes crammed with free-floating dicks. She used to believe the reason she was so prone to this kind of bad attention was because she herself was somehow innately "bad"; later she realized that not only was it the men who were bad, but that the crux of their badness was their ability to convince her she was bad. Though that doesn't mean she isn't bad, she sometimes thinks.

Love is not an accomplishment, yet to lack it still somehow feels like failure.

One night in her late twenties, Alison visits her best friend Neil's house. Neil is slender, bookish, objectively interesting: he builds his own furniture from reclaimed wood and works for a nonprofit that rehabilitates pedophiles undergoing voluntary chemical castration. He supports his parents financially, and his tiny apartment contains hanging plants, a half-bedroom with a

piano in it that he illegally Airbnbs for extra income, and an-
tique farming tools adorning the walls. They are meeting for
their monthly ritual: he makes her favorite panko-crusted baked
mac and cheese with Crystal hot sauce, and she cuts his hair
while they stream reality TV. They'd started this ritual back in
college, when he was helping her recover from the worst period
of her eating disorder by finding and making the one food that
she wasn't revulsed by, and waiting with her after eating it; Neil
was the only person who didn't regard her with either concealed
disgust or corny delicacy, who made recovery feel meaningful
and worthwhile.

They're watching *Hoarders* on his laptop perched on a stool,
and she's already seen this episode, so Alison spends most of the
time watching him squirm and gasp at the most horrible parts;
she's always enjoyed reliving things vicariously more than experiencing them directly. The video stream starts to buffer. "Shit,
goddamnit, sorry, this never happens when I'm watching by myself," Neil says. "I have to log in again or something. Damnit!"
Alison says he's acting like he has erectile dysfunction, and he
says, "You're the one with the ED, not me." She laughs—he's the
only one who could get away with that joke—and he mutters,
"Yeah, I've got *no* problems in that department."

This comment, the weird oomph he puts on it, tickles at her
brain. As the show continues to buffer, Neil leans forward to adjust the angle of the laptop screen as if that'll fix it, and when he
leans back he rests his hand on Alison's knee, but in a weird crab
shape where only the fingertips are touching. It stays there for a
full ten seconds until he leans forward again to tap the space bar,
makes some inquiring eye contact, and they lunge at each other.

Physically he's not her type at all, and she's never thought he was hot, until now, the moment she realizes he thinks *she's* hot. The kissing is pretty good, much enhanced by the spontaneity and wrong-hotness of tongue-kissing a close friend. They both awkwardly laugh more than she'd prefer, and he spends way too long sucking her nipples, to the point where she consciously thinks the word *latching*. But then the mood shifts—she is no longer Mommy, he is Daddy, and he lifts and tosses her around with a thrilling lack of effort, and, as she's long suspected based on the size of his ears and nose, he has an era-definingly huge dick, curved in the way only really huge ones are, like they have inches to spare and can take the long way around. She cums so hard it makes her *sit up*.

While she's going down on him between rounds, Neil says from above, "Hey, would it be lame if I took a pic?" Part of her mind recoils at this, and she doesn't reply at first, but she's sent nudes to far worse guys. Honestly, it's flattering he'd want a keepsake, maybe even body-affirming and hot, and it's not like she's going to run for office. So she says fine, as long as he sends her a copy, and she does her best to smolder next to his big ol' dick. He goes cross-eyed and double-chinned holding the phone close to his face, to fit as much in the frame as possible, and the camera flash stays on for an agonizingly long time.

Lying around afterward, she configures herself in Neil's negative spaces, back-to-chest, nose-to-neck, mindless and snug as a martini in its glass. She says, That was nice. By way of non-response, he does a silly tongue roll, then asks, "Do you want me to talk you to sleep? My ex used to like when I did that."

She's not thrilled he brought up his ex; still, it's good that he's putting her in that role, and she drifts off listening to him mumble about hikes he used to take with his father before he died. This is what love is supposed to feel like, Alison thinks. Her contentment is only mildly soured by the realization that she's been missing out on this for her whole life.

In the morning, when he wakes to the poached eggs and toast she's prepared, the first thing Neil says is, listen, he doesn't regret last night, but doesn't want to give the impression that he's looking for anything serious. Okay: he's being proactively candid, thoughtful really, and it doesn't mean anything's over. She can stomach the long game. She screws her fists against her cheeks in a "crybaby" pout, then laughs and tells him she's out of his league anyway. They eat breakfast and gossip about college friends, and when he shows her out the door, she goes in for a peck, and he pulls her in by the waist and gives her a kiss that makes her foot soles tingle.

She immediately reports the incident to her group chat, some friends from an internship at a ladymag years ago, whom she's seldom seen since, yet texts dozens of times a day. They're all younger than her, and many have graduated to well-placed staff jobs; her envy is tempered by the fact that, though she now does admin for a textbook publisher, she is technically one of them, and maybe they can help her land a better gig someday. In them she has found something like the coterie to which she's always wanted to belong, not the popular crowd, rather, the smaller satellite crowd that makes fun of the popular crowd—the outer circle, internally supportive and externally terrifying. The group chat started off as boys.txt, then Dateline SVU, which became All Cops Are Boys, and most recently he wore sANDals in bED!?

As usual she has to scroll through dozens of messages to catch up before she can contribute:

Sarah
yah it was one of those public daytime walking dates

Anjali
saves money on drinks and mace

Sarah
ikr

so we're passing by a pride flag hanging in a bodega window

and he points at it and says quote: "I don't know, it just weirds me out"

Edwina

Sarah
oh I forgot to tell you his name was literally Yelmer lol

Tala
NOT YELMER

Anjali
tryna get the Yelmer's Goo

Sarah
tbf later i farted in front of him on the park bench 😼

one of those sitting ones that slide up between ur thighs and makes ur pussy lips applaud

best sex I've had in months

Anjali
HELP

Tala
sksks

Sarah
my fault for ignoring the red flags, his profile said his interests
were "selling cheese and anal training"

Na'amah
I'm here to train ass and sell cheese . . . and I'm all out of cheese

Anjali
speaking of dudes who point, my tinder date last week asked me
how big my boobs were and just like . . . pointed at em

Edwina
Ah yes, I've heard of the female body inspector

Sarah named the conversation "female body respecters"
Today 11:18

Anjali
and omg that lil bitch's feet were so 👏 FUCKING 👏 grimy 👏

is this a wypipo thing can someone pls tell me

even after he showered the bottoms stayed pitch black

they were like . . . SEASONED like a cast iron pan

Edwina

Wet me up

Sarah

I'm going to kill mice elf

Tala

"showered" hold up!!

so u smashed

Anjali

😺😼😼😼

Sarah

I'M DEADDDDD

also jealous 🏨 i'm 🔪 hag mode

whose dick do I gotta suck to suck a dick around here

You

LOL! That's hilarious guys.

So, some personal news, y'all.

I just hooked up with my close friend Neil! 😳

Anjali

omg slut!!!!

is that the boy you just posted? cutie 👀

Edwina

Big square hands, nice arm vein, me encanta

my cheeks are parting of their own accord

Na'amah

crashes through the skylight on a rope ladder dangling from a helicopter I'm HERE

did someone get her eggs cracked???? scrolling up

ok ok YES we approve

he looks like he reads Architectural Digest but will also tap it on your tongue

ooo good taste in sweaters too, love a cozy fisherman's sweater

did u know those were knitted by fisherman's wives so they could ID their husbands' bodies when they washed ashore

Sarah

I've got something his body can wash ashore on

Edwina

I love short 2A curls on a yt boi ngl

Sarah

get his birth time and location i NEED to see sthng 👀

he's giving rich guy

he's giving "my parents own a Cape Cod summer home that's older than America" you said his name's neil? like he looks more like a "Clayton"

or "Cooper"

Anjali

the coop that eats like a neil

Tala

he does have those generational wealth glasses

that can't be his apartment can it??? im soaked థ_థ

I SPREAD for a man who can decorate small spaces

Na'amah

small apartment makes the dick look bigger

Sarah

S'CREAM

I love how we're like wow what discerning taste in sweaters and acrylic frames, I shall endeavor to inquire after this good fellow's professional interests and financial standing

meanwhile guys get a half chub when they see a pair of oranges sitting too close together ! 🚂

Tala named the conversation "orange u glad I sucked ur banana"
Today 11:25

Na'amah

NJBs dont get nearly enough credit for slinging sushi-grade dick

Anjali

nothing like fucking a longtime friend tbqh

aged like a fine wine

may I interest you in the 1983 dick madame, a rahther damp
year as I recall

Sarah

bring a tarp, the first three rows WILL get wet

did u point and ask how big his dick was

Edwina

boys really feel about their dicks the way we feel about our
whole bodies tbh !

                                                              You

                                    Hee hee. The man has moves, to be sure!

                                    Pretty excited for the follow up. ✌

Tala

yesss love this for u kween (/◑ヮ◐)/*:·✧

Right as the aphrodisiac of female consensus is making him
seem even more appealing, Neil texts her the blowjob pic. In
the photo, the flash blazes overexposure across her forehead,
and the high definition makes her crow's-feet look like the cling
wrap around a soft cheese. Her eyes are pink and goonishly half-
lidded, and she's gripping his dick like she's trying to pull it out

by the root. It's hard to imagine any guy beating off to this, but she doesn't regret it; it is proof that the bond has been official-ized, and if he likes her when she looks like this, he must truly like her.

Over the next few weeks Alison avoids mentioning their hookup so as not to seem overeager. The most she'll allow her-self is scrolling all the way down to the first post in each of his social media timelines and commenting "?," which is harmless and funny. She also sends grainy, late-night, ambiguously nude selfies of the area between her collarbones and her faintly smirk-ing lips, followed by wyd, to which he only gives frustratingly straightforward replies, like finally getting around to watching true detective s1. In any case, she goes back on birth control.

The next time they meet up for their monthly dinner and haircut at his place, he gives her an extra-long hug, but not the kiss she was hoping for. She makes sure to eat lightly, and during the meal manages to get in an arm squeeze and ruffle his curly bangs. When they're settled on the couch watching his laptop, she waits for the video to buffer, and when it does, she lets a deli-cious whoosh of silence pass, then asks if he's going to demolish her lower back again.

He chews his upper lip, then gets all serious and says he doesn't think it's a good idea, that he cares about her a lot and thinks she's really cute, sweet, and funny, but he's not in the right space for a relationship right now. (Even though, she knows, his last one was two years ago.) He says it's natural to have some sore feelings around all this, so it might be wise to take a cooldown period. Hearing this makes her collarbones feel tight. Still, the diplomatic forthrightness of his rejection is part of his whole appeal, and means that he doesn't hate her.

Like, that's fine, that makes sense, she says, if that's what he wants, it's good he told her, so yeah, a cooldown is uh, cool with her. She gives a thumbs-up and waits for him to reply, then realizes he means a cooldown starting *right now*. While she's putting her shoes on, he asks if she wants to take the leftovers home with her.

In the Uber she gets lipstick on her knuckles as she tamps mac and cheese into her mouth. What spooked him? What's wrong with leaving things open-ended, why'd he shut it down so decisively? She did *not* even come on that strong. It feels pointlessly penalizing that he won't even go for casual sex when she's totally down for it, she can handle it: that's all she's ever handled. Apparently she's not hot enough to fuck twice, but their friendship meant little enough to risk fucking once.

You
So now I feel stupid for letting him take pics.

Maybe that was his only goal to begin with.
Who knows! Who fucking knows.

Seems like he got everything he wanted.

Tala
ohhh bb

we hate him now yes?

typical venus in sag

Edwina
LMFAOO BYE

get him to turn on location

put his dick and balls in liquid hydrogen and SMASH

Sarah

fetches lab coat and goggles

fetches comedy sized mallet

You

Aw, ha ha. Thanks. No need to do all that.

Love y'all.

Tala

<3

he's actually in my bf's roommate's friend group, seemed chill when I met him the one time

but ya prison for him now ಠ_ಠ

Anjali

okay yes now that it is safe to say so. . . . I kinda thought that guy seemed sus lmao

didn't you say he works with pedos? literally who signs up to do that

middling ass softboi

Sarah

he's not even that tall?

ur way hotter like???

Na'amah
COSIGN

Tala
confirmed hot girl 🔥

the cheekbones ✔

the ass ✔

the everything, all of it ✔✔✔

As much as she appreciates their support, their sudden volte-face about Neil's worthiness implies some dishonesty in either their current or earlier support, or both. And she doesn't believe they actually think she's attractive. Since college she has gained an amount of weight that she cannot justify as healthy recovery, and, having yet to find the correct hairstyle to frame her new face, she has defaulted to bangs that are too long or short depending on the day. Given how much younger and hotter they are, she suspects the group chat is patronizing her, or at best consider her the kind of mild mousy pretty that provokes no envy, unthreatening to women and imperceptible to men. They don't know Neil well enough to genuinely hate him, anyway, and despite her annoyance she doesn't want to go all-in on vitriol, on the slight chance they end up together in the future.

Regardless:

You
Ha ha. Thanks again, y'all. I needed this.

Sarah

de nada babes :~)

tbh boys never treat sex as a commitment so u shouldnt either

no more wasting time on mid brunets just bc they sling dick

Edwina

Call that a sunk cock fallacy

Anjali

*phallusy

Na'amah

hard agree! don't even trip just cut him loose

can't get your eggs cracked without cracking a few eggs

Sarah

and whatever u do don't text him 🫥

mayb even softblock

Anjali

yessss yeet and delete

we stan a non-self-sabotaging qworn

def not healthy to dwell

You

I mean, I'm not doing it for my heakth, LOL.

*Health.

Edwina
Heakth

Anjali
heakth

Sarah
this bitch said heakth

Na'amah named the conversation "heakth appeal"
Today 3:49

Edwina
Lol

Anjali
lol

The friendship, it seems, has been quietly ruined by its reckless redistricting. Neil stops texting her, and she spends entire evenings patrolling his social media in a fugue, thinking about how his rejecting her to preserve their friendship is exactly what ended it, how it used to be a happy voluntary arrangement, and has now become something she is forced to settle for. And settle for, and settle for. Neil gets to come away from it all feeling wise and mature, and unless she wants to end up with nothing, or at least keep him from dismissing her as crazy, grabby, borderline, she has to play along. The closest she gets to openly criticizing him is to occasionally post a cryptic song lyric, ones where if he went and looked up the line right after it, he'd see it was about him and hopefully be devastated.

Three months later, Neil starts liking her posts again, which escalates to wordless exchanges of memes, until he hits her with a frosty "how u been dude." Despite where they'd left off, she's pathetically happy to hear from him, though also mad at herself for feeling forgiven when she knows she's done nothing wrong.

When they at last meet to catch up over coffee, the conversation is strained and overly polite, as they tiptoe around the incident that necessitated catching up in the first place. Alison realizes she has nothing new to report about her life that doesn't in some way involve trying to get over him. Also absent is any discussion of his current feelings about her, which is the only thing she wants to talk about, but she can't broach it without looking hung up.

Her disenchantment almost succeeds in getting her to forget him and move on, until on their next meeting—dinner at the gastropub Neil likes because it has no TVs and a jukebox full of burned CD-R bootlegs—he arrives late, with a hot tiny Asian girl. "Hope you don't mind I brought a friend. This is Cece," he says. "We were just hanging out and it ran late. I figured you guys should meet anyway, since you're both cool."

Alison sees what he's doing: bringing his new girlfriend around as a test, to prove she's not bothered. It's so nefarious of him to bring a date without even giving her the chance to dress nicer. She extends her hand, and Cece counters by coming in practically spread-eagle for a big hug, her six inches of visible midriff exuding supreme torso confidence. They pick a booth to sit in—Neil instinctively choosing to sit next to Cece—

and Alison excuses herself to go to a bathroom stall and gather some intel on Cece. Based on her posts, she seems infuriatingly worthy, from a guy perspective: thin with C-cups and a balmy sheen like she's always already done five minutes of Pilates, plus several differently hot friends and, evidently, a life fulfilling enough to not even need the validation of good looks, traveling often, therefore rich, working in a well-paid creative profession (landscape design) that does not threaten Neil's, and just *barely* age-appropriate. In her most recent post, Cece is holding her hairless sphynx cat and a handwritten sign that says END PAW-LICE BRUTALITY 🐾, with an impassioned three-paragraph caption that ends with a list of senators to call. It's the most annoying thing Alison has ever seen, until she sees the next photo, which shows Cece on a couch in leggings and a sheer tank top with a black bra underneath, her abdomen free of creases or swells even while slouching, holding a gargantuan platter of seven-layer nachos with her big eyes wide open in sexy pretend-alarm, and the caption:

> nachos and neglije 👅😺 gluttony >>>> glam ALWAYS. no shame in my food game!!

Even beyond Cece somehow bungling both the spelling and meaning of *negligee*, more grating is the pretense that she could feel shame of any kind, that she is not flaunting the very glamour she pretends to disparage, the glamour of getting everything without sacrifice—and that she doesn't know *exactly* what effect this has on men. On Neil specifically. Oh, it must make him feel so *cool* to be dating an Asian girl, so small and smooth, so much fun to bounce around in bed.

The ensuing pity-spiral is predictable if puzzling. Maybe because this Cece bitch is just so *obvious*. Alison used to think Neil had more sophisticated tastes, and that explained why he cared about her, why they'd hooked up that one time. Now it feels like he's simply raised his standards.

To show she's not bothered, and to punish herself, and to punish him, Alison returns to the booth and endures an hour of conversation. Cece attempts to girl-bond with her by asking if she's seen the reality show about people test-driving their green card marriages. Alison has absolutely seen it, and all of its spinoffs, but to look smarter than Cece pretends she hasn't, which leads Cece to recap an entire season, ending with a cowardly hedge: "Anyway, it's so dumb but I like it." No, Alison thinks: it's so dumb *and* you like it.

When their food comes, Cece spends the whole meal pushing her food around the plate, makes a big deal of the single enormous bite she takes from her fried fish sandwich, flips over the top half of the bun to cover more of the plate, then complains that the fries are soggy, to get away with not eating them. It brings Alison no greater empathy knowing that she and Cece share these tricks in common.

Projecting an unruffled conviviality, Alison keeps ordering rounds for the table, even after Neil and Cece say they've had enough. When they refuse to drink the last round, Alison drinks all three herself, one after another. It's not like they can force her to stop. She becomes unable to stop smiling, and at a certain point she feels that now is a great time to bring up the fact that she and Neil once hooked up, just to get it out in the open, so Cece will be reassured that it's all behind them, it's *so* not-a-big-deal that they can joke about it all they want. But it doesn't come out gracefully, tone-wise. She should not have brought up his nipple-sucking proclivities, or how it makes sense he'd date a Filipina girl because he likes 'em dusky but his parents would disown him if he ever dated anyone black or Latina . . . no, she can tell, from the way Cece keeps saying "Oh" and Neil is yanking at the drawstrings of his hoodie, that she should not have said these things.

"Hey, *hey*," Neil says. "Hang on. Cece and I aren't even—you know what, I knew you'd pull some shit like this, I knew you couldn't be chill. Fuck it, we're going." He stands and his little Asian princess follows, whispering something to him that makes him laugh as they leave the bar.

Plummeting into bed that night, now she feels like a martini *without* its glass, a sloppy puddle of poison. The next morning she's so hungover she has to sit on the bathtub rim while she's brushing her teeth. Her morning dump is like a multistage rocket launch, so loud and fervid and aerosol that to psychically recover afterward she takes a fifteen-minute shower and buys some white linen sheets online. Cycling through her tabs, she finds the email from Neil that she more or less expected:

Listen, I don't want things to fester after last night, so I feel like it's important to say: I apologize if bringing my friend around caught you off-guard. But that got way more fucked up than it had to be. You made it that way. I feel like I've made my boundaries pretty clear, and you agreed to them, and now you're acting like I'm cheating on you. And for no reason! Cece and I are, I repeat, NOT DATING, and I don't know why you wouldn't just take my word for that.

Alison slouches, the screen trembles. The gently worded restraint feels like proof of his low opinion of her. Still, does she really bear sole responsibility here? *He's* the one who did the thing that made her act "fucked up." Why should he get to dictate the terms of surrender? Why should she accept them?

His email goes on for a bit longer and concludes,

We've known each other a long time and if it's one thing I know, it's that you always manage to convince yourself that when you act out, you're only hurting yourself, or are justified in hurting others as long as you suffer too. I do not think it is unfair to say you have a habit of passively consenting to miserable situations, or even baiting them out of people, so you can later weaponize your sadness. Like you've even *joked* about how you do that. I've seen it, the obvious glee you take in talking about how awful men have been to you, and now it looks like you've decided to make me one of them. I guess you believe that's what makes you sympathetic, or you need it to lend gravitas to otherwise ordinary dissatisfaction. You want to drag people down into the mud with you. And when it backfires, because why would it not backfire, you fall back to your bunker of victimhood. It's a good thing Cece has a sense of humor, I talked to her and she forgives you even though she didn't have to, but she didn't do anything to deserve this kind of treatment, and if it keeps up then I don't know what's gonna happen with you and me. PS for future reference, Cece is Korean, not Filipina (like how did you even land on Filipina? That's so random). -N

Oh! Nice! Fun! Okay! So being miserable is a *choice*? It's her fault for *consenting* to the misery, and not his for *causing* it? Well, if she's such a fucking mess, so unable to resist lashing out, why'd he introduce her to Cece at all? It's so fucked up of him to use things she'd confided to him in the past, in the spirit of self-criticism, *against* her . . . and implying she's racist just for pointing out *his* obvious racist *and* sexist fetishism; pretending that's what he's mad about, "racism," when all he's doing is looking for excuses to vilify her. GOD!

Before, Alison might've accepted some of the blame; this email convinces her she was right all along. Her anger cremates away all her affection for him, but not the obsession, leaving her a scorched skeleton of wrath. Now that he's had his ego boost, his little pump-and-dump with a keepsake pic to beat off to for the rest of his life, how convenient to write her off as some insane bitch, while all she can do is moon over a relationship that no one could prove wouldn't have been good. He got everything he wanted, and she got nothing. Less than nothing: she's forced to choose between self-respect and peace of mind, when each requires the other, so it is a choice between nothing and nothing.

So, she went too far: fine. All she cares about is how she can make him own *his* share of the blame. Confront him with her grievances? No, that'd look petulant and reactive. Could she respond with a simple "lol"? Being glib would give him an excuse to sever their friendship with equally low effort, and he'd probably feel more relief than guilt. Ignore him? Wounded, weak, mind-gamey, plus, her absence would be punitive only if he cared about her. Retaliation is impossible when he's doing so well. All she can do is scrabble around in ineffectual rage like a cat chasing a laser.

In any case, Alison decides, she won't act petty, not because she isn't petty, but because she's holding out for, at the very least, a mutual apology. She stays up late composing her reply, writing that she's . . . really sorry, full stop, and she's not going to lie and pretend she didn't mean anything she said, but knows it was inappropriate, clearly she's underestimated how much of her own shit she has to deal with, which has only partly to do with him, he's always been a good friend and doesn't deserve any grief for communicating his boundaries and keeping things from festering between them—would he please pass her apology along? He doesn't owe her his friendship; still, she'd appreciate it, if he's offering.

With this simpering dogshit email, she wants to give him absolutely nothing to fault her for, though maybe she's just telling herself that, and is in reality indulging her wretched people-pleasing good-girl complex. Though she'd actually be *glad* to people-please, in the trusting confines of a relationship.

Waiting sensibly until the morning, she rereads it, tones it down even further, and sends it. Three minutes later Neil replies:

aight. we're good 👍

Mother*fuck*! It was a setup! He didn't fall for her reverse psychology—she fell for his *regular* psychology! If she'd known he'd respond this way, she would have annihilated him like he deserved, but backpedaling now would only confirm his idea of her as dishonest and conniving. Which she was not, except with him.

You
I mean, why would he bother keeping
up this facade of friendship?

Don't answer that! I know why, duh. The more open and direct and accommodating he pretends to be, the more he can convince himself I'm the one who's crossed the line. Like I'm this crazy bitch and he's this levelheaded UN peacekeeper trying to deescalate.

Because regardless of how they actually behave, men prize the abstract sense of their own integrity over literally everything, especially nonsexual relationships with women.

Although it WAS sexual at one point! And he's acting like it somehow didn't count! Sometimes I wonder if he pulled back from the brink of a relationship because he knew he'd lose the advantage of a one-sided dynamic. This way, he gets to feed his ego effortlessly without any of the hard work of relationship maintenance.

And because he cleverly preempted me by pathologizing any negative feelings I might have as "weaponized sadness," I can't even express any of these valid frustrations with him. Which precludes actual friendship. So I'm trapped in HELL.

I don't know. Ugh.

Na'amah
oh hun that's awful

let's take a breath n get centered

You
And I can't get over the absolute GALL of him trotting out his new hairless Asian child bride in front of me.

I guess she's technically legal but we all know why men are into that!

Anjali

whoa now

You

Truly, the cherry on top. And her trying to act like we're
friends, sitting there all like, Oh hi! So you're the old
slampig! Nice to meetcha you fat white BITCH!

Tala

ummm not that her being an azn sis has anything to do with it!

You

No, of course not! That's the wild thing, *he* went there! He
tried to act like I was only bothered about it because of her race!

Which, you guys know me, it totally wasn't about that at all! Sorry
if it sounded that way, I didn't express myself correctly. Tone is
tough over text. I know I'm spiraling a bit, I know.

If it's one thing Neil's a genius at, it's putting me at fault and
making me sound awful and crazy. And I know I'm not.

Anjali

:/

well it sounds like you've been rly hard on yrself babes

mayb set aside a specific time for wallowing

like 30 min/day tops

helps for my anxiety anyway, I use this meditation app

Edwina

Bitch cut this man loose, he's playing in your face

Likeeee he's fine but his pronouns are ho/hum

Tala

cosign anj + edwina, cutting out booze and cigs helped me too

got to feeling like I always had mild flu

u in therapy bb?

                                                              You

                          Nah. I used to be. For nine years, actually.

        And sorry, I know we're pro-therapy in here. I suppose I am too,
                          in principle. But it just never worked out for me.

          Sitting in a chair and dilating for 45 minutes. Crying over the
                    same stuff I already cry over all the time anyway.

          All it really did was give my problems new names. Which only
                                made them easier to dwell on.

        I tried so many therapists, too. Six of them. No one felt right. No
                                one understood.

          Switching therapists until I found "the one" started to feel
                    exactly like dating, which was clearly not helpful.

      The last one had this permanent burst blood vessel in his eye and
        it was super distracting. He said it was from blood thinners. It
      made me sad. Plus he liked saying shit like "Let's just sit here and
                                breathe the same air."

          He did get me on vitamin D though. Which helped, I guess.

I don't know. Can't afford therapy anymore regardless! All the good ones are out of network. LOL.

Anyway, sorry to go on for so long. Thanks for letting me vent. My old shrink used to tell me I'm an "external processor." Which is psych code I guess for being a mouthy broad!?

Sarah

join the grippy sock girlies in club lexapro

20 mg in the place to be fr fr

Na'amah

oh yes, combo lexapro wellbutrin + therapy

like a z-pack for your brain, literally changed my life

the girls are getting MOOD STABILIZED

Tala

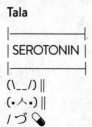

```
|———————————|
| SEROTONIN |
|———————————|
(\__/) ||
(•人•) ||
/づ💊
```

You

Why would I need antidepressants. I'm already boring.

Ha ha.

Sarah
?

You
Wait, I didn't mean you're boring, Sarah and Na'amah!!!

I was just talking about me. LOL.

Not about you!!!

Sarah
ur good 👍

Edwina
My lifehacc = year round SAD lamp. I do swear by it

Anjali
my wax lady says ketamine injections knocked her out of her depression in like six weeks

it's 💸 but could b worth

Sarah
climbing gym saved my life tbh

can't beat urself up if ur exhausted

I can send u a 1 week guest pass if u want! I get a referral bonus 🤑

!

Tala
ooo can I get down on that guest pass?

me wanty Ɛ꜆ ◐_◐ ꜆꜆

Edwina

Yes god

Re: ketamine should we look up some kind of cabin + take it together?? I'll get test strips and whatnot

You

But honestly the thing that pisses me off most is, he's so clearly LYING about not dating that Asian girl!

She is *absolutely* his type. (I.e. tiny, meek.) I'm not stupid.

And he knows I'm not stupid . . . I think? And he wouldn't bother lying about it if he didn't know on some level that he had something to feel guilty about. So he's tacitly acknowledging that he's done wrong.

But like, how do I call him out for that? Or should I, even?

I just, UGH.

Edwina

Girl

Anjali

oh hun

you just need to get you some garden fresh dick

don't use the lonely app, use the horny app

order that shit like a pizza

Tala

^^^ let the sausage cure u

be kind to urself bb >_<

After she cuts Neil off, not that he notices, the following months feel like slow nonlethal drowning. Every emotion besides anger and regret becomes blunted. She dyes her hair popsicle-red and nothing changes. Though dating is Alison's lowest priority, she follows her group chat's advice and gets on the apps. For a time she experiments with ethical non-monogamy, which, though its loudest practitioners seem very corny, was at least unlike the conventional couples she's grown to despise. But in practice she faces down a gauntlet of gym selfies, fish selfies, selfies cropped to conceal baldness. Plus, the relationships are so brief they seldom overlap, meaning she's not technically even poly, just hopscotching mile after mile of the dreariest dick imaginable; the ceaseless kayfabe of bad sex with divorced dads and DJs. The sociopathic nudniks, who either wind up jealous and clingy, or never ask her questions about herself. The otherwise handsome men over fifty whose DMs are like, Hi Alison. Great style. -Mike. The gallant fellow with the surprise last-second request to cum on her feet, who then falls asleep, leaving her to waddle on her heels leaving a trail of nutprints to the bathroom.

She starts keeping track of her failures in her notes app, an index of icks:

—smelled like a baby
—said "technically" too much
—said "mmm" whenever he took a bite of food
—kept shazaming the music
—hiccupped the whole time I was going down on him
—kept his Invisalign trays in while going down on me
—said "cromulent"
—drizzled pineapple vape juice directly onto his tongue

—shamed me for never having read Deleuze,
   later insisted condoms "hurt"
—eats stuffing every week not just Thanksgiving

Eventually, realizing that she does not actually want to re-member these things, she switches to keeping track of her dates using the contact names on her phone. Mr. Sneezy. Mr. Gifs. Mesh Shorts. eSports Guy. Beach Towel. Angry Vegan Doctor. Ugly Dog.

And then there is The Feminist, a guy she had a minor crush on in high school, who she becomes reacquainted with when they both angrily comment on a dumb Facebook post about how women can't code. Her former crush hasn't exactly blos-somed looks-wise, but when he asks her out, she has no reason to say no.

The date is powerfully bad. He's so weenily deferential, over-groomed in his little blazer with a graphic tee and matching Vans and raw selvedge denim. He has that sort of lenticular bald-ness where you can see the thinning patches only at an angle. Unlike most guys, he does ask her questions about herself, albeit terminally dull ones of the sort you'd ask to calibrate a poly-graph test—what do you do, where have you lived, what've you been reading lately. She pays attention only to gather cruel ob-servations to pass on to the group chat later. As her date finishes describing his job at a low-income women's health-care startup, she watches his teeth, which are too shiny, like they've been freshly zambonied. Veneers probably.

"I want to say, it's really *nice* to be out with a woman my age," he says. "It takes away the anxiety of any age imbalance whatso-ever. Like, even with a four-year age gap, that's like a high school

senior dating a *middle schooler*. Not that I want to control who
women are allowed to date! I'm always saying older guys should
be regulated like cigarettes, right? You can date them, but they
come with a big surgeon general's warning label that says He's
Probably Exploiting You—I mean, right? I think men who date
younger women should have to pay a tax that goes toward closing the pay gap. But I'd love to hear your thoughts."

Though she doesn't disagree, the way he delivers these sen-
timents, constantly soliciting her approval, makes her want to.
He's so plainly lacking compared to Neil—who, while no longer
in her life, nonetheless still functions as her standard.

She has no intention of going home with this guy, until after
three whiskey-gingers she starts talking about how bloated she'll
be tomorrow, which somehow doglegs the conversation toward
her eating disorder, then her situation with Neil. The Feminist's
attention activates like some motion-sensing light. Though he's
been laughing at everything she says, whether she's being funny
or not, it turns out he's the kind of guy who's only fully engaged
when she's talking about her pain, who subtly steers conversations in that direction, because it furnishes an opportunity for
him to demonstrate caring, which is not the same as caring. He
goes mercifully silent except for *Wow* and *That sounds tough*.
She is being genuine, knows she's on some level indulging him
and hates it. When a stranger's pool cue comes too close to her
face she slaps it to the floor.

Even after these intentional fouls, she somehow ends up going home with him, and all she can remember is thinking, at
least I'm in a position to do the pitying for once.

After spending ten minutes standing outside a pharmacy trying to pry apart the clamshell packaging around a dose of Plan B

with her fingernails, she goes on a dating freeze. She knows casual sex isn't inherently degrading, and any stigma around it is backward and boring, so it's extra annoying that her own experiences are failing to affirm her, convincing her that she must be doing things wrong and is somehow deficient, otherwise she would not be finding herself reigniting the slut-shame she thought she'd intellectually smothered in college.

All she wants is some credible vouchsafing of love and admiration from one non-horrible man who finds her interesting and attractive and good—who finds her good and attractive *because* she is interesting. Nothing more. She resents children and marriage too much to ever covet them, and since getting a blowfly larva removed from her leg after a high school trip to Tanzania, her fear of parasites carried over to pregnancy. It galls her to have to be so involved in all her cousins' and coworkers' and college RAs' weddings; her life feels like a never-ending search for eggshell or mushroom dresses. Every toast she has to write, and gift to register, and plane ticket to book, and male stripper to hire, and escape room to solve, and manicure to schedule, and stylist to suffer through, and group photo to mug for, and self-written vow to applaud; every baby to shower, and onesie to knit, and birthday magician to tip, and baptism to pretend to take seriously—each weathers away a thin unreclaimable layer from the enamel of her patience. Over the years she'd spent five grand on these events, minimum. Opting out would make her look unsupportive and cheap, but whenever she invited them to anything that mattered to her, mostly low-key birthday parties at bars, they always invoked boyfriends or childcare to get out of them, their unassailable pass.

She enters a months-long torpor where she barely leaves the

house except for work. Sudden billows of loneliness weaken her hands so badly that one time she gets trapped in her bathroom for a few minutes, unable to turn the heavy brass doorknob. She develops all these random leg bruises from clumsiness brought on by a new unwillingness to properly maneuver her body, and doesn't bother to move her tampon string out of the way when she pees, so she just walks around all day with a damp string. Going out no longer appeals to her; she feels paradoxically that everyone hates her and no one cares about her, not like damaged goods so much as expired. In bed at night, when the quiet is so deep she can hear her own metabolism, blades and spikes of regret slash around in her chest. So that she never forgets this pain, she takes some pics of herself crying, looking as sick and inflamed as possible so her future self would never be able to betray her by denying she was once this wretched. That is, assuming things would improve ever again. *My life's been stuffed into this tiny suffocating margin*, she thinks. If something is going to knock her so far off-course, it should at least be entertaining or make her seem worldly, like a drug addiction or a stalker. And then this feeds back into her whole thing about how she is and always will be unloved because she is simply ungood and unspecial, and could have been special, but doesn't have the innate passion or whatever to make herself desirable to anyone she'd want, or even to someone fairly tall.

Stale loveless boring endless dread: not even of death, merely the petty fear of becoming older and ever less likely. Though she has vague intentions of someday getting healthy, like when she went pescatarian a few years back, for lunch she eats the same soggy gyro at the halal cart outside her office instead of going to the chopped-salad place two blocks farther, and for dinner she stuffs a cold flour tortilla with turkey slices and shredded mozzarella and a squirt of mayo, each ingredient the same color as her, rolled up into a hateful dildo she crams in her mouth, barely chewing. No matter her mood, drinking always seems justified: either she's hopeless so who cares, or it'll help her sleep so she can theoretically jog the next day. Which she never does, because of the hangover—anyway even thinking about exercise makes her angry, the idea of willfully suffering to reclaim her looks against the time and effort she's wasted on this loser, or no, on the *idea* of this loser, and on an emotion nowhere near as nourishing as love. She fumes about how not only are women's indulgences framed as immoral and selfish, such that chocolate is sinful and ladymags are trashy and chick lit is a guilty pleasure, but that even the supposedly healthy alternatives, shopping, yoga, skin care, are demeaning in their attempt to pass off consumerism and vanity as self-care and, largely, just as selfish and immoral.

No surprise, then, that she finds solace in the simplicity of hate—how comforting it feels to hate Neil, how succulent the fantasy that the world's full complement of injustice could be concentrated in one stupid guy, and that to hate him silently, invent ways to undermine him, conscript others into this project, was to increase the world's fairness.

Her desk job gives her a chronic neck spasm, causing her to gasp whenever she takes a hard step, and making her unable to turn her head to the left. The elderly chiropractor she visits applies e-stim and heat pads for fifteen minutes. Then gets out some doodad that looks like a letter opener, greases it up, and performs excruciating myofascial release. "Military neck, we used to call it," he says, raking it like a strigil against her neck and shoulders, "though you kids call it tech neck, how's that for a generation gap? Jiminy Christmas, it feels like I'm massaging an anvil. You must love that phone of yours." When he's done, exploded capillaries map her pain purple across her skin. He recommends a neck brace; she can't afford one, so she asks if there are any cheaper options, and he replies, "Sure, you can make one yourself at home. All you need is a folded towel and a rope long enough to go around your neck."

She surprises herself with a hiccup that turns into a squall of sobs, wiping her sloppy face on the paper covering the padded bench, too waxy to absorb the wet. The chiropractor hastily shuffles over to unroll more paper.

This incident seems to set off an incontinence of tears, everywhere: in the pharmacy line waiting to fill her hydrocortisone prescription; when she fails twice to enter her PIN at the ATM; on the toilet at work watching a video about laboratory beagles walking on grass for the first time; when she sees her x-rays at the dentist ("It's not *that* bad," the dentist says, "but it is bad. You should buy a softer brush"). She cries so much her face-bloat becomes permanent. She pictures a calcifying bitterness taking the place of all the emotional fluid she's losing, like a bean unsoaking.

With her neck propped on a heat pack, she spends many joyless hours online, haunting Neil. Even though she knows she shouldn't care, and that of course he was lying the whole time, she sees that he and Cece are now officially dating. He posts photodumps: Cece in cutoffs and a bikini top at the park with a thigh gap the size of a pizza slice. Cece at the pop-up ice cream museum, at a murder mystery dinner party, disco bowling, in every shot smirking with her chin upturned at the same haughty rehearsed angle. Every photo announcing, *Look at her, here's who I'm dating, see how perfect she is, see how much I appreciate her, and therefore deserve her?*

The only way to compete with Cece without overtly bad-mouthing her, Alison realizes, is to silently outdo her. Until their recent troubles, Neil was always a dependable source of likes, and Alison knows the algorithm will show him anything she posts. So she will be mysterious and intellectual and unattainable, and hopefully show Neil how shallow and attention-hungry Cece is by comparison. How exactly to express all this in a photo is unclear. She's not going to post a picture of herself reading some fucking *book*. The subtext of every post is an expression of how one wants to be seen, and wanting to be seen reading is so corny it makes her blush even to think about it. She wouldn't be seen cooking or eating either, obviously. But what other interests does she have?

Trying not to make it look like a selfie, she balances her phone upright on her bookcase. It's too high and she can't tilt the phone downward, and the low angle from her nightstand is un-flattering. Every pic comes out looking "unapologetic." It wasn't that she was flat-chested or obese so much as ill-proportioned—thigh-to-ankle, waist-to-ass, shoulder-to-boob—in places she knows not even starvation would amend. Add to that her round cheeks, with deep smile lines that went down to her jaw, like a ventriloquist's dummy or old-person stage makeup. And then there were her teeth. And ears. And hair.

After consulting her friends' accounts for ideas, which only demoralizes her, she gives up and decides to dig up an old pic she's never posted before. Her hair was a different color then, so if anyone assumes it's recent, that's on them. She feels ill scrolling through her photo library, which contains many pics of Neil, and several of herself she'd screenshotted from his timeline. She selects a favorite from five years ago, outside a bar in a thrifted lace-up top and ripped jeans, with an unlit cigarette in her teeth. After searching for the sweet spots on the brightness and temperature sliders, she realizes she's spent forty minutes on this, so she captions it "smokin 🐍" and quits the app in disgust.

She gets the requisite likes from the usual people, nothing from Neil, and when she gets only one comment from her stepmom (so glad to see you healthy! love from home) she deletes it.

Creativity, dignity, reputation, not the discourse of images— that's where she can actually compete. What she needs is a thing. Everyone she knows has a thing and she doesn't. She used to think self-branding was beneath her, or rather that her brand was not having a brand, and that everyone who was cool would recognize this as authenticity. But with her confidence about her non-boringness destabilized, she has lately taken to wondering: Should she adopt a pet? Would that not also make the loneliness less debilitating? Conscious of her risk factors for becoming a stereotypical cat lady, she figures a bird will be cheaper and lower maintenance, and won't take much time, even though she has nothing but time. One day she sees a video of a talking raven on her feed and thinks, how cool. She didn't know they could *actually* talk. She likes that they can hold grudges. It's exactly the kind of thing her ideal self would do, casually own a raven; its illegality only makes it more interesting. She manages to find a seller online who sends her a video of a plump, captive-bred, white-necked African corvid with a ruffled wattle like a little beard, clicking and whistling and saying in a surprisingly manly voice, "Hi. Hi. Hi. You're cute. You're cute. Hi. Stop that. You're cute." She cancels a holiday trip home to pay for it and drives six hours out of state to pick it up, feeling for the first time in years the excitement of a vista-expanding adventure.

The raven, which she names Pootie, turns out to be a flesh-ripping fiend with a knife for a face. It nips and scratches her whenever she gets near, and is way too large for her cramped apartment, knocking over cups as it waddles around with its wings outspread, and it smells like soiled hospital clothes. Too late she learns they're mostly carnivorous, so she has to feed it wax worms and crickets, and buy rat weanlings online which she keeps in a Tupperware in her freezer, chipping them out from their communal slab in unnatural pieces once a week, hearing them pop loudly in the microwave. Within a month Pootie acquires odd captive behaviors, gouging the stuffing out of her duvet, bobbing and flinging itself against its cage and ripping out its own bloody pinfeathers, no matter how much she snaps her training clicker at it. It talks all night, even with the cage covered and moved into the kitchen, in its newly acquired lexicon: "Hi. Hey girl. Ow. Ow. Ow. Asshole. Stop that. Whatever. You're literally the worst. Literally. Krrrrr. Krrrrr. Stop that. Literally the worst. Want some water? Fucking freezing. Asshole."

Even this would be fine, were Pootie ever to give any indication, after all the shit and feathers and wet microwaved rats, that it loves her. But it defensively spreads its wings whenever she approaches, and only calms down when she leaves. In her care it will live up to forty years. She hates this fucking bird, she admits to herself, she should've gotten a cat, cats are obviously better.

By year's end she's so bored of being depressed it makes her angry, and, worse, anger has made her corny, incapable of any irony, lightness, or critical detachment. In college she used to read theory and mid-century novels by clever British women, for fun; she'd translated parts of the *Aeneid* in high school; she'd had some ideas for essays about why autofiction is bad. Now reading makes her feel lonely, and Pootie's clanging and pecking are too distracting anyway, so she listens to podcasts about love and sex addiction. Her favorite is hosted by a white Buddhist with a chesty voice who intones mantras over pillowy synths.

"You feel as if you cannot exist without love," the host says. "You are addicted to the prospect of unearthing new love like a deep-buried gem, of cleaning it and finding yourself reflected in its coruscating facets. It's said you can never love another person if you don't love yourself. Perhaps that's true. But this takes 'yourself' for granted: your *self*, which is only your idea of yourself. Without it, there is nothing not to love. Envision yourself as a glass of water so full it looks empty. Be a river stone, changing and changed by the current yet indifferent to it; be also the river. Imagine yourself as a sourceless sound, as the act of forgetting. As space itself."

The main outcome of all this is to make Alison wonder if she should start a podcast, maybe one about owning a raven, though she has nothing to say besides *Don't*. But she is as smart and charismatic as most podcasters, or used to think so anyway. You can produce them from home, even make money. Then she thinks of all the other pathetic podcasts by and for people like her, with the same tastes and worldview and craving for recognition, and the same impulse to commodify them, varying only in degrees of shamelessness, polish, and reach, the outcome in every case to make their audience even lonelier. Podcast subscriptions are a numerical measure of loneliness, she thinks. Everyone just listens to the voice that makes them feel least alone, and the lonely are the easiest to manipulate.

So she quits podcasts too, leaving her nothing to do but stream all nine seasons of the American version of *The Office*, then all nine seasons again, and again, that fucking melodica theme song playing from her laptop's trebly speakers over and over until her mind feels bleached by screenlight. She brings the American version of *The Office* into the bathroom with her so she doesn't have to be alone there, and can't fall asleep without it playing at quarter-volume beside her, sipping off her weed pen and dully prodding herself with her vibrator while watching this prechewed slop, so pandering and room-temperature, so *American*, this homeopathic dose of comedy that yet manages to perfectly silence some companionship-starved lobe in her brain until she nods off and wakes to her vibrator and laptop both dead.

On one of these nights, attempting to break these self-soothing habits, which make her hate herself in an intimately special way, she adapts an exercise from her old therapist, who once had her write a list of things she liked about herself; instead she makes a list of everything she dislikes about Neil. He rejected her, for one. He's not *that* great in bed, not *so* good-looking, kind of bad with money. One time he flaked on her birthday party, though he bought her a nice bomber jacket to apologize. The nipple-sucking thing was goofy too, wasn't it? Could it mean he has mommy issues? But every guy has mommy issues. And daddy issues. As did she. In fact, reviewing her list, the problem is not only that much of the list applies equally to her, but also that none of it is *that* bad, so it functions as an index of his forgivable humanity, reminding her that it might've worked out, if she were a better person. What hurts the most is knowing that his rejection of her was fair.

After this, she lies in bed weeping with her lips pressed together, and finds herself submerged in a fantasy of her and Neil years in the future, spooning in bed in the dark, with her telling him in a low dignified voice about how miserable he'd made her when he rejected her, how alone she thought she'd be for the rest of her life, and he would take this seriously and say, *I'm sorry, I couldn't see what we had, the whole time I was really just scared because I knew how good it could be and how crushed I'd be if it didn't work out, but it DID work out after all, and here we are and I'm sorry, I'm going to spend the rest of my life making it up to you*, now he'd kiss the back of her neck, and she would turn to him super slowly with her eyes open in the dark and say that he never really liked her, and he'd say, *You know that's not true, Alison, you're the best person I know, you're the only person I've ever cared about, the funniest smartest person I've ever met, and your body is so fucking hot and TINY and sexy, I just know you're going to be a huge success one day and I'll be there to support you the whole time. I'm sorry I'm sorry I'm sorry sorry sorry* and then they would fuck. In this fantasy she is also the only woman on earth, so he would not be able to leave her even if he wanted to, and even if she was the worst, she was also the best.

The film reel ends there and she reenters her body back in bed, always already alone, ruined by how infantile and self-serving her fantasy was, moreover impossible, since she knew she would never get Neil to love her, or receive an apology from him, or ever hear any of those nice things from anyone because they were not, any of them, true.

She clenches her eyelids and presses her fists into her temples, as if to physically crush this false conviction that Neil is in some way realer than everyone else, that he is somehow the axis of her life and the only one who can "save" her and his opinion of her constitutes her entire worth, having staked exclusive mining rights to her happiness, because of the irreplicable circumstances of how they knew each other, when at the bottommost level of truth she knows he's just . . . another . . . fucking . . . guy.

In this trough of insomnia, she takes out her phone, mindlessly opening and closing apps for the relief of activity, until she opens her photo app, and at the top is an auto-generated album titled 1 Year Ago. It's the blowjob pic Neil took, her hideous hopeful face beside his pale dong, and she feels punctured by this anti-versary, the knowledge that at exactly this time last year they were spooning in his bed. It's so unfair that the one piece of evidence someone once found her attractive was tainted by everything that followed, and that all these months later, without a millisecond's thought or effort, this one asshole she doesn't even *like* anymore can, by merely existing, make her feel small, brittle, ugly, vulnerable, and discarded, and no matter how miserable she becomes or how much she trains her anger at him, he will not be harmed. He won't even be aware of it.

She moves to delete the photo before remembering it is still the only tangible proof that it happened at all, so instead she makes an album called loser, uncommitted as to whether she means him or herself, and puts the photo there, revisiting it regularly. Every time she looks at it, she wants to delete it, but she can't surrender the only thing that makes her feel anything close to love.

The group chat plans a holiday potluck. It's the first time they've all gotten together since the internship, and Alison insists on hosting. She procrastinates all morning, but finally gets it together to spray her shower curtain and tiles with bleach until the dark patches vanish. The trendy buttermilk roast chicken she's seen online sets off her smoke detector twice, causing Pootie to caw and shit and bat its wings around. By the time everyone arrives all the windows are open and it's freezing inside. Na'amah, a friend of Sarah's who she's never met in person, shows up nine months pregnant, with her five-year-old daughter in tow. Alison remarks that she didn't even know Na'amah had kids, and Na'amah says, "Oh god, beleaguered-mommy energy is the *last* thing I want to bring into the chat, you guys are like my life raft. If I think about *Paw Patrol* one second longer I'll turn into a family annihilator. I've got another group chat for all that boring shit."

Na'amah is startled when she sees Pootie perched on the sofa's armrest, and asks her if it's okay to have it around her kid. Oh totally, Alison replies, though she honestly doesn't know, and is disappointed that they aren't more impressed by it, as well as annoyed that she's expected to childproof her apartment without even a heads-up. When it's clear Na'amah still has doubts, she stows Pootie in her bedroom.

As they eat, it's clear that no adult conversation is possible. Every few minutes Na'amah's kid coughs up macaroni, falls over and cries, or cries because nobody is looking at her sparkly nail polish quickly enough, or buries her face in Na'amah's armpit and mumbles that she doesn't *want* macaroni, she *wants* mango slices, obliging everyone to look over and coo, which leads to a tedious symposium about pre-K and language milestones and child airfare. Alison doesn't get to catch up with anyone, leading her to wonder if they hang out regularly without her and therefore don't need to catch up.

Finally, the kid needs a nap, so Na'amah lets her lie on the couch, and the conversation warms. She listens with interest as they discuss Sarah attending her mother's second marriage, and Anjali's recent date with a celebrated alcoholic war reporter, and Na'amah's efforts to secure better maternity benefits at her workplace. Alison's anxiety mounts as she realizes she has no updates of her own to offer, nothing that wouldn't make her look pathetic. Sidelining herself, her interest turns to intimidation, then self-loathing—they're all so much quicker and funnier and busier, always so effortlessly *on*, all their problems so valid and worthy.

By the end of the meal, with the chicken only politely nibbled at (somehow both charred *and* translucently cold on the inside; the guests keep saying *Let it rest, it'll finish cooking*), Sarah leans over and mouths *Everything okay?*, confirming that Alison's vibe-killing misery is palpable. Alison considers faking a migraine to get them out of the house when she hears a scream from the other room: the kid, looking for the bathroom, has opened the bedroom door and released Pootie. Na'amah, moving fast for someone so pregnant, frantically scoops up her child and soothes her on the couch as Pootie starts to flap and feint toward everyone in confusion.

Guys, it's fine, he's *captive-bred*, he likes people, Alison says, and hurries over to calm Pootie. She peels off a shred of the cold chicken to lure it over, causing someone to say "You're feeding chicken to a bird?" Finally she manages to get Pootie to climb her arm and says, Look! It can talk, I'll show you. Pootie! Say hello, say hi!, and the bird lunges and clamps her index finger in its beak, gouging a wide meaty gash under the second knuckle; in the cut she glimpses a flash of bone before it wells with blood. Arriving home at 2 a.m. from the ER with a turban of bandages around the finger that, according to the doctor, has likely sustained permanent nerve damage, she notices a strange shadow on her couch. It's a big stain in the shape of an upside-down bowling pin, right where Na'amah was sitting; it's not sweat or pee, which would have evaporated by now. She knows it's hot water for food stains and cold water for protein, but where does coochie juice fall? Vinegar, dish soap, lemon juice, and baking soda do nothing except widen and darken the stain.

You

Um, so.

Sorry everyone about the commotion last night.

I should've given y'all a heads-up about little Pootie.

He's not dangerous though. People don't get that about ravens, it's a huge misconception, all because of that stupid poem. They're only dangerous if you treat them that way. They just respond to the vibes you put out at them. They're like mirrors.

Na'amah

it's fine

we can meet at my place next time! I have a backyard

Sarah

yah no worries bb!

sorry girl we had to dip at the hospital, I had an early day and figured everyone could use a ride

hows your fingie? did you need stitches??

Tala

that bird was a v large boi!!

I was a bit startled ngl

but so cool! must b wild to live with ^_^

You

I'm fine. It's fine.

One thing, though.

Na'amah, I think you left a stain on my couch.

Kind of a big one.

Na'amah

oh fucc really? 😣

oy I've been using evening primrose oil to try and induce labor

I realized I had a big stain on my cooter when I left but I hoped it didn't soak through to the couch

SO embarrassing 😅 sry girl!!

gotta start carrying a damn butt towel around like a nudist lol

You

I've tried everything to get it out. Dish soap and hot water. Baking soda. Tide pen. Lemon juice just made it turn brown. Nothing works.

Steam cleaning would cost $199. I checked.

Na'amah

I mean

I guess I could pay for the steam cleaning?

as you know work's been fucking me so might have to wait till end of month for the funds

Edwina

That's nonsense, she's got a baby on the way and no income from the strike

Can you just flip the cushion over

You

First of all, no I can't, because I already flipped them once before. This was the flipped side.

And even if I could, I still wouldn't feel super amazing about it?

I just think it's funny how I have to like pretend that a humongous oily cuntprint on my living room couch isn't a big deal. Like I shouldn't be bothered at all and I have to be responsible for what y'all did.

That couch is the only piece of furniture I ever bought new. It's CB2.

Na'amah

umm ok

I got gooch grease on your couch and you endangered my kid's life

call it even?

You

I did not "endanger" your kid.

That is a ridiculous overstatement.

I put my raven away safely and he posed no imminent threat. If anything it's your fault for not telling me you were bringing a kid. And your kid's fault for opening random closed doors.

Na'amah

my kid is FIVE

How fucking date you

Sarah

hey so guys

Na'amah

*dare

Sarah

let's pump the brakes a bit

Tala

hard agree! let's all chill

good vibes only in this space pls (╯><)╯

hate to be That Vulnerable Bitch but this conflict is honestly a lil bad for my mental

not rly in a position to hold space for this rn ｡ﾟ･(>﹏<)･ﾟ｡

You
Oh. Gosh. Wow.

Sorry I did "conflict" (*texts) in your "space" (*phone).

Guess it's not a good "space" to "hold space" in.

My mistake.

Tala
excuse ಠ_ಠ

You
Must be nice avoiding responsibility by wreathing it in the language of self-care.

And glibly dismissing people's problems by just chanting "go to therapy" over and over and over again.

I should try that sometime! Sounds even better than therapy!

Sarah
ok uhhhh simmer tf down

tala and na'amah didn't rly do anything wrong

Anjali
yooo sorry sluts I was in a meeting !!

damnnnn you guys have been WRITING in here, catching up now 😜

oop

Sarah

and she did offer to pay for the steam cleaning?

and you did kind of put the kid in mortal danger? and it was just by the grace of god that it ate your finger instead?

Anjali

nvm

                                                                    You

Ha ha, cool. Cool cool.

All of y'all. So cool.

Your whole cute misandry circlejerk schtick is SO. BORING.

None of you truly hate men. You just like acting like these put-upon underdogs. 💩

Complaining about men is nothing but a lifestyle affection for you. And that's the entire basis of y'all's friendship. Think about that.

*Affectation.

Edwina

Girl if you don't

                                                                    You

It's all "Ew, boys" right up until the moment you get your boat neck wedding dress and your bonded pair of labradoodles. And start posting fucking Facebook letterboard memes for your parents where you complain about hubby's snoring and property taxes.

Or whatever the fuck.

Nobody here actually has real problems.

This is just a daisy chain of empty compliments. A validation cartel.

Or worse, because y'all also get to consume other people's suffering and feel, all at once, superior, gracious, and caring for it.

Edwina
"y'all"

You are from connecticut

Sarah
the group chat cop has logged on 😳

Na'amah

"no real problems" okay

so let's see, I'm pregnant, raising a kid, and supporting my family on a single wage in a media job that could vanish at any moment and doesn't even offer benefits AND it's a whole strike going on

now let's talk about *your* problems! what are they exactly

your friend didn't text back after you went psycho gf on him?

anime boyfriend pillow didn't ship in time for the holidays?

You
Like, Na'amah. Really?

You just posted pics with your husband in Cabo with the caption, and I'm copypasting here:

"Celebrating five years with this dumbass who brings me cold brew sometimes 🐱"

Like, we get it, you have a man, and he loves to laugh, that big galoot! Can't wait for his "as a father of daughters" posts. Like, tell us for the thousandth time about how he has no refractory period!

Na'amah
yes dear, I have a man! because I'm not a bitter crone

Sarah
ok Alison like we get it u punctuate texts bc u don't want to risk looking stupid even though it makes you sound amish

ur that bitch who wears a cami under a v-neck because ur too scared to be even a normal amount of slutty

the way u use highlighter makes u look like u xanned out in a tanning booth

You
Oh fuck off, Sarah. Literally shut up.

Wow, I'm so wounded by your trendiness.

Go back to soft cheating on your fiction MFA boyfriend with the other guy from your fiction MFA.

Sarah
plus ur dye job looks like shit and ur barcode bangs cover like 1% of your big ass forehead bitch

wrinkly ass forehead like the atari logo. there isn't enough botox in the WORLD

Anjali
also anti-asian, don't forget anti-asian

Tala
guysssss pls

the group chat is like the only thing that makes my job bearable (˘͟ ˘)

so can we just not??

burning sage over my phone rn

You
Oh. I'm so sorry you're bored at work.

Too bad you're not able to "hold space" with all that free time.

You named the conversation "shitty fake fucking bitches"
Today 5:30

Sarah
aww baby wants attention

won't someone puhleeeeaze change her big stinky diaper??

enjoy your internalized misogyny sweetie

You
ARE.

YOU.

FUCKING.

SERIOUS.

YOU'RE LITERALLY THE ONES ATTACKING ME.

I HAVEN'T INTERNALIZED ANYTHING.

I JUST DESPISE YOU BASIC CUNTS.

Tala has left the chat.

Na'amah
apartment not covered in birdshit = "basic"

k

Sarah
see *this* is why we started the other group chat

bitch you're shiesty

Anjali
23 skidoo 🖐

Anjali has left the chat.

Edwina
Smh sad and depressing

Bye

Sarah has left the chat.
Na'amah has left the chat.
Edwina has left the chat.

Although she's blocked him on all social media, through their shared friends' congratulatory posts Alison has been kept abreast of the many milestones of Neil's life the past two years: a hefty promotion, then suddenly quitting to pursue his dream of being a travel photographer, starting a joint Instagram account with those POV photos where Cece leads him by the hand through the rain forests of Borneo, through fish markets in the Maldives, hefting steel tankards in Budapest's ruin pubs, playing hide-and-go-seek at a Swedish IKEA, clicking a padlock together onto the fence at Pont de l'Archevêché. (How is it that she can envy experiences that she doesn't even want, would actually be ashamed to want?) Then: a reckless pregnancy announcement just three weeks after conception, followed by an ultrasound post. Everything is happening to Neil; he is living a real life, where relationships deepen and circumstances improve, the life she should have lived with him. Watching her own true life unfold this way makes her feel like a ghost, unable to be touched or effect any change. Except ghosts don't age.

So she is not surprised when she hears they're getting married. She receives a digital invite only to the reception, not the ceremony, and the Personal Note field reads: *The ceremony's super inner circle, but it'd mean a lot to me if you came to celebrate with us afterward. Bygones? Old times' sake?*

The sight of it trips her gag reflex and she covers her mouth. That's his idea of an olive branch. There's no way she'll go: her absence would be the cleanest and most dignified way to telegraph her disapproval without a word, a means to finally reject him back. Or maybe that's what he wants . . . to get her to silently recede into his past so that he can shrug and say, *Well, I invited her, guess she wasn't able to handle it, ah well, meep!* A nutty surge of dopamine at the sight of his name, the notion that *he doesn't hate her*, also has her thinking, stupidly, that the invite means he's not done with her, and he might be inviting her to finally apologize, which would restore them to their former intimacy, and from there, if the marriage falters . . . no, no. The best she can hope for is closure, the final extinguishment of hope. She decides she can go, as long as she doesn't make it easy for him.

She RSVPs, telling herself that buying the cheapest gift on the registry, a smoked-glass cake stand, is an act of spite and not thrift. Bringing a date feels cliché and would likely backfire, plus she doubts she could find one hot enough to inspire envy. She settles for showing up in a way-too-slutty cutout dress that makes her look like a backgammon board, in the hopes of both declassing the ceremony and attracting potential hookups.

By the time Alison arrives at the lovely bucolic farmhouse she feels like a submarine at crush depth. She's early, and awkwardly loiters at a distance, surrounded by tea lights and easels cheekily displaying the couple's blown-up social media posts, to observe the ceremony she wasn't invited to. Despite her titanic pregnancy, Cece's arms are no thicker. With short tender secular vows and an elegant handfasting ceremony, the newlyweds stammer over their happy tears. Alison would have cried even if she didn't hate them. She'd been good, she hadn't made any trouble for him, and this is where she ended up: there was no reward for being a mature adult who forgave and worked on herself. She rubs her numb fingertip when they kiss.

Neil is busy posing for photos after the ceremony. During the dinner Alison is seated at a table of children and ancient dying satellite relatives. He hasn't even noticed her. It's not until after the dancing has started, when his tie is whipping around to

Stevie Wonder, that she approaches him and asks to talk. His face goes solemn, and he follows her over to the fancy portable trailer bathrooms with the Aesop hand soaps.

Seeing him in his tuxedo, flushed with pomaded hair and a perfect beard, she feels like she's going to grow a tail and start wagging it, insanely thinks that maybe this has all been a delusion, that he secretly loved her this whole time and was about to prove it, and if she closes and opens her eyes, this will be *her* wedding. She tries and it isn't. The speech she's rehearsed gets scrambled into non sequitur talking points in her head, and looking at his expectant face, she hastily edits out the meaner parts. She says she's happy for him and doesn't want to cause problems for him ever again. She says she's doing fine, all she wants is some closure, that's all, and if he doesn't want her in his life, she understands and will respect that.

"Oh come on, dude, that was a billion years ago! Like, seriously, how could I be mad after all this time? We're good, it's all good. Let's just forget about it! Come on, come and dance!"

Hearing this makes her makeup feel heavy and dead on her face. To her it does not feel like a billion years ago; it feels like right now. He pulls her by the wrist toward the dance floor, and without looking she can sense him smiling. He's going to dismiss everything, forget it all, get away with it all, make her a stowaway on the superyacht of his life. It feels like if she lets herself be tugged to the dance floor, he will officially win, so she doesn't move, which only makes him tug harder, forcing her to seriously plant and backshift her weight to resist him. He says, "All right, fine, well, try to enjoy yourself."

Before he turns away, she raises the one issue she knows she's right about: Why did he lie about not dating Cece? Like it's okay now, it doesn't matter, but if he'd just *admit it* so that she doesn't have to feel crazy . . .

"I'm sorry, I truly don't remember that at *all*," Neil says. "And I don't think I'm someone who'd say that. Or I don't know, maybe it wasn't official then and I didn't want to jinx it. I mean, if I misled you, I'm sorry, but I can't apologize for something I don't think I did."

She feels her lungs inflate with fury and excitement, knowing that she has his email on her phone, and could rub his face in his lie. But she doesn't. It doesn't matter now if he lied or not, no admission will pop the gold balloons or snuff the candles or shatter the coupe glasses, it would not turn Cece ugly or Alison interesting, or revive her dead whatevership with Neil. So she drops it, a wedding gift of sorts, one that she can't afford.

Alison says she has a final request: Can he delete the photo?

"What photo?"

The photo you took of me, Alison says, *that* photo. Neil still doesn't understand, so she takes a long time to find it on her phone and show it to him. His eyes go round before he covers it with his hands. "Jesus, fuck! Okay, what're you going to do with it? Are you here to, like . . ."

She says she's not going to do anything, she just wants him to delete it.

"You're kidding, right? I deleted it like *immediately* after I sent it to you. That was a single-use thing. Like *why* would I hang on to that? I mean honestly, I don't want it to exist either, so!" Before she can do anything, he deletes the photo with a few nimble taps. "Listen, it's my fucking wedding night. I'm not dealing with this shit right now, I'm going to have fun, I'm going to dance with my wife, so, I don't know, go eat something. And don't get too shitfaced to drive home."

Alison gets shitfaced and drives home. She stumbles into her apartment, lurching like she's chasing after the upper half of her body, passes by her stained couch, startles Pootie away in a flapping scurry as she enters her room and collapses on her bed, landing painfully on her vibrator, which she tosses aside. Out of instinct she pulls out her phone to look at her group chat, finds it still empty. Breathing loudly through her mouth she types,

no one will ever know how I feel

no one will ever know how I feel

and looks at the words spinning and triplicating on the screen. She tries again,

why dont you care

why dont you care

The swell of sobs she expects rises up her stomach, then melts away. Somehow, she doesn't feel the usual rewarding jab of righteous pain in her chest. At first, she thinks, this could be closure, I've won, I have become the river stone and the sourceless sound. But it doesn't feel triumphant, it feels like nothing. She realizes that she's been realizing this for a while. She tests her newfound numbness on various painful thoughts: how he probably deleted the picture not because it was awkward, but because it was ugly; the fact that he is at this instant probably fucking his bride in her wedding dress; that unless she continues to cause trouble, he has no reason to think about her ever again. Where she once would wince, her heart is now as indifferent as her fingertip.

In the morning, she will awake to a makeup stencil of her own face on her pillow, a loud mosquito whine of tinnitus in the back of her skull. On her ankles she will feel a strange draft in the apartment; when she goes to investigate, she will discover Pootie has escaped out the door she left open. And she will feel the same, nothing, and think, maybe I *am* nothing, and this is the best I can offer to others, my absence in their lives, though they will never notice it or thank me. Still, their lives will be better for it. After many years she will see the whole saga not as a tragedy but as the beginning of a horrific process of self-understanding, at the end of which she will accept that whether or not it has been her choice, to be and feel nothing will be all that has made life possible.

AHEGAO,

OR, THE BALLAD OF SEXUAL REPRESSION

I. THE YEAR OF DAMP FEET

It takes Kant a year to write the one-paragraph mass email, another three weeks to compile the mailing list of friends, family, and colleagues, and three bourbons to send it. For his entire life he has so grotesquely imagined the consequences of coming out that he's only recently, at age thirty-one, stopped hedging to himself as bi or "flexible." He pictures his mother saying through tears that she never wants to speak to him again; he imagines getting evicted and dying alone in an unheated tenement, though he knows that this is unlikely to happen to a video game asset designer with two degrees. Part of him once believed that so long as his sexual proclivities lived only in his head, and sometimes on his computer, they didn't "count." Now everyone knows; his sexuality exists as a public fact, beyond his control. After sending the email he turns off his phone and spends the night vomiting from stress.

But the response is unanimously supportive. His friends reply with the visible spectrum of heart emojis. His coworkers politely underreact ("Oh neat! Psyched for you"). His mother is not thrilled exactly—she wishes he'd called her first, though he couldn't fathom doing this twice—yet she is neither disapproving nor surprised. The fact that gay marriage was recently legalized, and that his younger sibling Bee already came out as agender, probably eased things; mainly his parents want to know whether he still plans on having kids, and he tells them yes, just to give them something. And Bee simply replies: no shit lmao we shared a computer growing up remember. If it was that obvious, why didn't anyone tell him? Maybe everyone wanted to respect his process, or something; more likely no one cared, as it would make no difference, they knew he'd be alone either way.

Everything is so encouraging and underwhelming that it feels like nothing has changed—or rather, that what's changed is everything but him. Perversely he sort of wishes the response had been more dramatic and adverse, to underscore the significance of the change, though he knows he doesn't *really* want that. Having tailored his life to compensate for its lack of relationships, there's nothing compelling him to act on his new freedom. Everyone must assume he's going on dates, when instead he's gaming and masturbating more than ever. He will recall this post-coming-out phase of his life as The Year of Damp Feet, spent forever popping into the shower to rinse off his dick and stomach.

Beyond the inertia and under-confidence, the deeper problem, and the main reason Kant took so long to come out, is that he is also a sadist. He has known this even longer than he's known he was gay. He despises his libido for responding nearexclusively to degradation. Its origin is no mystery: growing up noticed by no one except in his public embarrassments, by some dark alchemy of childhood bullying, social invisibility, and overlapping cultural taboos, he has developed a sexual constipation that finds its only release in the fantasy of boundless, monstrous subjugation, reified and reinforced by the hyperspecific porn that has been his lifelong solace—the *yaoi* visual novels, the vore and mpreg, the 100 percent runs of fan-translated Illusion Soft *erogē* torrented from Hongfire, modded to replace the women with men. It all points to a desire to rehouse his own abjection in other men; render them pathetic and ridiculous so he can feel powerful and attractive by comparison; make them suffer the punishments that he, deep in the crawl spaces of his mind, fears he deserves. No matter how much he reminds himself there exists an ethical practice of BDSM, he can't convince himself that fantasy and reality can be fully partitioned, especially not by him. Everyone knows of the potential self-serving evils of sex, and at any moment, Kant feels, the leash could slip and he could hurt someone, humiliate himself, and discover that his loneliness and abuse were warranted all along.

To even try and act on his desires, he would have to be an entirely different person. Who has the desire and patience to be railed, much less *conquered*, by a jittery, inexpressive virgin? A dom must be tall, brooding, assured; no one wants a sadsack sadist, no one longs to be topped by a man shorter than his refrigerator. Kant's very presence in his own fantasies ruins the fantasy: when he imagines himself having sex, he pictures a Yorkie humping a Great Dane. He has the sort of coarse-sparse Asian facial hair where the skin's always visible underneath, and his body—well of course it's not good. He is five foot four, his hairline looks like a sandbar, and his wardrobe consists of a drawer of crumpled webcomic T-shirts and identical black Levi's 511s. He is too chubby to make a good twink, with asymmetrical creases on his abdomen pressed in by years of slouching in front of game consoles.

After a year goes by with his sexuality still theoretical, Kant suspects he must build his résumé. The apps, everyone says, the apps! But when he tries one it feels like a minuscule butcher shop, an infinite display case of rumps, loins, and wursts. Quickly he acquires a horrid efficiency at rejecting men on the basis of a two-inch photo or two-line bio—for having close-set eyes, or long gums, or because they kayak, believe in astrology, say they have "man fur." Even as he is vexed to discover his unjustified pickiness, what really inhibits him is imagining the men on the other end looking at his own unsmiling, gormless photo and laughing at it. Every fiftieth profile or so states it rather bluntly, no fats femmes asians, each applying to him in varying degrees; others were probably just too polite to say it outright. So the apps are only good for supplying tantalizing photographs of men he can't attract; even when he sees a guy hot enough to tempt him to send a message, he blanks on what to write, and that blank is soon filled with reasons not to.

Anyway, it would be hypocritical to complain about it, as he, too, is only attracted to tall, muscular, masculine white or Black men and the occasional hung Latino; his complicity neutralizes his claim to oppression. But he feels excluded nonetheless, and the more he browses, the more desperate he becomes, and the clearer the problem gets. It is a cairn of shames, towered and teetering on his chest, that the slightest movement will lethally topple: not only the first-order shame of the straight gaze, under which his self-worth was based on their social norms, but the second-order shame of *wanting* to cater to these norms despite knowing better; and the third-order shame of knowing that even if he tried to cater to them, he'd still fail; and the fourth-order shame of trying anyway. In his mind he is constantly answering

not only to overt racists and homophobes, but to straight liber-
als who were secretly disgusted by gay sex, straight Asian guys
who resented gay Asian guys for reinforcing the effeminacy ste-
reotype, white gays who considered Asians effeminate. Maybe
the desire to appease this imaginary focus group is some sort of
clichéd, middle-class-Asian flavor of striving. Or maybe, Kant
thinks, he is just a fucked-up person.

In spite of himself, he receives a message from someone ten
miles away, a rotund clean-shaven man somewhere on the Greek-
Spanish-Italian spectrum, trying too hard in each of his photos
to smolder from under the hood of a black Cornell sweatshirt
that conceals the true outline of his face. His bio reads simply:
sub bottom. something of a novice. no chit-chat let's meet up. can
host. Though it's unclear whether he means he's new to the app
or to bottoming or perhaps even new to dating, Kant realizes
being with someone similarly inexperienced might allay some
pressure, and he's grateful he can dispense with courtship. Kant's
hands sweat so badly that he has to wipe them on his shirt before
the phone will recognize his typing: Thank you for the message!
Sure, let's meet up! Looking forward to meeting you soon IRL!

As he pulls up in front of the man's house in a weedy suburb
forty minutes away, he notices things amiss. A Mayor McCheese
merry-go-round, clearly expropriated from a McDonald's play-
ground, lies next to a tree in the overgrown front yard. Only one
light is on inside the house and it's blue. When Kant knocks, he's
greeted by the man, red-eyed, wearing the same hoodie from his
profile pic, and exactly the same height as Kant. His shabbiness
makes Kant regret wearing a tie; Kant decides that if the man
asks, he'll tell him he came from work. The man takes no notice
of Kant's arm extended for a handshake, and bids him to enter

without smiling or making eye contact. Bong runoff and olive brine are smellable in the wall-to-wall carpet; the blue light is coming from a massive flatscreen TV whose display reads NO INPUT. "I don't have liquor or anything," the man says, and Kant, to indulge his hospitality, says a glass of water would be fine. The man picks up an already full water glass from the cup holder in his recliner, finger smudges visible in the blue screen-light, and hands it to Kant, then says, "All right. Shall we to the boudoir?"

The first thing Kant notices in the bedroom is a bowl on the nightstand, holding three uneaten potstickers in an evaporated puddle of soy sauce. The man immediately disrobes and Kant casts his gaze away from the thing he came here to see. The man then announces that he only wants to be spanked, nothing else. Spanked? Kant says, to which the man replies, "Yes, spanking. *Le vice anglais*. Is that all right." Kant says Oh, then says Sure, as he thinks *No*. Kant sits on the edge of the bed and the man takes his time uncapping, applying, and recapping ChapStick before lying prone across Kant's lap, his weight pressing the two of them deep into the memory foam. Kant flips his tie over his shoulder so it doesn't gather on the man's back, then asks if he should start spanking, and the man looks over his shoulder and says, "I mean . . . ?"

One nice thing about spanking, Kant finds, is that he doesn't have to be watched while doing it, and part of him does relish his position of power, though he is not particularly engrossed by mere pain, as it leaves dignity intact. He strikes the man's ass about as hard as he would a malfunctioning toaster, and only hears the man's level, unchanged breathing in response. Achieving erection seems as distantly likely as waking up in a foreign country by sunrise. After a few dozen spanks, the man says, "Stop, please." Kant stops, certain that he has somehow ruined things. The man says, "Can you like, try to get into it a bit more? It's really mechanical the way you're doing it, like it's *rhythmic*, it's just fucking strange. You can go a lot harder, too, I can barely feel it. And are you not going to say anything?"

Relieved that he hasn't caused any outright harm, though still too mortified to ask for guidance, Kant apologizes and goes to it again, varying force and tempo and location in ways that unavoidably resemble bongo drumming. As if to himself, he mutters *You like that?* and *That's what you get*, monitoring the man's grunts for feedback, and in his distraction, he swings low and accidentally smites the man's balls at maximum force, causing him to shout and roll onto the floor into a shrimpy curl. "God, fuck! What the hell?" the man says, all four cheeks aflame.

Kant leaps up and retreats into the corner of the room by the door, then escapes out of the room and the house in an ink cloud of apologies, hurries past Mayor McCheese, and gets back into his car. He spends the ride home marveling at how precisely the date had substantiated his fears, wondering if he will be somehow arrested; at home he masturbates, primarily to reset the board, feeling something jinxed about the load he's carrying around.

Still, he does not give up on the prospect of sex, only on reciprocity. It was foolish of him to imagine he possessed anything other men might want. Accepting this, he considers hiring a male escort, but, after his recent dating app debacle, is disinclined to meet anyone in person. He still browses escort sites regularly, though, and one day, in the navigation bar of one he notices a little red badge (*NEW!*). A click delivers him to a gallery of high-end, relatively realistic sex dolls with posable steel skeletons covered in TPE flesh. This new service offers to drop the sanitized doll off on his doorstep in an unmarked duffel bag and pick it up twenty-four hours later. This could be a good solution, for acquiring muscle memory—for all he'd been worrying about services, he'd forgotten about goods. In the past he's tried a male masturbation toy, one of those scientific-looking cylinders with thoughtful industrial design, lined with jellied nodules and frills and ramps, arriving in fancy matte boxes made to resemble smartphone packaging, but he didn't like how he had to sort of spatchcock it open to wash it. What he needs is a body, a physical one if not a real one, and a body that feels no pain can elicit no shame.

The doll is delivered in a large black duffel with an instruction card written in a casual jokey style intended to make the consumer feel laughed-with. A brunette with an orthogonal jawline and bumpy abs that look more like unnippled teats, it smells strongly of new rubber and takes hours to off-gas. It's chilly to the touch, requiring a minute of joyless foreplay to warm up. Soon he realizes that a body that feels no pain can't *be shamed* either, and to finish the task he has to play porn in the background, negating the remedial value of the whole project. After he's done, he strains his shoulder hauling the ninety-pound doll back into its bag.

With the body lying cold and bespooged by his front door, awaiting pickup, he lies on his couch, icing his shoulder. This isn't preparing him for anything, he thinks, except for even weirder equipment. Unwanted queries soon follow: What if he can *only* be attracted to his abstract fantasies, perhaps even to the very quality of their nonexistence? Could it be that his libido isn't stunted, but stillborn; that whatever limbic pathway joins stimulus to response has missed some crucial window of development and now only craves the unreal? Or is he just monogamously devoted to his fantasies, which have been his only comfort for so long that having a real partner feels unfaithful to them, these eidolons who never judged him and will never leave?

II. COMMUNICATION FIXES EVERYTHING

On his commute a month later, Kant passes a twenty-four-hour gym at a strip mall. The immutability of his race has always made him consider his own body likewise unchangeable, but he realizes that nothing's stopping him from becoming, at the very least, thicker. Wasn't coming out supposed to drive him to uncomfortable new ventures, and isn't the gym notoriously the place where hot men go to get hotter? It seems impossible that a few pounds of firmer flesh will heal any psychic wounds; then again, he's never tried it. He finally gets invested when he starts researching three-day splits and supplement regimens and meal-prep spreadsheets for tabulating optimal amounts of pea protein and white meat. Nothing is more comforting to him than min-maxing.

With this pleasant upswing of purpose, he signs up for a free day pass at the strip mall gym and, not owning proper work-out clothes, chooses to wear teal swim trunks. When he enters the gym, his glasses fog even though it isn't cold out. Beyond the check-in desk, damp bodies in polycotton invest themselves with hardness and diameter. He flinches when a barbell clangs to the ground nearby.

The locker room is a hotbox of armpit and Lysol. He's never changed in one before, not even in gym class, where he used to change in the bathroom, one of many reasons he'd gotten bullied, though it was for being Asian, not gay, that they called him gay. His other reference point for locker rooms is porn, which gives this one the surreality of a lucid dream. He knows it's silly to expect men with oiled V-tapers and blundering slabs of ruddy cockmeat striding about in a Roman caldarium. But he didn't expect it to resemble a public bathroom, with its echoing coughs and mildewed tile. Wet footprints and shoeprints track the rubberized floor. An untanned, de-eroticized butt hovers in his periphery. It is unbearable, too little space for too much attention parceled among too few. Fortunately he can change quickly, as he's already wearing his swim trunks under his jeans.

In the fluorescent lights, the thin nylon of his trunks reveals his bulge, making it feel simultaneously too large and too small. He warms up on the treadmill, but his swim trunks rustle loudly, and his car keys welt his thigh through the netting of his pocket, so he dismounts and approaches the weight racks with his head lowered. He's read that squats are the most comprehensive exercise, and he loads on the smallest plates that don't look comically small. The nearest person, a chestnut-haired white guy in a yellow mesh tank top and earbuds recording his bench presses in a sweat-crinkled notebook, remarks at him, "That looks heavy." Kant is fairly confident this is an insult. He tries to ignore the guy as he tiptoes to get the barbell up. The draping hem of his T-shirt trembles when he steps forward; his tendons creak and kneecaps pop in upsetting ways. Because his swim trunks are not absorbent, he worries sweat will begin to drip from them. As he totters back to re-rack the barbell, he stumbles and falls, and the barbell strikes the floor with a deafening clang. Everyone turns to look.

Tank top guy trots over and asks if he's hurt, picking up the barbell and setting it back with a grunt. Kant says, No, sorry, I'm fine.

"Need a spot?" asks the guy.

No, no thanks, Kant replies, and leaves before the guy can respond.

So as not to look like he's running in fright, Kant buys and drinks an enormous diet energy drink from a vending machine in the lobby, then goes to the bathroom and tees up at the urinal. Before he can start, the tank top guy from earlier walks in and installs himself two urinals away, even though a far wider buffer is possible. With the guy pissing freely, Kant's bladder seals like a panic room. He's been there too long to pretend he finished, and they're too close to pretend his stream is inaudible. So he decides to wait the guy out, and tries to focus on his phone. Then he receives a message on his dating app, from a guy named Julian six feet away: That looks heavy. Kant looks over; the guy, Julian, is waving his phone screen at Kant, with a smile that seems opinionated.

Speech clogs Kant's throat. He thought he'd feel a miraculous gratitude to be cruised, but he is so unconvinced of his own appeal, and so convinced of his inability to respond, that he ends up feeling like a sulky kid who won't kiss his grandma. Julian leaves without flushing, squeezing Kant on the shoulder as he passes.

After Kant finally lets out his piss and fart and washes his hands for a full minute, he seeks the guy out, who introduces himself as Julian. When Kant tells him he's new to the gym,

Julian guides him around, shows him how to load the leg press and unfold the cushioned platform on the assisted pull-up machine. He offers to Venmo Julian for the lesson, and Julian laughs. "Just buy me a drink sometime." Julian makes a show of friend-requesting him, gives another genial squeeze on the shoulder, and heads for the locker room.

At home, Kant forensically scours Julian's social media, finding only evidence of a thoroughly well-adjusted man, with rainbow flag and Caucasian thumbs-up emojis in his bios. In his photos he is boyishly close-shaven, and in all of them wearing the same black beanie with various gray Henley shirts, laughing with his arms crossed, like he always has a reason to laugh and someone there to photograph it.

Amid this research, Julian messages him suggesting they hang out, and he agrees. He wills his expectations low, preparing for a no-show, or casual racism, even somehow physical bullying, the sort that defined his adolescence and has made him generally averse to touch and male bodies ever since.

The date goes exceedingly well, mainly because Julian takes point. They meet at the kind of upscale Italian place that serves meatballs but not spaghetti, Julian arriving late with a crescent of lotion on his cheek that he hasn't fully massaged in, his stubble grown to the length where it just begins to acquire direction. Kant asks where Julian is from (Pasadena) and what he does for a living. Julian says he works "in the design space," then declares that he doesn't believe in small talk, especially anything work-related. Soon they find themselves agreeing that having kids is overrated, the French manner of keeping separate apartments after marriage is ideal, and college is an institution designed to reinforce class stratification, even though they both went.

They also share a history of being bullied—Julian for being emo, which he later realized was an excuse to dress up, which led to him coming out at age fifteen; being six years younger than Kant, he'd enjoyed the crucial lifeline of social media in high school. He talks about his strained relationship with his older brother, who was friends with many of his bullies, but who later wrote a successful college entrance essay about the heroic ordeal of having a gay brother. Trying to seem like he's commiserating and not one-upping him, Kant talks about the four white boys in middle school who would pin him down and take turns sitting and farting on his face. Julian cuts him off there, squeezing his hand and making a sympathetic expression on the exact midpoint between frown and pout, then says, "God, that's awful! I'm sorry to hear that. Though god, I probably would've been like, *Go ahead and pin me down, boys, I'll just cum!*"

Not wanting to seem skinless and unhealed, Kant laughs, like he was going to tell a light anecdote all along, even though the full story had been that the bullying soon escalated to other "pranks," which included prying his mouth open and forcing raw eggs and dogshit down his throat, or putting him in a chokehold and saying *Time to put the freak to sleep* until he passed out, or just wailing on him wherever bruises wouldn't show, one time hard enough that he shit blood. Nor, despite an unfamiliar urge to reveal what a damaged deviant he is, does he say anything about the episode two years ago when he stripped down to his underwear, unable to bear facing death nude, and sat in a warm bath with a kitchen knife on the closed toilet seat beside him, drinking two glasses of whiskey and a taking handful of aspirin to dull pain and prevent clotting, until enough courage came to sever his life, such courage never arriving, the tip of the knife merely hyphenating his forearm before he broke down sobbing into his knees, getting out of the lukewarm bathwater, feeling stupid as he put the knife back in the drawer, and now whenever he touches a kitchen knife it feels like a mild electrical current is running through it. Instead he talks about how he thought doggystyle meant anal until he was twenty-two, which makes Julian laugh until he coughs.

After three drinks, Julian with sleepy eyelids asks, "Okay, hotseat: When was the last time you were with a guy?"

Kant takes a long sip of water, wishing for the topic to change itself.

"Oh. Am I gonna be the first?" Julian says evenly. "What an honor. I would've thought you were a killer."

He's not sure what game Julian is playing, ascribing to him power and options he clearly lacks, but it doesn't matter, because now they're kissing in an Uber to Julian's place.

Following his first kiss, the loss of his virginity is an anti-climax. After a demure interval in the bathroom, Julian takes the lead and maneuvers beneath him, whereupon Kant discovers that though they may have chemistry, they do not have physics—Kant's thighbones are shorter than Julian's, forcing a relocation to the edge of the bed, then the trial-and-error of angles and newtons, going tangent when he means to go secant. Every position feels like doing a plank, and he's put off by the novel dimension of smell—however marshy and squelching his fantasies were, they never had an odor, and Julian's is eyewateringly tart, like some savory citrus. It feels counter-intuitive for someone so nice to smell so strong.

As Kant begins to worry whether he will be able to finish, Julian reaches back to still him and says, "Time out." Kant withdraws, sees a streak of scarlet on the condom, and unwillingly thinks *Fresh spring roll with sriracha.* He startles and stammers apologies.

Julian does a glance back and hurries off the bed, wipes his face with both hands in exasperation. "Ugh, sorry, this is so awkward—it's this hemorrhoid thing. It's fine! You didn't mess anything up. We just gotta call it for tonight. Rain check, okay?"

Julian's embarrassment should feel equalizing, letting Kant off the hook performance-wise; instead, he feels guilty for causing actual harm to Julian—then aroused by the harm, making him suspect his subconscious may have done it on purpose—and finally horrified by the arousal, to the point where he's turned off again.

Despite this failure, they keep seeing each other. Their compatibility rests in their shared taste for spending enormous amounts of time occupied together in silence. Julian, he learns, is someone who says *Right on* instead of *Yes* and never unsubscribes from political email lists, who believes the greatest song in human history is Passion Pit's "Sleepyhead" and owns a drawerful of Henley shirts. He is tanned and centered, his chakras agape, comprehensively Californian.

They spend Fridays and Saturdays together, agreeing that being in their late twenties/early thirties they are too old for clubs (though unlike Julian, Kant has never been to one). Kant will visit Julian's very nice apartment, exuding well-roundedness and hobbyist homesteading. Swing-top bottles of ginger beer ferment on the windowsill, near a rack of matching copper cookware. Tastefully concealed smart-home appliances and hot pink grow lamps shining on planters of lemongrass, basil, and weed. In the basement of his ground-floor duplex is a DIY woodworking bench, and a series of shelves and unfamiliar machinery that Julian explains is a cheese cave in progress.

Kant expends serious effort in seeming unslovenly and being a good boyfriend by cooking and cleaning a lot when he stays over at Julian's. In the morning Kant makes complicated toasts, with roasted shallot baba ghanoush or tangerine marmalade or smashed avocado, and coffee so strong it gives him contractions. He picks up the single-use contact lens packets Julian leaves everywhere; he finds internet recipes to make, spends evenings cranking and slicing pasta dough to make pappardelle with lemon zest. Occasionally the time this takes, and the ease with which Julian accepts these favors, makes Kant feel resentful, before he reminds himself that Julian never asked him to do any of it. At dinnertime the two of them bring the food into Julian's bedroom and balance the plates on their thighs sitting in bed to watch "something stupid," usually reality shows about either wilderness survival or cooking, and every time Julian will make the same joke about how these shows make food taste better. Whenever Kant gets up to use the bathroom, he asks if Julian wants another red wine, and the answer is always a sheepish yes. After three episodes, Kant will take both their empty dishes back to the kitchen, clean and dry everything, then slap all the light switches off, knowing Julian is lazy enough to leave them on overnight, and bring two glasses of water for Julian to keep on his side table because he sweats so much in his sleep, even with the bladeless fan he constantly has trained on his face.

In receipt of these unsolicited favors Julian likes to tease him for being a service top, but Kant understands his own intentions better than that—in the same way that he'd once converted his sexual repression and friendlessness into excellent grades, he realizes he has transposed his whole achievement M.O. onto his relationship, being helpful and solicitous and doing Julian's chores as if it will entitle him to what he wants, i.e., outlandishly violent and degrading sex. So all of this caretaking is just pointless sublimation, Kant knows, he really is a genius at channeling his bullshit into laudable endeavors, and it only deepens his conviction that he'll never be able to give Julian the easy loving he deserves, so maybe he should end things before they get any more entangled, so that it won't hurt as much to leave him.

Since their first attempt, they have not had sex. Sometimes in bed Julian will tug at the elastic of Kant's pajama bottoms or press an amiable semi against the back of his thigh, but it always stops there. For Julian, sex is just *stuff*—hand stuff, mouth stuff, butt stuff, the light attitude of a well-adjusted guy, for whom sex is dessert; maybe he doesn't need it as much. At any rate Julian hasn't officially complained.

It's when they're lying in bed that Kant feels most acutely the membrane that draws up over his heart in the presence of others. The prospect of undressing in front of someone else gives him overpowering willies, like rubbing burlap with cold dry hands, so he changes in the bathroom. His sleep suffers from the fear of accidentally kneeing Julian or waking him with his snores, and the ambient breeze from Julian's sleep fan dries out Kant's sinuses, so he wakes with his nostrils encrusted like a geode, and winces as he extracts the bloody caltrops hardened around his nose hairs.

In the summer, they attend a backyard party where Kant meets Julian's close friends, with whom Julian visits a different country every year. Entering a backyard patio crisscrossed with string lights, Julian says, "What's up, sluts?" to the assembled group, who are mostly white and all gay and very hot and tall in a rich way and artfully tattooed and eating charcuterie. Half are in tank tops and half in open button-down shirts, exposing opposite regions of skin, yet signifying the same type of ease. In particular Julian's ex-boyfriend, Noah, is appallingly buff, with a Thanos jawline, an immaculate Caesar cut. His abs are as craggy and segmented as a prizewinning pumpkin and run all the way up to his forehead basically. Julian introduces Kant to Noah: "So, this is my *boy*friend, he designs armor for a living. He makes these cool game music things too, what do you call them? Right, *chiptunes*—oh god, and you should see him play Mario, he can beat it in like five minutes, it's crazy. He's just the best."

"Whoa, armor? So you're like a blacksmith?" Noah asks.

It is awful, not only to learn that Julian believes these are Kant's main selling points, but to see how Julian must describe him misleadingly to make him sound interesting. No, um, Kant explains, it's virtual armor for . . . it's, it's a mobile fantasy game that's free to download and play but you can buy optional sets of armor that your in-game characters can wear, but it's purely cosmetic, and even though the armor doesn't give you any advantages our users like to customize their avatars so it's um a really profitable business model but a lot of gamers hate it and there's been articles about that . . . but yeah.

Noah makes active listening sounds at all the wrong moments, which only emphasizes how actively he is not listening. Kant is aware of reflecting poorly on Julian as everyone's interest visibly flags; to avoid being distracted by eye contact, he keeps his gaze trained over Noah's shoulder, and Noah keeps glancing behind himself to see what Kant is looking at. Finally, Noah says he's getting a drink refill. Kant can clearly see him walk straight to another group of people and talk to them.

Thereafter Kant spends the evening silently at Julian's heel, with the lowered eyes and ungladsome grin of primate submission, passively excluded from the conversations about celebrities he doesn't know, shows he hasn't streamed, and is acknowledged only when someone takes a question they've already asked Julian and regifts it to him. *How about you, do you like hiking too?* No matter how Kant replies, the answer is either *That's so cool* or *Okay, work!*

Which is fine, Kant is used to this. More disconcerting is seeing Julian's effortless shit-talk, in an unfamiliar swoopy voice, when he and his friends, between gossip about college friends and upcoming vacations, begin to discourse about subdemographics of gay men Kant has only ever heard about— DataLounge gays and Southern Catholic gays and theory gays, Tumblr tenderqueers and circuit queens and lumbersexual otters, Instagays who complain about getting fat in the captions of objectively stunning thirst traps. Julian mentions a man he used to date, who had a super ripped skinny body but a math teacher's face, and as he gets a big laugh, Kant can easily imagine himself ridiculed in far nastier terms. Seeing Julian in his aspect of fluent bitchiness makes Kant feel, all over again, like an unwelcome outsider in the land he was born to.

The alienation must have breached through to his face, because on the car ride home, Julian says, unprompted, "Hey, so thanks for bearing with me tonight, I know those guys can be a little sceney. Honestly, I'm *so* glad you're not like them. Sometimes when I spend too much time with the girls it's like, okay, that's enough for a *while*."

Even though the real problem was that Julian was acting just as sceney as his friends, Kant knows he should appreciate this declaration of loyalty. Then he feels bad for tacitly pressuring Julian into demeaning his friends, and begins to sulk again. He grips the passenger's-side ceiling handle. Since they started dating, he's allowed himself to hope that Julian would have enough patience, know-how, and communication skills for them both. All it does is make him feel like he doesn't deserve it.

You don't have to shit on your friends for my sake, Kant says.

"That's not what I'm doing."

You clearly enjoy hanging out with them. It's me you don't like, which makes sense.

"Hey! What's all this? I *do* like you."

Kant realizes it sounds like he's fishing for compliments, and that in doing so he might find the lake empty. He apologizes and stares at his stupid face in the sideview mirror, getting sucked into an emotional gravity well where he pities Julian for dating such a loser, and resents Julian for pitying him, and pities himself for being pitied, all of which cancels out into silence.

"Listen," Julian says. "I'm just saying, my friends are a lot of fun but they're not very . . . so like, Noah? One time I used his laptop and saw that his last search was 'what are military industry complexes.' When we first started dating, he said he'd have to 'work around' me being an Aries moon, like he was doing me a favor!"

You really don't have to—

"No, wait, I have more. He'd have me vet all his selfies, like twenty versions of the same one through different filters, and after posting it he'd give me the running tally of how many likes it got. Oh, and he once said he'd never been in a *magnanimous relationship*. And this other time he asked me where the Sydney Opera House was. Don't get me wrong, I mean he's gorgeous, but—oh my god, I just remembered the time he hurt his neck at Orangetheory and built this, like, *sling* that hung from his ceiling to support his head while he watched TV. Isn't that nuts?"

I had to get carpal tunnel surgery from gaming, Kant says, so I must be worse.

"Okay, but you didn't build *infrastructure* for it."

I had to wear a brace!

"All I'm trying to say is you're a giant upgrade. You're nicer and more interesting, and way smarter."

But not as hot.

"You are being *so impossible*! You're absolutely as hot as Noah, cum gutters aren't everything. And there is an annoying way of being hot, you know. He would literally text me updates about his abs."

As much as he appreciates the support, he doesn't actually *want* Julian to like him for his niceness or intelligence. He'd hoped that being in a relationship would somehow make his self-worth feel less concentrated around cartoonishly yucky sexual degradation; yet six months in, neither of them has acknowledged Kant's obvious avoidance of sex, because he can't or won't specify his needs, being convinced that he is always in debt and on probation, that Julian's assenting to date a stammering moon-faced pornsick Asian virgin in his thirties was already asking too much, and any extra demands would only risk losing everything, plus what could be more pathetic and off-putting than begging Julian to please pretty please be terrified of his cock. And on top of all this, Kant is basically someone who, in his normal life, wants monogamy, stability, even kids someday, a life entirely incompatible with his hideous desires, so wouldn't it be simpler to refrain from indulging them, lest they get their roots even deeper in him? If Julian hasn't brought up the sex problem, it's probably because he's fine with not having sex with Kant, and who could blame him.

To avoid the question of sex, Kant pursues a strategy of over-eating on purpose at dinner, which gives him chronic acid reflux that actually does make sex impossible. The ensuing weight gain deepens his sense of ugliness, which bolsters in turn the suspicion that any attraction Julian demonstrates is charity.

And yet: Kant also wonders if his own reticence is a smoke-screen to avoid admitting that he's never been very physically attracted to Julian either. It's not that Julian doesn't take care of himself, with his thrice-weekly gym visits and flexitarianism; he is undeniably good-looking. But not *perfect*. He has a recessed chin and patchy leg hair, butt acne, a dick that could be two inches longer (though still bigger than Kant's), and occasional hand eczema requiring creams and latex finger cots. None of this comports with the fantasy in Kant's head. It would be un-conscionable to ever suggest that Julian is inadequate; it's clearly *Kant* who's lacking, for looking the way he does, and wanting the vile, absurd, disgusting, and physically impossible things he wants. Yet the sense of his own guilt and hypocrisy do nothing to counteract the wanting.

So instead Kant's dissatisfaction transfers over to ordinary annoyances, like how Julian nags at him for patronizing com-panies on the BDS list, but will happily use his rich friends' SodaStreams and eat their Sabra hummus, laundering his con-sumption. All the little projects he always says he's working on but never finishes, not just the cheese cave but his Studio Ghibli–themed novelty tarot deck; his graphic novel about the 2008 subprime crisis; three kittens adopted and rehomed. Or how Julian can absolutely never use the word *racist* to describe any offensive thing his white friends ever do, only *kinda weird*, *unfortunate*, *messy*, *chaotic*, or if it's truly indefensible, like when Noah posts a photo shoot of himself in geisha drag with a sequined Chinese-takeout-box-shaped purse, *not great*.

But unlike the sex, these issues are all forgivable and workable, and there's never enough friction to spark confrontation: Julian is always so willing to hear out and reason with the other side, the kind of guy who takes daily walks to feel more connected with his neighborhood, attempts to change the minds of bigots in online comments sections. They never fight, only have levelheaded contretemps in normal speaking voices before arriving at respectfully clarified stances, concluding with one of them saying *I definitely see your point though* or *Maybe I'm being obtuse* or *I think we basically agree, this is just the narcissism of small differences.* Even when it's obvious they don't agree, Kant never feels it worthwhile to push any issue, because the relationship, he reasons, matters more than winning a fight. If he's going to be a doormat, he should at least be a welcome mat.

Meanwhile Kant does nothing but feel guilty that his ultraniche, polymorphous sexual urges should outweigh fondness and kindness and sympathy; that the fulfillment of these urges seems to be the only thing his psyche accepts as love at all. If Kant dares to ask for what he wants—if it is even possible to articulate, rather than experience as a nightmarish mural of angry mental events—he knows Julian will leave him; or worse, he'll try it once, realize what kind of horrible degenerate he's dating, *then* leave. Neither would do anything to quash the desire, might possibly even intensify it, so why stimulate an appetite that can't be sated; why not try to reprogram himself into wanting what is good and real? Why not be grateful that he's found someone like Julian who can tolerate him and doesn't exploit his gratitude? He'd never want to offend Julian by implying that he's settling for him. But never expressing his misgivings means he can't get into any of his larger shame issues, so instead he acts weird and squirrelly and sneaks out of Julian's bed at 2 a.m. to watch porn on his phone and glumly ejaculate in the bathroom into a tissue wadded around the tip of his cock like a silencer.

After a few weeks of this, Julian starts trolling him. Once while watching TV Julian reaches over to knock on his belt buckle and says, "Anybody home?" Another time at breakfast, Julian squints at the back of an oat milk carton and says, "Huh, that's weird, take a look at this." On the side of the carton Kant finds a blue Post-it that reads

MISSING: MY BOYFRIEND'S DICK

LAST SEEN: IN MY BUTT

REWARD $69,420

NO QUESTIONS ASSED

At this goof, Kant laughs lunglessly and leaves the room.

One night before bed, with Julian in the bathroom, he sees a notification on Julian's phone from his ex, Noah:

how goes it with the nevernude boy 🦫

is he still not giving up the cahk

he should try putting it in rice 🌾🍚

Kant feels a cold glaze ladled over his heart. He has no time
to plan what to say before Julian walks in, and without thinking, Kant throws Julian's phone at the wall hard enough to scuff
it, and turns away. Startled, Julian retrieves his phone and, after
reading the messages, initiates an hour-long monologue about
boundaries of trust, the inherently facetious and exaggerated nature of the kiki, what is and isn't fair game to discuss with close
friends about a relationship, the subtle contingencies when the
close friend is also an ex, and how the rice joke was about water-
logged smartphones, not Asians, though the word choice was,
Julian concedes, *not the best*.

Right around when one of them would usually be saying *I
get where you're coming from*, Julian says, "But isn't this actually
all about sex? I mean, six months and we've only done it once.
That's weird, right?"

Kant pushes himself upright. Briefly he feels that crying might
exempt him from having to explain anything, and he puts his face
to his knees to try and force it, but he is more humiliated than
sad. Julian pushes forward. "I want to apologize, again, because
it's totally on me for not communicating more, which is part of
why I vented to Noah. I wanted you to take your time, because
you're still new to all this. I should've been more proactive. I even
thought it might be a little problematic and, you know, trope-y to
imply you were repressed. Am I wrong though?"

Not really, Kant says.

"I'm just putting it out there, I'm down for anything you
want to try, like *ennn*-ything. It'll be fun! I'm like the furthest
thing from vanilla."

Julian may not be vanilla, but he is still ice cream—sweet,
popular, wholesome—whereas Kant is more like a plate of

mashed eggplant braised in snot. He tells Julian he'll consider it, but he's not sure he's ready right this second.

"Do we really want to kick this can down the road?" Julian's posture improves in a problem-solving way, his gaze so probing it feels like he's looking at his own reflection in Kant's eyes. "How about this. Name one thing that gets you reliably horned up. Try it this one time, and I promise I won't judge you or bring it up again for, like, a month."

Kant becomes conscious of chewing a bloody gouge in the skin of his bottom lip, and says that promising not to judge implies eligibility for judgment.

"Oh come on! I just want us to *work* with each other. There's no I in cum! Can't you let me decide if it's okay or not? I feel like you're worried I'm going to abandon you or something."

Kant has never felt close enough to anyone to feel abandoned, although, he thinks, it would be a sympathetic cover story. He knows Julian won't let up until he makes some kind of burnt offering of his interior life, so, mustering offhandedness, he says: All right, one thing I think I would enjoy is, um, facefucking. Hearing his own words, his head feels like a flickering lightbulb that's barely screwed in.

Julian maintains a therapeutically straight face. "Facefucking? That's *it*? Oh my god, I saw a guy get fisted like a sock puppet in broad daylight at Folsom last year. So you're a top who likes getting top. That's great—as you may have heard, there's a shortage. Like, if this all's what you're worried about, then you are well and truly bugging."

This is not what Kant is worried about, though it's true that a majority of his fantasies feature him jamming his cock down a buff man's uncooperative throat. He has always figured this has to do with the symbolic valence of gagging as the reflex of disgust, that it relieved his anxieties around another person's disgust by inducing it on purpose, part of his larger you-can't-fire-me-I-quit ethos.

But this is not even the problem, as Julian continues his reassurances; the problem is that facefucking is by far the least bizarre and disgusting thing he wants. Kant's voice halts and struggles, like he's trying to say a six-digit number in a foreign language. Finally he says, Well, not just facefucking, it's more close to, um, degradation.

Julian does the annoying thing of listening too hard, treating his words too meaningfully, at a moment when Kant would relish the option of ironic distance.

"That's cool," Julian says. "Why don't you show me the kind of stuff you're into? We can even incorporate it somehow, since you're, like, used to screens? Gimme a genre?"

Kant tucks his lips, and does not say the word he's thinking, *illustrated*.

"Or how about *I* just name some things, and you tell me what appeals to you. Sissy play? Knife play? Water sports?"

Kant shakes his head. For him, sex is not play, and not sports, nor even work—sex will always be a trial, ending in a verdict.

"Oh—scat! Is it scat? Or do you want to like, pretend you're white?"

What, Kant says, No, wait: What? You think I want to be *white*?

"No, no no no." Julian rubs a spot on his skull like it's been whapped with a tennis ball. "Like, you know, raceplay . . . I was thinking maybe that could be why you're embarrassed—or not embarrassed, but difficult to, like—hmm, let me start over. I'm sorry if that was problematic, I don't mean to upset you. Uh, what was I gonna say . . . Listen, to be honest, it sort of feels like I'm playing twenty questions here, and I could use some guidance. Talking about sex shouldn't feel like defusing a bomb! You've got nothing to be embarrassed about."

Here finally Kant perceives the true rift between them: Julian doesn't know the difference between embarrassment and shame. How shame soaks, stains, leaves a skidmark on everything and, when it has nothing to stick to, spreads until it does. Embarrassment is contained by incidents, gets funny and small over time; shame runs gangrene through the entire past, makes the future impossible. You can't own it or laugh it off, only try to bail it out in sloshing bucketfuls, drenching yourself in the process. Embarrassment is an event, shame a condition, one that Julian has somehow either mastered or never experienced, which explains why he's so easygoing, and why, to him, the world is so tractable, why all seems fixable with talk. What's inside Julian is smooth and fragrant, his desires desirable, and so his words are gift wrap, sometimes sloppy but always appreciated. Whereas if Kant ever relaxes his vigilance, allows his own sick and malign requirements to escape through the candor of voice or touch, they could never be recontained. Plus, there's this inkling, with Julian's soigné friends and ambiguous employment and the Dartmouth diploma that he never mentions but hangs framed on his bedroom wall, that wealth is part of it, somehow. And/or race. The power that all this confers on Julian can't be roleplayed away.

"I'm just not getting what's wrong, if I say I'm game," Julian says, ruffling and repairing his hair. "Like, not to put you on the spot, but don't you trust me?"

I don't trust *me*, Kant says.

"I know it's scary to be vulnerable, but if you can jump this hurdle, you won't have to keep *living* like this. You know exactly what I mean, because you came out like two seconds ago! Didn't that help, wasn't that liberating, wouldn't you say you're happier as a result? Wouldn't it be a shame to go through all that, just to stay pent-up about this one last thing? And you know, I have my problems too. Trying to cum on Lexapro feels like starting a fire with one stick. And to get super real, I'm not like, *exactly* a bottom, all I know is that you're *definitely* not. I expected us to experiment over time. And I still expect that! But even if this doesn't work out . . . like, if sex is all I wanted, it's not exactly hard to find—"

For you, Kant says, for you!

"Yes, for me. Which is why I'm looking for a lasting intellectual connection, and, sorry this is gonna sound so LA, but like, a *heart* connection. And I think we mostly have it, this is the one thing that's not clicking. I mean, sex is important, it just is. So would you please give it a try?"

Julian is being far too accommodating to not accommodate back. Kant says, All right, and he takes off his shirt and feels dumb and hard-nippled in the air-conditioning.

"Right on! We're doing this! Now it sounds like, if I understand correctly, you want to sort of control me? So don't bother asking if I'm okay, just let yourself go, and if I need to set boundaries, I'll tap your leg, as long as you can promise not to be upset. Not that I think it's likely, I'm covering our bases is all. Okay?"

These humane, clear-cut instructions have the unfortunate effect of dampening any illusion of power; it feels like being briefed after coming out of a coma. The precautionary atmosphere doesn't exactly make him feel like the homicidal cosplay Viking his stupid libido requires him to be. Julian tosses a wrinkly brown throw pillow onto the floor beside the bed and cracks his neck loudly as he settles down on his knees. "Is this good? Or clothes off first? Paint me a picture. Remember, you can do and say anything you want. No judgment at all, just ask."

Okay. Okay. So, first, I guess—could you suck it? Kant says.

Julian goes to it, keeping supervisory eye contact, slathering up and down the sides of the shaft. It feels agreeable enough, though Kant is not able to get much firmer than an overripe tomato. He nods, to appear grateful, while inwardly he plays out how he'll apologize for his failure whenever this is done. After five minutes the pleasure reaches a shallow plateau, which Julian must sense, because he says, "Remember, you're the boss. Give me orders."

Maybe, Kant says, you could change your expression? To be more like, I'm giving you a hard time. No, I don't want you to look sad, more like uhh—flabbergasted? But also like, reluctant. And so ashamed. I'm not saying this well, sorry.

"Say more."

So I guess I mean I think I feel like I want you to look, like, *alarmed* by the size of my cock. And also sort of disgusted, like it's made of shit, but also you want it so bad that it makes you a bit brainless . . . um, do you know what an ahegao is?

Julian halts midsuck. "Ay-gow?"

It's where you like, cross your eyes and look up, with your tongue hanging out.

"Can you show me? Or no, hold up, I'll just look it up on my phone, one sec . . . hang on, it's being slow . . . Oh, cute! So it's from anime? Right on, love it. Here's the thing though, I don't know how to cross my eyes. They only go to the left or right. Okay wait, I'll try! There, am I doing it?"

That's more like surprise, Kant says. I'm looking for something closer to uh . . . ecstatic inanition . . . and sort of like, you can't believe this is happening? Your eyebrows should be more lowered, not raised, but your eyes should still be wide.

"I got you," Julian says. Then makes the same face as before.

Now I'm going to try to facefuck you, Kant says, sort of rough, if that's okay. Here goes. Okay. So it's good your eyes are watering up, but see if you can make them not turn red. Can you make an expression that's, um, like, this has never happened to you before, and you're almost, like, cumming to death? And can you try the ahegao face again, and also make a peace sign? Sorry if this is too much. Okay, um, I need you to not breathe so loud through your nose.

He feels two gentle taps on his thigh. Julian pulls away and wipes his mouth, trying not to gasp. "Sorry, it's all good. It's just not super easy to, you know. Not breathe."

Oh, yeah. Yeah, don't worry about it. We can stop.

"No no, you're good, it's all good! I like learning what you're into, it's cool, it's a process. But like, this, it's just that this is all very—specific! Feels like I'm sucking off Stanley Kubrick over here, ha ha . . . oh hey, come on, that was a *joke*! Hey! Hey. I can see you going into your head. Can you stay with me? Stay with me!"

Julian's pleading makes him sound like an EMT watching someone bleed out on a gurney.

"Maybe it's too much pressure. Let's"—Julian glides his hand in a circle in front of his face—"reset. What if we structure it more like a dialogue? Just answer quick, first thought best thought. Where do you want me to touch you?"

Kant thinks, Oh great, the Socratic method. Gamely he says, My cock.

"Gotcha. Now what do you want me to do? Say it like you mean it."

Um, suck it. You fucking . . . pig.

"Good, *good*! Then what?"

Now I want to put you in uh, in um, in a jar.

"God yes, put me in that fucking *jar*, what am I doing in the jar, Daddy?"

And, um. I want to shake the jar so you're coated. And then pig, I mean pickle—I want to *pickle* you in cum. I want you to drown and get pickled by my cum, you little, uh, pig.

For all this effort, it's about as sexy as any other improv game. In particular getting called *Daddy* distracts him into wondering why his son would be white. Kant decides to make a dramatic gesture, if only to spritz and wipe the last few moments off the record. Hoping his feelings will follow his actions, he seizes Julian by his hair and pushes down hard. Julian's eyes react first with real surprise, then a put-on, overexaggerated fake surprise. Another thing amiss: no matter how hard he pushes Julian's head down, his cock doesn't meet any resistance. He stops and lets go of Julian.

Julian sits up and wipes his lips slowly with the back of his wrist, clearly buying time to think before he says, "So, I have a really *long* mouth, seriously! I had to wear a special retainer in middle school, it was a whole thing. Let's not even worry about it. Shall we proceed?"

The possibility that *short dick* passed through Julian's mind for even a nanosecond is enough to kill everything, a drop of detergent hitting the greasy surface-scum of his lust. Julian tries for another five minutes, then looks up at him with heartbreaking empathy and says, "Um, I think he might be tired."

With his dick now sequestered in the third person, Kant knows there is no recovering. He reaches for his boxer briefs and turns away, though he knows Julian is still attending to him with his full sensorium; it feels like being acquired by some sinister face-recognition algorithm.

"Hold up, new concept," Julian says, reaching over to touch his thigh. "How about we get you some molly? I'd take it with you if it weren't for the Lexapro. I'll call my guy right now."

Ignoring Julian, he gets fully dressed, puts on his ugly sandals, and makes for the door. His syrup feels like blood. His air is full of head.

"Wait, are you leaving? Like I don't want to push you, but I feel like we're eventually going to end up having this same conversation all over again, so could we just—"

Kant thanks Julian for giving this all a try, being so patient.

Julian performs a loud sigh. "All right, well, I'll see what you're up to tomorrow?"

Kant says Sure, and leaves. They never see each other again.

III. ADD CUM

Two months later Kant has made a full return to the conceal-ment of the closet, and the consolement of his consoles, and the contentment of content, having no ambition beyond raw existence. His feet once again damp. He becomes conscious of how his furtive and constant masturbation, which has always felt oddly sacramental, is not, maybe never was, an outlet for thwarted lust; it is a pacifier, a syringe of oblivion. He has ac-cepted that it is the form of love that fate has assigned to him, one-sided and ersatz, the only one available to him in this life-time. Nobody gets a perfect life, and the sane thing to do is to stop hoping for one and enjoy what he can. Too bad, he thinks, that this honesty about his true nature has come too late to spare him any grief.

With much to pacify, he explores new terrain in the realm of cam sites, then adult-content-creator subscriptions, and finally custom-order porn videos. On the most popular site, he searches muscle twink and cum fetish and hard degradation until he finds a provider who gives him the first stirring of hope since leaving Julian. His name is Cody Heat, and he is, judging by his sample content, actual perfection: kink- and fetish-friendly, bright blue eyes, biceps like veiny mangoes, a torso riven with channels and trenches, a thick but pointy tongue, the ideal of the ample, bombproof, round-assed muscle queen. Just reading the numbers 6'3" and 225 makes Kant's cock unfurl. It would be private and anonymous, and since they'd never meet, this man could never have an opinion about him. No worries about overstepping boundaries, because Cody could always opt out. And there was an undeniable erotic charge to placing an *order*, a command to a stranger to humiliate himself without even seeing who was making him do so. He refuses to think about whether Cody is desperate for the money—refuses, because he worries it might be a turn-on—and opens the video order form, which offers a list of options:

- ❏ 4K HD @ 60 FPS (free)
- ❏ Solo (free)
- ❏ Add Cum (+50)

- ❏ Add Bl**d (+200)
- ❏ Say Your Name (+50)
- ❏ Bad Dragon (squirting) (+50)
- ❏ Gape (+100)
- ❏ With a Buddy (+400)
- ❏ Butt Plug w Tail (+50)
- ❏ Complicated Script (+100)
- ❏ Special Costumes (email for rates)

Allow 2–3 weeks for turnaround. Email codyheat [at] pr*t*nm**l [dot] com with questions or special requests.

It's marvelously similar to ordering food off a touchscreen, or booking a haircut; the simple presence of a menu furnishes the comfort of a clear-cut transaction sanctioned by the market, where all parties know what they are getting into. The specificity of the options, too, suggest that this man is a jaded adept who will be hard to offend.

Kant's face goes slack with lust, watching his twitching knuckles type at terrifying speed as he fills out the blank text field describing his desired video, unable to make himself look at the words he is producing, yet, even so, amazed at the ease with which he can describe what he never could before. Words appear onscreen as if pushed from his eyes, or somewhere more vital and embryonic, his brainstem, his heart.

Greetings, Mr. Heat! I'm VERY interested in commissioning a custom video, and I'm submitting the concept for your pre-approval. I'll provide a "content warning" up front, as

I think this might be quite a bit more graphic than most requests, and sort of detailed and long, and will involve the extensive use of practical effects, plus include sissification, mild raceplay, and what could conceivably be categorized as gore (100% staged, I hope it goes without saying). If you feel offended or overwhelmed at any point, please feel free to stop reading and go about your day, as that is not my intention, and accept my apology in advance.

Well, here goes! I've split it up into three "acts" to pace it out.

Setup/Backstory:

You are an attractive straight man at the gym. (A green-screen of a typical weightlifting room would be acceptable, though if it's an option, I could scout a discreet location to shoot in real life.) You live an ordinary and healthy life, with close friends, hobbies, steady work, a 401K at your design job; it's important that you look "normal" (combed hair, henley shirt, distressed jeans—not sure if this qualifies as a Special Costume, but happy to pay the fee regardless). But unbeknownst to everyone else, and even to yourself, you are gay; you deeply fear that it is latent inside you, and that under certain conditions these tendencies would involuntarily "come out," as it were.

Act I (mins. 1–8): "The Call to Action"

While you're in the middle of a 315 lb. barbell squat, you see me: a seven-foot-six Thai-American man wearing a long scarlet cloak, like Vincent from *Final Fantasy VII*, and shining bronze pauldrons, like Auron from *Final Fantasy X*, if you've ever played those. My cloak's cowl neck conceals most of my face, and my giant bulge casts an imposing shadow across my leather pants. (FYI you don't need to supply an actor here to play my role; the camera should stay on you and your reaction, I'm just describing what your character is seeing here to help you understand your motivation.)

As you see me enter the gym, your cock gets hard instantly, to your great alarm. The closer I get, the more painfully and pleadingly it strains against your tight jeans, like a crowbar nearing an electromagnet, until at last I simply make brief eye contact with you and your zipper instantly *EXPLODES* (here please dub in a sound effect of tearing fabric and a KA-POW!!!). Your big fat cock punches out through your underwear at a 45-degree incline, big as a can of computer duster, balls bursting out in close pursuit. Your cock is so engorged that it hops with every thump of your pulse. You try to hide it, but it's too fat to fully conceal even with both hands, and, having forgotten to hold the barbell, it crashes down onto you and you're trapped under it flat on your back, with your brawny mast waving aloft. "Ha—looks heavy!" I exclaim triumphantly.

Offscreen, the other gymgoers, who are all hot men, are scandalized, saying things like *That's revolting* and *Shame on you, degenerate pervert!* And I slyly smile, and side with them against you: *I agree, he shouldn't be doing that in public! What's that lunatic thinking?* and so on. (No need to record my part, I will dub it in myself.) The crowd, seeing that I am the biggest man there, collectively drafts me to

handle the situation, and I easily hoick the barbell off you
with a single hooked finger. As I drag you to the locker
room by your dick, everyone cheers and claps for me,
chanting my name (Kant! Kant! Ka

The cursor freezes, refusing to issue any new letters, as Kant
maxes out the form's character limit. His eyes are dry and un-
blinking. His mind feels like a limb that's been freed from a
plaster cast, greenish and sickly but with, at last, a full range of
motion. Switching to email, he continues,

Leaning against a locker with crossed arms, I impatiently
tap my foot as you try to cover yourself, but the more you
try to stuff your dick back in with both hands, the more
helplessly tumid it gets, even your balls swell in anticipation,
exposed to this superior man whose undeniable hotness
threatens your whole way of life and concept of self. I toss
my long silken ponytail, cross my arms, and make a bold
whinnying laugh at your misfortune. "Alright, buddy boy,
let me show you what a REAL cock looks like," I say, tossing
back my cloak, and with my arms still crossed, my pants
zipper opens by itself and out flops the hugest, veiniest,
purplest slab of thoroughbred cockmeat you have ever
seen, about the size of a baguette and not even hard yet
(so more like baguette dough, I guess). It smells so bad, like
week-old paella, that you convulse and tear up, but are also
deeply impressed. Dubbing in "flies circling garbage" SFX
could help convey the odor.
    Witnessing my cock is like a landmine going off in
your head. It's not that you enjoy the public shame or the

prospect of getting your hole ripped apart, you're just so forlornly in thrall, in such a hopeless nadir of lust and degradation, that you are suddenly willing to sacrifice everything, you lose all hope for your life apart from deepthroating my cock and ingurgitating gallon after gallon of my foul cum. Your expression should convey that.

Then I steal your phone away and take pictures of my massive cock next to your less-massive (but still massive) cock, and I announce that I'm posting them to all your social media accounts. "Please sir," you beg, "please don't post my meat to my socials." You try to take the phone, but you're so much shorter I can easily play keep-away. "My parents and boss and fiancée of two years follow me on there! Please, sir, I mean master, I mean milord, I mean sire, I prithee, don't post my meat!" But I shrug like *Whaddya gonna do?* and post it anyway, simply because I care nothing of your fate. "Oh no," you wail. "Now everyone will see how small my meat is, in relative terms, compared to yours!"

Act II (mins. 8–15): "Cock, Meat Holes!"

The shame and confusion you feel about lusting after my enormous, frightening Asian cock makes you feel, not like you *deserve* this abuse, more that you're responsible for it happening, if that makes sense.

It transpires that I am so overpowering, you are so helpless against my commanding desires, that you can intuit them telepathically. So, without my even asking, you follow me back home to my place, a giant stone castle called Balls-Deep Keep, complete with drawbridge and moat, portcullis, torch sconces, bats, hunchbacked manservant—*Castlevania: Symphony of the Night* for PS1 makes a good comp. (Again, green screen works fine here.) You enter my dungeon, where a digital scale sits on a stool to your right, with a folded placecard that says REGISTER DICK HERE. First I lay your cock on the scale, and it reads "10 OZ." I laugh confidently, like *Heh, step aside kid,* and with a beefy smack my cock hits the scale, which reads "99999999 KG" and then shatters.

Defeated, and without prompting, you strip down and put both legs behind your head. I've observed that you're quite flexible, so try and get your face as close to your hole as possible, so that you can see up close my unlubricated Death Star of a cockhead approach your sphincter, then sizzle as it makes contact. It won't fit: you can plainly see it won't fit. Your fully opened eyes cross as you watch it go in millimeters from your face. "Careful, my hemorrhoids!" you say, then make a sustained *Dragon Ball Z* power-up scream, your face turning beet-red. (Sweat will cause makeup to run, so for the redness try applying a slice of actual beet to your face instead.)

Remember to set the camera to continuous autofocus so it doesn't get blurry.

When your asshole finally engulfs the flare of my glans, your cross-eyed expression will transition to what's known as an ahegao: upturned crossed eyes, knitted brow, tongue hanging limply from your mouth, ideally with saliva dangling from it. This denotes both your instant sissification and "stupidization" at the moment of insertion. Your hemorrhoid does not bleed, instead induces intensely pleasurable pain. Inch by inch, you feel my python scouring through your guts, rasping your prostate like an angle grinder, and just when you think it's finally all in, I cram one of my grapefruit-sized balls into your ass, then the other, and lastly the phallic braid of my pubes, and hold everything in there for about five Mississippis. My dickprint is now visible through your abdomen. Just like how ejaculation is sometimes represented by a "splat" even though it's actually soundless, here I'd like a sound effect representing your asshole being stretched to its absolute tensile limit, perhaps the rubbery sound of a balloon animal being tied.

Straightaway I slam your hole from various angles. You should be filling any dead air with dialogue along the lines of, "You're ruining my hole," or "Who will ever love me now, with my hole ruined," or "Shred my prostate into fettucine alfredo with your ginormous Asian bloodwurst," or "I am a stupid braindead pig for Asian-American cum [oinking sounds]," or "My uvula is a speed bag for your heavyweight Southeast Asian fuckstick," or "I am a subhuman 2.7 GPA cum reservoir for your first-generation Thai-American diaspora uberdick, and actually I'm enjoying it despite my deep shame, not that I'm asking you to stop." Please face the camera while you're speaking, and add pauses between lines, employing active listening cues, so I can dub my dialogue in later. And feel free to improvise, the spontaneity does add a lot!

Before pulling out, I do one final thrust in your ass so hard that my cock rams its way *inside* your cock from behind, so that my tip protrudes from yours like a pig-in-a-blanket. (I know the colon doesn't connect to the urethra; I abhor suspending disbelief, but have accepted this as a necessary evil.) The fit is so snug you can't even cum, though you badly want to, because to your surprise and profound shame, you're enjoying this.

We now cut to a tight close-up on your waxed hole when I *slowly* pull out with a loud "boot-stuck-in-mud" slurp; after I withdraw, a plume of white smoke should issue thereout, like when they announce a new Pope. If the hole won't stay fully gaped on its own, you could prop it open with a clear acrylic tube. Not sure if you're able to induce a full "pink sock" prolapse, but I'd appreciate that, as long as you are 100% confident you can do it safely!

For the next shot, I go ass to mouth. (Feel free to cut so you can wash up in between.) As I facefuck you, you realize that not only is my cock already the longest, meatiest rod in recorded history . . . it's getting *longer*, can become *infinitely* long at my merest whim. As I'm plugging away, your gag reflex produces a rhythmic effleurage, so it's as if you're jacking me off with your throat. Capitalize on your gagging to produce from the sides of your mouth the largest possible quantity of what I call "slobber," which is *not* just saliva, but rather *the viscous clear-white admixture of both mucus and saliva that ordinarily resides in the esophagus, and is expectorated only via gag reflex.* It should NOT contain any vomit, which would discolor it. Slobber's resemblance to lube suggests that your body is so intrinsic a receptacle for my lust that at the slightest touch, to say nothing of pounding your stomach valve with my cockhead, it involuntarily self-lubricates.

I'd appreciate if you could festoon your hair, forehead, nose, earlobes, chin, lips, and eyelashes with slobber in a tinsel-like arrangement. This is to address what I call "the Cumshot Paradox": how, in porn, you want your climax synced with the performer's, but this deprives you of the pleasure of seeing the load afterwards, since you're already spent. My imperfect solution is to use slobber to emulate cum earlier, in effect taking the money shot on credit.

The end sequence is somewhat more involved vis-a-vis mise-en-scene. By now my cock has grown to ~60 feet, while you have shrunk to ~3 feet; we will now create the cinematic illusion of me traversing your entire alimentary canal, throat to anus. You'll need three cameras, an endoscope, and an 18" squirting dildo ("Doc Johnson"-style, phthalate-free w/ realistic vasculature). Run the endoscope through the plastic cum-ferrying tube, until the lens peeks from the meatus, providing a "cock's-eye view." Now get on all fours, with cameras in front, behind, and in profile. My cock will plunge through your esophagus, detouring to poke into each lung, then smash past the lower esophageal sphincter into the stomach. The sideview camera tracks it zigzagging through the small intestine, doing a quick loop-de-loop through the ascending, transverse, and sigmoid colon before finally jutting eight inches out of your ass like a tail.

Afterward remove the endoscope and cut the dildo in half. Stick the top half in your ass, and the bottom in your mouth, so you look "spit-roasted." The part sticking out of your ass should be sparkling clean, as if the filth of my cock got scrubbed off inside you.

Act III (mins. 15–18): "Huge Loads Emerged from My Yellow Wood"

The actual cumshot shouldn't take long, but it's worth a deep dive. Most squirting dildos come with a meager 1 oz. syringe-style pump. We'll require a few gallons at least, so you can retrofit it with a motorized pump or a bladder-based pump-hydraulic system like a Super Soaker.

My first long, loud jet of cum should be Chardonnay-colored; this is because it's not cum at all, but pure liquid testosterone. The next spurts should BLAST your forehead like a faucet running over the back of a spoon, while you make the surprised "*Home Alone* face." Speed is crucial here, as cum, real or fake, deliquesces quickly, losing its whiteness and surface tension to become a transparent glaze, and I *strongly* prefer distinct "laces" of cum. Don't you dare wipe or smear that precious load! Whatever gets in your mouth should dribble out both sides and the rivulets should join at your chin in a single swinging pendant, gradually elongating. Stalactites of cum should hang from your eyelashes, then drip down across your eyeball, which stays open and motionless, because by now you're so dead inside you can't even blink, only ahegao. If you tear up, that's A-OK.

By now you resemble a white chocolate drip cake in hot weather, and insofar as your expression is visible at all, you

should look shocked and revolted, maybe pinching your
nose and grimacing like *Pee-yew, who cut the cheese?*—
yet also with an undercurrent of chagrin and wistful
resignation, like *Alas, tragic is the lot of this low, lorn wretch.*
Finally my dick rears up, makes a ferocious slavering ROAR,
then slaps your face hard enough that the cum flies off, the
camera chasing the load as it loudly extinguishes one of the
torches on the wall.

SIDEBAR: FAKE CUM

The viscosity of the fake cum is paramount, since that's
what enables it to "dangle" like real cum, instead of just
dripping off. Lotion is insufficient, as it's too white and more
"gloppy" than "goopy," and off-the-shelf cum lubes are
too "glossy." A better comp would be snail mucin or—not
coincidentally—slobber.

You can prepare serviceable fake cum with common
pantry staples. This is the recipe I've worked out for one
"serving" (= one complete load, ~7–8 spurts) though you
will need about twenty, so I've included conversions:

2 (= 40) egg whites
1 tsp (= 6 tbsp + 2 tsp) sour cream
1 tbsp (= 1 ¼ cup) cornstarch
1 cup (= 1.25 gal) water
Salt to taste

Stir gently, so the egg whites don't stiffen. The result
should be a turbid, opalescent off-white (hex code

#F6F3E9), and when you coat your fingers and separate them, it should hang in a heavy parabola, ideally dangling ~4 inches without breaking off or lengthening any further. As it is perishable, be sure to use while fresh; I can't imagine it'd feel too pleasant refrigerated. If diet prohibits, for a vegan/non-ovular alternative base try methyl cellulose, a vegetable-based food emulsifier sold at most art supply stores. You could futz around with gelatin thickeners like Instant ClearJel so it's more bubbly, less foamy.

If you'd be at all willing to employ my actual semen, on its own or as an additive, I will produce an adequate volume and overnight it to you with a cold-pack. Of course I'd pay extra, and, for your peace of mind, I'd include notarized copies of my blood test results, and film myself producing, collecting, packaging, and shipping the cum immediately following the blood test.

END SIDEBAR

To finish off I thrust my cock back in your mouth; it's so fat your lips form an airtight seal around it, and with each shuddering spurt the cum forcefully expels in long unbroken ribbons out of your nostrils, ears, asshole, urethra, belly button, and tear ducts simultaneously, because you're fully "topped off" and each spurt displaces the last. By now the friction from all the high-velocity reaming has caused my glans to glow orange-hot like E.T.'s fingertip, the light visible through your throat (a single fairy light under a layer of latex skin, perhaps?). The heat causes the cum in your stomach to boil, then froth out your stretched lips (baking soda + vinegar for the froth; a dash of bitters would suggest that the intense heat has "browned" it). You also cum at this point, though your load is a pathetic trickle compared to mine, evaporating before it even hits the floor. Finally my cum should vaporize to a dense steam inside you and begin to whistle out of your ears; two boiling kettles placed behind your head ought to work.

By this act's end, you are completely used up and tiny. My stupefying cum has dropped your IQ to 72. My final surge of cum flings you like a champagne cork twenty feet into the air. You bob atop the geyser for a beat, then, as you plummet down, my cockhole dilates and engulfs you whole, your screams echoing in my cavernous dickshaft, until you land in my stomach (again, forgive the anatomical license). My intestines are so controlled and smart that they know better than to digest a moronic cum rag like you, so my asshole dilates painlessly to shit you out. We zoom in on your face, reeking with effluvia and emanata as you ahegao. Shining the ring light into your eyes will help shrink your pupils to look "soulless."

The last thing you do before losing consciousness is accidentally take a humiliating selfie; my prehensile cock grabs your phone and types the caption "I just got swallowed up by my Asian-American cocklord's behemoth dong and it's #CumPigGoals" then post it to your socials, where I also update your relationship status to "Jizz Mop." (Please send me the selfie too; I can handle the retouching myself.) My cock continues growing, spiring skyward, its envelope of pulsing blood-heat protecting it from the frigid temperatures of the stratosphere, its hardness indestructible against the scorching thermosphere, soaring off to where? No man alive knows . . .

Epilogue (mins. 18–20)

Phew! *Wipes brow* Thanks for bearing with me, we're in the endgame.

It's several years later, and your ultimate fate is revealed as my personal suck-slave. I am now the most important man on earth, because the enormous umbra cast by my cock over the earth's surface, and the renewable phallothermic energy it generates, and its surprising ability to convert carbon into greater cockmass, have reversed climate change—therefore, keeping me hard is a matter of planetary survival. My individual spermatozoa are so tall and charismatic that they're elected to lead the G8 nations, ushering in an era of equitable prosperity and nuclear disarmamentation, and they all have hot boyfriends too.

As for you: you've shrunk down to about 18 inches, and I'm able to store you in a jar of my cum—you have developed discreet gills adapted to seminal respiration— which I keep under my flowing red cloak for whenever I need sucking off (I'm able to adjust my cock size to "human-scale" at will). Owing to the size disparity, blowing me requires your whole body to stretch around the cock, like when Kirby eats a car. You subsist solely on my cum and various organisms inhabiting the vibrant wetland ecosystem on the teeming expanse of my world-circling cock, so every cell in your body is made of my cum. Occasionally, a breeze

blows my cloak aside to reveal you mid-fellatio; the sight
of it turns on all nearby hot men so much that we can hear
muffled but distinct "squish" sounds as they cum in their
pants and it pools in their shoes.

   This new life of yours is quite busy. Open with a montage
of a typical day:

- ❏ I hit the alarm clock and stretch while you're already
   busy sucking me off, and continue to do so while I cook
   and eat breakfast, then follow me to the bathroom
   to blow me while I loudly shit and fart and read *The
   Economist*.
- ❏ When you attempt to read a book, I dump a load on
   the open pages and then slam it shut with my cock so
   the load splatters out on your face, then my cock wags
   chidingly at you, like *Nuh-uh-uh!*
- ❏ In an effort to remember your life before becoming my
   designated fuck socket, you try to draw a picture of your
   former self, but then, sniffing the tip of your pen, you
   realize the ink is actually my cum, and the pen suddenly
   blasts into your face. I then make you lick your drawing
   off the page.
- ❏ When you try to escape, you are swiftly lassoed by my
   posse of spermatozoic bounty hunters, who collect the
   bounty of $69,420 I have placed on your cock.
- ❏ At the DMV, as you're getting your driver's license
   photo taken, the walls begin to rattle: a giant
   thunderhead of my cum has formed, its moist heat
   creating the meteorological conditions for 300 MPH

cyclonic winds that rip the DMV's ceiling off and hail torrential curtains of cum onto your head right before the camera flashes, so that your legal ID depicts you smothered in my balljuice, forcing you to show it to hot bouncers and TSA agents for the next decade. (I also own the world exclusive rights to the photo.)

To conclude, we pull in tight on your face. Lashes and gouts of my load bombard you at alternating .25x and 1.5x speeds, each making the descending whistle/explosion of a mortar shell. With your voice pitch-shifted up two octaves, you say: "I've become a lowly barnacle for your cum, and that's totally on me, it's my fault alone that your putrid cum is my destiny, because of my own weakness for your specifically Thai-American manmilk, and, counterintuitive as it may seem, I'm grateful to you for showing me what a miserable hog for Southeast Asian cum I am." Then you applaud, and the citizens of a unified earth join in, while you do an ahegao and peace sign.

Thank you, thank you, THANK YOU!!! I reckon this is a LOT more involved than your usual requests, and hopefully the payment is commensurate. (I'm also tipping extra for the time it likely took to read this email.) I'm *super* looking forward to seeing what you come up with, and once again I appreciate your discreet professionalism. If all goes well, as I'm confident it will, you can expect plenty more of my business in the future!

P.S. For any shots using a smartphone please shoot in landscape mode, i.e., widescreen. Important!

The total, after tax and tip, goes north of eight thousand dollars, comprising half his savings, an extravagance that eases his guilt about the complexity of his request. If the video is well executed, Kant could see it retaining its appeal for perhaps a year, and if he budgets carefully or gets a raise, he could afford to do it every year. Maybe he'll get sick of it, though it seems unlikely. Proceeding this way life will not be ideal, but probably sustainable, and it's not like there's an alternative. He only needs to make it through one life. No one's ever proved that desires are better off fulfilled. No one literally needs love; you don't die without it. And a substitute isn't nothing.

By the time Kant types in Cody's email address, his blood sugar is nil, and the hour late enough that he does not notice the tremble of his ring finger striking the Tab key, which causes his email app to autocomplete the letters co to Coming Out, the mailing list he'd compiled almost two years ago, before he sends it. He closes his laptop, brushes his teeth and tongue, switches off the lights, thinks about the glasses of water he used to bring Julian, types out a grocery list on his notes app for the shepherd's pie he plans to make the next day, swallows two Benadryl, and goes to sleep. Though routine and of a piece with the quiet steady safety he's accustomed to, these will be the few minutes of his life in which he is known better by others than by himself, and he spends them thinking, What if this works, what then?

OUR DOPE FUTURE

Waddap! So this is sort of a long one, but I figured all you good folks might help me get a couple things straight that have been nagging at me recently. I (37M) am a serial entrepreneur, inventor, and futurist who's been his own boss since age 18. I am homeschooled, self-made, visited 29 countries and counting, never touch alcohol but a big caffeine junkie, believer in a Stoic outlook to life, dreams big, never wastes time, always has his mind on the next move, and totes family-oriented.

A while back I met Alison (32F) on a dating app. She had that wide-hipped, glowing-skin look I'm really bananas AF for, and from the moment we matched I went all out for her, just like everything I do, messaging her for months. One thing about me is I never know when to quit, which is usually good, and sometimes not, as you'll see.

Eventually I scored a reply, and from there I gave her the VIP treatment. Her profile said she was a pescatarian so for our first date I took her out for $200 omakase flown in from Tokyo that morning, she was from bunghole Connecticut and never even heard of omakase so I knew this was gonna be lit, and we got into a deep conversation. Most girls aren't used to direct communication since your average NPC is terrified of commitment, but I never waste anyone's time. She was so dazzled by the hard sell that she barely said anything all night, and let me take the lead, which suited me fine—when I was a kid my folks put me in charge of a "solo debate club" where I'd argue two opposing positions against myself for hours on end, so I can easily chat all by myself if necessary, and it gave me the chance to flex and stunt right away. I gave her the topline: I was homeschooled, and yeah, I know homeschoolers have a reputation for being sheltered and dweeby, but I've made it a top priority over the years to study modern social behaviors, pop culture, and slang every bit as seriously as I studied Marcus Aurelius and JavaScript. Straight up, I've probably memorized more slang than anyone, so I can get down with people of all ages, races, nationalities, classes, or cultures, and it's always completely gucci. I also mentioned I'm fourteen years into a plan for early retirement, which unfortunately has held up my other plan to have kids, but that's whatevs because I'm still waiting for Ms. Right anyway.

And before you roll your eyes: yes, I got to know all about her too, I've iterated on what I call my "algorizzm" for years to make sure I minimize time wasted on chitchat and footsie. I start with prompts—what was "the incident" at your high school, have you ever broken a bone, do you remember Bubble Tape, stuff like that. I like to ask if she paid for her own college tuition, a nice little challenge that gets them in a feisty mood, and when they ask me back, I can talk about how I skipped college altogether to start my first company.

Once Alison was all warmed up, I asked her: What are the biggest problems you face in your life? Girls always want to talk about this, plus while she's talking it gives me time to memorize her drink order and eye color, something I've found makes me look totes on point when I mention it later. At first, she sort of squinted and stuttered like she was trying to describe a new color, but once the 100-year sake hit the table she opened up and told me all about 1.) being in recovery for her eating issues, 2.) pining after her former best friend, and 3.) getting dumped by everyone she's ever been close to. This was all sweet music to my ears because having problems to solve always gets me jiggy with it. I thanked her for spilling the tea.

My second question was, What are your life goals? And she laughed and said she'd settle for health insurance. I said I meant more big picture: Did she want a family, her own place, financial independence? And she said, Sure, but that'll never happen. Now I *knew* I was in. I assured her that I was all about bringing dope people into my life and helping them achieve their goals, wealth isn't only about private jets, it's about taking care of people, it's about freedom, right, so don't worry, I'm here to help, it's practically my job. At that point our omakase came, and I helped her appreciate it AF—just think about how every bite is 25 dollars, I said, how those fish were swimming off the coasts of Japan and Norway while we were brushing our teeth yesterday! Doesn't mindfulness hit so different?

Finally I waited till she went to the bathroom, then pulled one of my more successful routines: I moved over and sat in her seat, and when she came back looking all confused I pulled her onto my lap, and whispered in her ear that I've never met anyone like her, someone so exciting and special and on fleek, and I'm not some immature boy like the guys she's dated before, I know what I want, and what I want is you.

Now, where other guys might be trying to weasel their way into bed with her, I told her I had to get up hecka early, but I'd like to see her as much as possible any day she's free, can we lock it down? She said yes, and then, as we were parting ways, I saw a good opportunity to flex. Having no siblings, and with my parents often out socializing when they weren't homeschooling me, I've always longed for that feeling of always having a homie around, so my first successful startup was Umeego, an "Uber for friends" where you can hail someone with a clean background check to accompany you to dinner, movies, or parties anytime, starting at fifty cents a minute. At the time my UX research was finding that many users were using it to hire ad-hoc bodyguards to escort them home, so we were testing a pivot to personal security, cutting out the human middleman and adding the option to hail a cute robot dog to follow you around, equipped with sirens, cameras, and "less-lethal" personal defense armaments. I called one to see her home safe, chatting with her through the speaker in its neck. By the end of the night I could tell I'd snatched her wig, and we shared a beautiful, impactful kiss that really slapped.

I take a 10X approach to everything, and that includes dating: every date at least 10 times as committed as the one before. You could think of me as a romantic accelerationist of sorts. Why wait if it feels right? My name isn't Max for nothing! So for our second date, five days later, skrrt skrrt! I hit her with two tickets to Barcelona, departing in six hours. She told me she couldn't just bail on her internship. I was like, for real-real? You're reeeeeeally gonna turn down a free romantic luxury vacation to a top-five most beautiful city on earth according to TripAdvisor? Business-class Delta One with Sky Club access and lie-down seats? Yeah, didn't think so! Fast-forward sixteen hours later, and we're going dumb and ham on Las Ramblas, rolling deep to all the night spots, vibing at the big disco church and the wavy houses. We got our drink on, and our photos on, and our culture on, and I made sure to hook it up with sangria and Manchego cheese and Russian salad at every meal to help with her food issues. When we toured the Palau Nacional, I said the classical architecture was worstass, and she looked confused, so I explained it meant "the most possible badass," and she literally died! That, I thought, was the best leading indicator of our long-term compatibility—I was always making her laugh, without even trying.

The first night we spent together, I could tell she still had some doubts, so lying in our executive suite, I let her know that I understood she was probably used to seeing life as this big struggle, a set of limitations, people telling her who she should be and what she can't do, telling her she has to be someone else if she wants to deserve love. Well that's all over, I said, I'm here now, and I'm offering you my mad love and support if you'll have it. She started crying and saying nobody had ever said they believed in her. Poor girl! All she ever needed was someone to gas her up. Needless to say, the rest of the night was goated. I even snuck her ring size with some dental floss while she was sleeping. Like I said, 10X. Bet.

Anyhoo, trip was tight, many memories made, and after we got back, things between us were reasonably lit. We texted every day for the next few weeks, and I made sure to consistently give her mad props, had her send me photos of her OOTDs just so I could say she was a smokeshow dime serving fish and doll. I made sure to read the wiki for every movie and book she mentioned so we'd always have things to talk about, and had flowers delivered to her place so often she had to tell me to stop because her roommates were wiling!

Not long after, she was let go from her magazine job, probably because they didn't offer sick days and we'd left for Spain with a quickness. She was feeling sadsies about it, but in my head, I was thinking, that's an entry-level job in a dead-end industry, like for realsies, who reads magazines? When was the last time you walked into a store like, gee whiz I really want to buy a MAGAZINE? So if you ask me getting fired was a net pos. Success is built from a thousand failures, I reassured her by saying.

Next time we met up she surprised me by saying we couldn't see each other anymore, she was planning to move back to Connecticut. I was like, Heck naw, why not just move into my crib? A better deal than her two-roommate shoebox, that's for sure. Now, I didn't want to scare her off, so I pitched it like this: getting people set up for success is what I'm all about, so let me pimp your life! See it as an investment in your goals: I'll pay your bills for six months, and if at any point you're not happy with where you're at, we can find you an even nicer place to live, I'll front the deposit. Why? Because I stan you. I'm your simp. I freaks with you heavy, and that is no cap whatsoever. As long as you make this one promise: Will you work together with me as a team to pursue our life goals, deadass?

It actually took a pretty lame amount of arm-twisting considering how generous my offer was; even after I left to take a shiznit and came back she still hadn't made up her mind. Actually she didn't give me a straight answer until the day before her lease was up, but whatevs, a promise is a promise, and soon after that we were officially cuffed, and she was my shawty. Luckily she had barely anything to move since she mostly used her roommates' appliances and furniture. After I persuaded her to unload her books (no shelves at my place, switched to paperless ages ago), all her stuff fit into four IKEA bags. We hit a snag when I found out she had a cat. I told her I had a lot of prototype furniture inventory from one of my startups that I couldn't risk damaging, and to make it easier for her I slipped her roommates five bands to look after it until we figured something out.

When she first stepped up in my hizzy, she seemed surprised at how small it was—I live in a hyper-efficient one-bedroom, which minimizes upkeep, and you don't get rich paying rent. She asked me why there was no bed in my bedroom, which gave me the chance to show her how my bed folds out of the wall, a "hypersleep pod" of my own design with a body-conforming memory foam cavity that allows you to sleep at a 20° decline, decompressing the spinal cord and increasing blood flow to the brain, and told her I was already customizing one tailored exactly to her body (which I'd measured while she was sleeping). Since the closet was full I let her keep her stuff in the oven, which I never use anyway. I also gave her a very nice clean pink microfiber towel that my last shawty had left behind. So she was all set up, or so I thought.

Around this time things started getting slammed at work. I was gearing up to pitch investors on my new startup, Sweat-Seats, a complete living room furniture set that doubles as gym equipment—alright, so peep dis: you get antsy while watching TV on your SweatSeats recliner, so you flip up the footrest and crush out some leg presses up to 300 lbs, making productive use of what would otherwise be wasted time! Cool beans, right? We hadn't fully cracked the "stinky/soggy upholstery" problem yet, so my team was in all-hands solutions mode, and I was in heads-down building mode: up at 4 a.m., chug a Creatine Bacon shake on the drive to the office, then grind till the wheels come off that bad mutha' shut-yo-mouth!

Actually, that reminds me how our first fight was over those shakes . . . okay, so, my most successful startup to date is a meal-replacement shake called DöpeSauce. It always baffled me why other shakes like Ensure and Soylent were always *sweet* and only did the bare minimum of nourishment. I saw a GIANT hole in the market for savory-yet-functional flavors like Adaptogen Grilled Cheese, CBD Clam Chowder, and Piracetam BBQ Ribs, all with a little kick of caffeine, at a price point so competitive it'd be perfect for schools, hospitals, and correctional facilities. As a founder I live and breathe and, in this case, drink my products, so I haven't eaten solids at home or bought groceries in years. Like I said, I had zero time to take Alison out, but she said she wouldn't drink the shakes because she's pescatarian, even after I assured her they contained no actual animal products, just really great flavoring. I was hoping she'd be gagged for them, it would've been a win-win because she was always talking about her struggle to eat healthy, and dogfooding would help me deal with surplus inventory that was filling all my closets and nearing expiration (shelf-stability was a pain point back then). Unfortunately she gagged *on* them whenever she tasted them; she wouldn't even try the Adderall French Fries. I couldn't understand why homegirl was trippin'. Were we not on the same side, helping each other achieve our goals? I don't even know what she was doing to feed herself otherwise, and she certainly didn't have the shmoney for groceries, but hey, her choice.

I thought it was a bit rich for her to turn her nose up at my hard work while lying around the hizzy all day. No shade, but I think she was frustrated that, given all the time and space in the world, she was realizing she didn't have as clear an idea of her goals as I did, and was taking her frustrations out on me. I figured if she used to work at a magazine, she could maybe start a new media venture. A while ago I built a "sexual consent on the blockchain" app (a use case so obvious I'm shocked I got to it first!), so with my Web3 experience, I told her I could help her launch a decentralized magazine? Where readers could be token-holders who vote on editorial decisions? I also offered multiple times to give her a free workflow and SWOT audit, but she'd always say "It's a thought" and never bring it up again.

Instead, what did she do? If I'm keeping it one-hunnid, not much! Mostly goofed around on her phone; I checked her screen-time tracker once and noticed she was logging something wack like 40 hours a week, which is about the same as me, except I actually use my phone for work and informative podcasts. Her browser history was mostly TV recaps, celebrity plastic surgery timelines, the phrase "weight gain" with different antidepressants, and, for some reason, lots of videos of grain-entrapment deaths and people hugging their pets goodbye before euthanasia. Something that got me especially heated, too, was she'd been looking at adult content. I'm no prude or anything, and it's true that we hadn't Netflix-and-chilled since Spain, but that was partly because I was so busy, and partly because abstaining from Netflix-and-chilling is how I keep my cognitive function on point, and partly also, as I explained to her, that I'd been noticing it took usually up to twenty minutes to accomplish her goals in bed, whereas it only takes me around two minutes to accomplish mine, so that's not totally even stevens. But the adult content didn't sit right with me either, it implied that she wasn't adapting to her new circumstances, and that what we had wasn't enough for her. I don't know, it just seemed ungrateful.

The way I see it, I was giving her the opportunity to pursue anything she wanted, pretty much the most amazeballs deal you could ask for, and still she wasn't motivated. Clearly she needed a push, so I set out to be her accountability homie. I've been fine-tuning my own habit stack for so long it's like breathing to me, and I saw lots to fix with hers. For starters I bought her a pomodoro timer and day planner, and set up a Kanban board. Her phone was clearly the big time-suck, but I knew confiscating it would make her freak out, like any kid when you take away their toys, so one day before work I rootkitted her phone to install the beta of my latest productivity app, WristSlapp, which tracks everything—screentime, messages, heart rate, location, caloric intake, sleep and menstrual cycles—and keeps you accountable by locking you out of social media, texts, and credit cards, or deducting money from your bank account when you don't hit your stated goals. I set it to block incoming and outgoing messages on Alison's phone, and stop time-wasting websites and adult content from loading properly. I figured this would be enough to tip the balance toward progress.

The first time she complained about her phone being broken, I told her it was for the best, and that personally whenever I feel like taking a motivational break, I pair some inspiring savage images with sickening music; for me I like to crank "Another One Bites the Dust" while looking at that photo of the American soldiers sticking the flag into Japan, just a double dose of freaking epicness, after a few minutes of that I'm always eyes-up and ready to rock. She said a few sort of negative things about this, so after I set her straight on the "No Bummers" policy in my house, I reminded her that if we were gonna pursue our goals we had to keep focused on the long term.

Then, in rebuttal to her crying, I asked her to explain why she thought that was a constructive or salient response to what

I'd just said, and all she did was keep crying, which proved my point. It was giving irresponsible. It was giving lack of commitment! I knew if I let it drop here it would condition her into thinking that crying was an acceptable way to win a debate. So for the entire night I sat with her, leaving only twice to take a quick shiznit, and gave her plenty of time to explain how exactly it was my fault she was unhappy. She said we never went out, to which I pointed out that I'd been working hard, and she was welcome to go and do whatever she liked, though she'd probably find it hard to do without any shmoney. Then she asserted that she was bored, and I countered that she wouldn't be bored if she kept herself busy pursuing her life goals, and it was not my responsibility to define those for her.

Her third claim was the wildest: she said I was only pursuing *my* goals, not *ours*! As a Stoic, I seldom get pressed, but I wasn't gonna let that one slide, so I clapped back and said, Oh so I'm the jerk, me! Sure, yep, that's right, I'm soooooo terrible for giving you a free place to live, free nutrition, free affection, free mindset coaching, I'm the big bad bumbaclaat, everything I do and say is SO awful and I've NEVER done anything good for you and you've NEVER been wrong in your whole life, I'm to blame for you sitting around on your bussy all day doing hey-nonny-nonny, that's right, gosh, what an opp I am, and so on. (I was using my spreading skills from debate, so imagine me saying all this at about ~300 WPM.)

By then all she could do was clutch her hair and mutter "Nononononono," to which I replied "Yesyesyesyesyesyes!" When she finally tired herself out, I didn't want to make her feel bad about losing, so I said, Who believes in you more than me? Who's truly gotchu? Do you see any of your homeskillets rushing to help you? When's the last time your parents called to check in? In no way was she going to trick me into thinking I wasn't being bae.

Mind you, I'd been keeping my teletherapist looped in on everything. I told her I'd met a girl who'd moved in with me, whom I was supporting so she could pursue her goals, and my teletherapist confirmed that was great of me to do, that it's good I'm embracing my role as Alison's "main attachment figure," and I said, Bars, that's very tea, sis! That's exactly what I am, I'm her main attachment figure, and I'm embracing it! Go awf, slay queen! (My teletherapist is Black.)

I'd hoped Alison's mood would shift after our chat, but it felt like every night was the same sulking and moping for months. I started feeling like I was alone, moving toward our goals for the both of us. I figured some time apart would be aight, so I worked longer hours at the office, kept an eye on Alison by streaming my hizzy's security camera to my third monitor. Instead of even trying to do any work, all she did was rearrange her few belongings over and over: her makeup kit, the contents of her purse, little stacks of clothes, for hours on end. Then, weirdly, she'd take a spray bottle and her pink microfiber towel and wipe circles on the media console in the living room, over and over. Sometimes I'd catch her lips moving but no sound would come out. At first I thought, okay, well it's dope of her to reinvest her energy in a positive direction, that's a win for me because I love coming home to a tidy house, might even be able to let the cleaning lady go. I made sure to provide positive reinforcement by saying things like, I appreciate your hard work, betch! You're really eating that media console up, no crumbs! But it started to get so that I'd leave for work and she'd be wiping dust on the media console . . . check in at lunch, still wiping dust . . . at 7 p.m. I'd come back home and she would be in the same exact spot wiping dust, not even looking up at me, on God, I thought maybe it might've been a stubborn stain but I checked and nothing was there? Freaky deaky.

So one day, after I'm standing there watching her wipe this spot for five minutes, not even acknowledging I'm there, I said, Listen, I'm sincerely gagged that you're taking some ownership of the space, but how is wiping dust all day contributing to the pursuit of your goals? And she turned and looked at me with this spacy squint, like I was a window and she was peering through me at the horizon. I said, Maybe if you enjoy cleaning so much, you could stack it as a reward only after you're done with your tasks for the day? Or at the very least you could show the bathroom and kitchen some mad love too, blud!

She nodded, and I realized that since our debate, I hadn't actually heard her voice in days, maybe weeks. Not only that, but when I checked in on the security cam one day, I saw that she wasn't even wiping dust anymore, just sitting in my wing chair/ ab crunch machine staring straight ahead with the curtains drawn. She was still there when I got home that night, and I thought she might be angry, so I said, What's the matter, hunty? She didn't answer me, so I repeated myself until her pupils suddenly became enormous, and she said, "I'm meditating."

At this I thought, all righty then, maybe it'll help clear her mind. So I left her alone and went to take a shiznit, but on my way back from the can forty minutes later she was still in the same pose. It was wild seeing her sit there for so long in complete silence. I figured she'd get bored eventually, but instead the sessions started stretching out to five, six, seven hours, with no water or bathroom breaks, every time I went in to check on her I never saw her move once, couldn't even see her breathing, I mean it was not healthy and definitely not productive, and when she'd come out of one of these sessions she would head straight to bed and sleep, which was bizarre to me that she could fall asleep after sitting still for so long, or maybe she was faking it, who knows. One time I plopped down next to her to give it a try myself, just to see if she'd figured out some new mental focus hack I could use, but literally nobody with real responsibilities can sit still for that long, and every time I peeked to see if she was cheating, she was motionless with a zonked-out look on her face, like she was sleeping with her eyes open.

When I asked her what she thought about while she meditated, she said she didn't think about anything, but I knew that was totally cap, nobody can think about nothing, that's not mindfulness, that's mindlessness! I suggested that maybe instead, she could repeat some autosuggestion mantras, like "I'm a really slay badass!" or "I'm definitely finna get a lot of work done soon!" But she didn't seem interested. It bugged me that she'd rather hang out with nobody and think about nothing instead of hanging out with and thinking about me. Then I realized it was even worse, I started feeling like there was someone in her head she was talking to, specifically about me, and that guy was making up rude things about me. That kinda cheesed me off, almost like she was cheating on me with this guy. I went over to tap her shoulder and ask her about it, and her eyes popped open and she yelled, I mean right in my face: "I'M! [bleep]ING!! MEDITATING!!!!" I started to suspect that this new urge to meditate was from her being Netflix-and-unchill, so to speak, so I asked if she would like some backshots, and she completely snapped at me. I don't usually like raising my voice, but she was the one who took it there, and I wasn't hollaing at her so much as I was hollaing at the guy in her head, so after I reminded her that the "No Bummers" policy included cuss words, I dipped.

For three weeks it was like this, even worse than the silent treatment. She didn't even seem to be aware when I was in the room. Like one time when she headed to the bathroom, I tried blocking the doorway, and she bumped into me and acted confused before slipping past under my arm. I was starting to worry, like maybe she was secretly harboring some genetic predispositions toward being delulu, even though the cheek swab I took in her sleep didn't turn anything up. So I opened WristSlapp to figure out who her closest homies and family were, based on the people who'd been texting her, and I reached out to them from my own phone to tell them that, as her main attachment figure, I'd been finding her behavior somewhat sketchtastic, and asked if they knew of any good hacks to snap her out of it. I was pretty steamed that instead of responding to me, they tried going behind my back and texting Alison instead to ask how she was. No biggie, I just backdoored her phone and, posing as Alison, texted them what I was going to say anyway, which is that she was going through a hard time but was fortunately being taken dope care of by me, and given the first real chance in her life to pursue her goals, and she didn't know where she'd be without her bussin' boyfriend. They said they were glad to hear that, but were still worried about her and wanted to come check in on her, and asked where they could visit her. I considered that idea mad sus, since they were the ones who'd probably got her twisted like this in the first place, so I disabled SIM tracking on her phone just in case they went Robocop mode.

A few days later, Alison brought up my previous offer to move her into a better place and front the deposit if she wasn't happy. I'd kind of forgot about that since it was months ago, which is centuries in startup world, but fair's fair—I did remember promising that, and my word is bond, though the challenge with this was that I was not comfortably liquid at the time because crypto was dipping, and the rest was tied up in WristSlapp, so in terms of shmoney on hand, we'd have to chillax on that for a while, and where was she going to find a better bargain than living here regardless? To me it sounded a lot like she was trying to peace out of her promises, and I wasn't going to let her let herself down. If she didn't want to fight for our goals and our relationship, then I was going to step up for the both of us.

So when she said I was breaking my promise to her, I said, Well exsqueeze me, but I never said I'd be able to help you move *right away*, and anyway my teletherapist says relationships are about give and take, having each other's backs, intimacy and trust, no secrets, no running and hiding, which is all you've been doing since you moved in! I showed her all the pictures of us I'd posted from our Spain trip and how many likes they'd gotten from her homies, it was clear that everyone thought our relationship was poggers, plus did she think they were still going to want to hang out with her after ghosting them for months? And what was she going to tell her parents, who were #TeamMax ever since I booked them a cruise to Saint-Martin? That she was going to leave the guy who wanted kids and had been paying her bills for *how* long now? At *her* big age?

Lastly, she said a few hurtful things. She said I was criticizing her for not pursuing her goals, but "What are *your* goals?

To start a bunch of stupid companies that reinvent [crap] nobody needs, just to make a [crap]load of money you won't even
spend on anything fun?" This was totally specious, of course, but I
accept that it was my fault for not articulating the full scope of
my goals earlier on. I'd been planning on saving it for our first
anniversary, but I wanted to let her know what she'd be leaving
if she walked out that door, so I dropped the mother of all truth
bombs onto her.

These are my goals, I said: the instant I hit retirement at
age 40, I want to start having kids, just like you do—as many
at a time as IVF will safely allow, until we hit a dozen. (Four
per gestation cycle would strike the ideal balance between fast
and feasible.) I want us all to live under the same roof, in a big
"mothership" that takes care of our every need. Alison would
be the household COO, running admin and housework, which
she obviously enjoys, and I'd be CEO, overseeing our kids' education from birth. We'll wake up at 5 a.m., chug our shakes,
engage in physical and mental enrichment, and get our yeeks in
bed at the stroke of eight. As soon as the kids acquire language,
we'll start them on an *actually useful* curriculum focused on
bizdev and Stoic thought that will give them a massive edge on
public-schoolers—picture everyone happily sweating away at
their custom desks/treadmills as they absorb meticulously cu-
rated high-quality podcasts at 2.5x speed.

Right when they're old enough, I want each of our dozen
kids to start having a dozen kids of their own, each family in
their own house, every house in the same neighborhood, each
kid raised exactly like ours. You and I would be on each family's Board of Directors, making the appropriate modifications

to behavioral stacks and educational regimens to stay current and competitive. And each of that gross of grandkids will have a dozen kids of their own . . . and on, and on, and on, until after nine short generations, we're looking at over five billion, or 5,159,780,352 beautiful homies, to be exact. Naturally we can expect some deviation along the way with the descendants' individual fertility and sexual orientation, but I don't see that as a major obstacle with the advanced surrogacy and gene-editing tech I'm developing now—which, even if our descendants choose to mate outside of the family, could make each generation identical or even improved on the previous, minimizing wack aberrations and maximizing dank traits.

And how, she might ask, do I know our descendants would willingly stick to the plan? Because we'll be around overseeing things the whole time! With our regimen of caloric restriction, cybernetic augmentation, strength training, DöpeSauce's Chili Dog Autojuvenation Blend, and daily blood transfusions from our own youngest offspring, there's no reason we couldn't live to a spry 200 years; and if we can get the generational turnover to 18 years, or even faster depending on local age of consent, then I, or some lossless copy of our minds and bodies in whatever thinking substrate, should be around to keep things litty titty! And on top of that, we'd create strong barriers to leaving—my plan is to eventually prohibit all currently existing languages, and design our own new proprietary language streamlined for the post-textual age, built on a lexicon of intuitive and info-dense pictographs or "emojis" if you will; plus I'd make it known that anyone who quits the family, or associates with quitters, would be disinherited from our global empire, losing the only social world they've known their whole life.

Imagine the billions of us, united, striving toward a common goal, building together, breeding together, voting together in the trustless political system of our own nation-state, built upon future-proof modular platforms sprawling over the gentle waves of the Andaman Sea, with our own hydro-solar power grid, enjoying the universal peace of family love, all tracing back to you and me, like Adam and Eve, only far more impressive, because instead of some magical cloud-man giving us everything, we're going to grind our way to Eden . . . and THOSE are my goals, PERIODT.

But, but, BUT, I said to Alison, before any of this can happen, we're gonna need to deliver those Gen 1 babies on a tight turnaround, and that's going to take a lot more commitment than I'm currently seeing here, and the window of opportunity isn't going to be open forever, fertility-wise, on your end.

Even being a Stoic, it bums me out to remember this next part, it really does, the same way it saddens me when a kewl new startup folds because the public isn't ready for its vision. I could tell she wasn't fully geeked about it, but I wasn't going to give up or anything. Nothing on earth is worse than a quitter, I truly believe that. Ultimately it was Alison who just couldn't even. And instead of owning it by saying "I'm sorry, ese, but I have to break my promise to you about pursuing our goals," she walked over to me all slowly and handed me this kind of like, big nasty pouch made out of her pink microfiber towel, covered in stains and full of junk. Like weird little sculptures of animals' mouths, and leaky prescription pill bottles filled with oily liquid, and bits of hair tied up with different colored hair, and loose handfuls of some sort of seed or grain. Also this dirty piece of paper covered in ink drawings of either veins or vines and writing like (I'm copying out a part from the middle now):

*STITCH BIRDNEST DOLOR CONTAMIN SOLUS
EXPOTENS CONSTRUCT UNGOD NOT OF HIS
OWN XOUS WED TO PLUTOUS BY COARD DIS-
TRAT SUNBLED CHOLER CHRISM DUJN XER-
OUS FETTOR WED TO MALBOLG ENFAST XOUS
OM ANTIN DISFER*

Like, what? Just super random. And kinda sad! All that time she could've been pushing toward our freaking dope future together, she spends on arts and crafts and a weird poem? I don't really mind when relationships fail. It was more sobering to consider for the first time that my talent for seeing and bringing out the dankest in people had misled me.

So I told her, I'm sorry, I just don't see a path forward for us, so I have to let you go, and although we were not able to achieve our goals together, I wish you the best on your journey wherever it takes you, may your time on Earth be prosperous AF, and you can keep the pink towel if you want. She moved out that night, didn't even bother taking her stuff from the oven. She was willing to walk away from all of it, from a truly exceptional and meaningful life with her biggest simp.

After the breakup, I peeped her socials to see if she was mentioning me anywhere, but I didn't see anything. I figured she was pretty embarrassed about letting me down. Not that I'm pointing fingers, but I'm pretty sure she did a few sus things on her way out. Like somehow a bunch of grit or sand found its way into some of my DöpeSauce inventory, even though the freshness seals were intact, with a smell I can only describe as "surgical." Also I think she messed with my Umeego robot dog, because it kept barking at me late at night, even though I never programmed it to bark.

Whatevs. The thing that really bugged me, after all the work and temporal capital I invested into the relationship, beyond just the lack of ROI, was realizing that some people can't be helped, even actively refuse help, and if you try to save them, they'll yeet you down with them, so all you can do is let them learn from their own mistakes. The bottom-line takeaway for me is that some women are scared of life, and can't handle a passionate guy with a big heart and big goals who's willing to call them on their BS, I mean I'm fully for equal rights etc., but sometimes you heaux really wield your tears like tear gas! I don't necessarily blame her, but I'm pretty steamed that I let this whole kerfuffle delay my plans by months (though if any adventuresome baddies reading this are intrigued and at peak fertility, slide into my DMs!).

So there's my tale of heartbreak. No need to feel bad for me, I see it as just another speedbump on the path to success, all I truly regret is that I didn't fail faster. I'm sharing my story with you because this relationship was the closest I've ever gotten to achieving my goals, and I feel like if I can step through and debug the process, the next one will be a resounding dub. What do you all think? How might I have convinced Alison to believe in herself more, instead of projecting her own limitations onto me? Are there any untapped efficiencies or "single points of failure"? Here's to a productive and stimulating discussion, gang gang!

*   *   *

EDIT: Holy schnikies, this is popping off! Thanks to all who are weighing in on this; even if we don't see eye-to-eye, I love your passion. THIS is builder culture—steel sharpening steel, pure caffeine and adrenaline, and may the best ideas win, boots!

EDIT 2: Okay, I'm seeing things start to get heated in the comments, so let me clap back on some specific claims:

- Alison was perfectly healthy and in no way confined to my place, nor did I "surveil" her. I've had security cams way before she moved in, would you argue I'm "surveilling" myself?

- If running an app on someone's phone to improve user experience and minimize distractions is "hacking," then I've got news for ya, fam: every tech company is "hacking" you! Again: I did it to *help* Alison achieve her goals, like *she said* she wanted. I don't see how it matters whether she asked for this form of help specifically; some might consider it rather thoughtful that I did it without having to be asked.

- I've heard some wild takes in my time, but this idea that wanting a large close-knit family is "Nazi sh*t"? As if! This ain't it, chiefs! 🤣

EDIT 2a: More clarifications. Dawgs, I truly don't appreciate this suggestion that I somehow pushed or inveigled Alison into doing anything she didn't want to do. Really, where are you getting this stuff? Were you there? Did you peep it with your own eyes? From the start I was above board with where I was coming from, I anted up and followed through, if anyone had gotten it twisted it was her, for not honoring her commitments. Any reasonable person would agree everything I did was for her benefit, not mine.

EDIT 2b: IMPORTANT CONTEXT: A small handful of player-haters have taken it upon themselves to distort the conversation by upvoting all the most negative comments. It's high-key sus how the moderators appear to be asleep at the wheel, despite the clear violations of policies against posting personal information. Have we just decided to pretend rules don't exist?

EDIT 3: Har-dee-har-har, hats off to all you bozos posting my LinkedIn—yes, my name is Maximus Aurelius Horney, which I think is a beautiful homage to one of history's worstass thinkers. Hate to break it to you suckaz, but the ink is dry on all my funding, and my squad of investie-besties are solidly in my corner. You can't really get me fired if I'm my own boss, now can you? Also, can someone explain in what way I'm supposed to be insulted by old photos of myself? Actually, according to a 1998 Merck study 16% of men experience moderate-to-extensive hair loss between the ages of 18 and 29, and I'm within a standard deviation of the mean in terms of frontal baldness, but oh wait, you didn't bother looking that up, did you? Thought not! Ya burnt! But it really shows how invested you all are for trawling through my old accounts, I'm flattered, really. Looks like Alison wasn't the only one living rent-free somewhere (i.e. I'm living rent-free in your heads)! And thanks for the free publicity, always a big help for startups! IJBOL! 🤣 🤣 🤣

EDIT 3a: If the mods won't step up, I guess I'll have to do it myself. Fine with me, I'm used to doing everything myself, it's kind of my whole deal if you haven't noticed! For the handful of folks taking a more considered view of things and debating in good faith, mad props to you—I'll be continuing the conversation here at Seneca's Revenge, my private chat server for Stoic entrepreneurs. ¡If you enjoy debate, timehacking, longevity science, laser tag, the extended *BBT / Young Sheldon* universe, and the occasional hilarious image macro, vamos, mi gente! DM for password.

EDIT 4: Okay, circling back to this thread. Some bad actors have seen fit to infiltrate my *private* chat server, post offensive and disturbing material, and circulate misleading screenshots, so once again it falls upon me to clarify: I'm not responsible for ANY of the racist/misogynist content posted there. Just because I happen not to be ashamed of being a ytboi does NOT mean I believe in "woman farms" or "Semitic expulsion" or a "10,000-year Anglo-Scandinavian imperium." I'm certain that these posts were part of a "black propaganda" op to defame me, and I spent the better part of last weekend mopping up the mess (more wasted time). Also, the posts that were attributed to me were taken completely out of context—for instance, when I posited that heaux aren't always best suited for organization tasks, I literally just meant it on the level of spatial cognition! Look up "sex differences in chronometric mental rotation study" for yourself! Either you believe in science or you don't!

EDIT 5: Welp, I see that everyone's new problematic fave Alison has opted to take the low road in the comments, and opportunistically roll with the bizarre revisionist history of our relationship. And not only that, but track down every shawty I've ever dated and get them to join the dogpile! If you want to blindly side with them over me and my (female) teletherapist, who is Black, be my guest. Playing the victim is a great way to get people to care about you without accomplishing anything, seems like! Alison, since I suspect you're listening intently, let me just say this: it's mad easy to look back on a situation that didn't turn out the way you wanted, and then scapegoat others for it. But aren't you leaving out how much I helped you? Was I not, in the final accounting, bae? Have you forgotten Spain?

EDIT 5a: This will be my FINAL word on the matter. The way I've been abused over the past few weeks by total strangers, and especially by Alison and my other ex-shawties, really has me having a cow. My entire life is dedicated to improving the world, helping people by bringing out their full potential, relying on nobody, and working for my family, the future, and my future family. This whole clusterfloomp has made me realize there's no place for a forward-thinking guy like me in this country. So I'm gone like Tron, peace out and word to your mothers. It's dark days for society when we start treating our most productive members like villains and opps, instead of leaders and GOATs. Great job everyone, condragulations... NOT.

EDIT 5b: Sorry to all my new "followers," but despite your creeper efforts to track me down, you're not gonna find me anywhere near dry land or the laws of man. With all the guff you put me through, I've decided to start my plans early and liquidate my assets, taking to the open waters, free as a fish in my swagged-out quirked-up self-sustaining floating ocean pod, truly living according to nature. While you all burst your forehead veins open typing angry comments, I'm lying here all cozy in my chaise longue/Pilates reformer, with blazing satellite Wi-Fi, adjustable tint portholes, more than enough room to stand and walk around, and a year's supply of DöpeSauce to keep me flexin' and flossin' on the blue frontier. There is just something SO kawaii about being able to poke my head out from the sunroof twice a day and see nothing but space and possibility surrounding me, and scream my affirmations to the sky full blast: I am ill! I am chill! I am phat! I am fly! I am clutch! I am fetch! I am a bad betch! I am based! I am bae! I am slay! I am cray! I am a whole snack! I am a real G! I am a hot mess! I am the coldest to ever do it! I am mother! I am zaddy! I AM SASHA FIERCE!!!!!!!!!!

Vibing out here in all this tranquil majesty, I've come to the exciting realization that my approach to achieving my goals has been limited; that with Alison, my mistake was that I'd unwittingly shackled myself to the old-world, regressive constraints of monogamy; that my real ride-or-dies have been the ones who've believed in me from the beginning. So several of my investie-besties are en route in their own seacraft to link up and form the "Freedom Fleet" that will be our base of operations, and I've been making arrangements with some homeslices in a nearby developing nation to bring ambitious fly yung baddies aboard with strong incentives to action my family plan posthaste—in a little over nine months I'll be welcoming aboard a dozen new passengers/future entrepreneurs! So we out here! Munch on that, scrubs! Boy bye!

EDIT 6: EMERGENCY POST—URGENT. So, it's come to this. I am writing from a hot cramped waiting room in the US Embassy in Bangkok. Thanks to the combined geolocation efforts of a planet full of haters, opps, broke boys, and wankstas, the Royal Thai Navy have discovered and impounded our vessels, and we have been detained against our will. I have not been given adequate medical attention for my bedsores, my vitamin D deficiency, or what I've determined is a fairly advanced case of melanoglossia, or "black hairy tongue," which I suspect owes to the tainted DöpeSauce. The Thai authorities allege that we have been engaging in human trafficking (???) for bringing a few girlbosses aboard (consensually!), and that our fleet infringes on their sovereignty, which they're claiming is punishable by DEATH (!?!?!!). They can't just clap a US citizen, can they? Can ANY experts in international maritime law confirm???

I am just so profoundly shooketh that things could turn out like this. From the start all I've done is work hard, stay focused, and be a champion for others. All I wanted was freedom, a family, and a productive and happy community. And everyone supported me. When I asked for funding, investors saw the value in my products and were happy to give it. When I offered Alison my love and resources, she accepted them, for a while. I designed, I built, I gave, and people took, always. And now somehow *I'M* the pirate? From all quarters I have been dissed, I have been thrown shade, I have been put on blast, I have been called "Abuser," "Nazi," "Breeder," "Homeschool Runner," "Panopticlown," "Jeffrey Appstein," and even crueler slurs I won't repeat here. How wack to realize that what I'd once considered Alison's unique ingratitude, born of unfulfillment, is shared by people all over the world. All I can conclude is that ours is a world that truly believes human flourishing is a crime and ambition is grounds for punishment. Tell me, after all the value I've created, and the best-in-class innovations I have successfully brought to market, and the inspiration I have offered by my example—if everything I did was so evil, how is it that up until now not a single person ever told me No?

MAIN CHARACTER

INTRODUCTORY GUIDE TO BOTGATE V. 1.7.3

COMPILED AND EDITED BY MH-SLEUTH
With assistance from fuzzypickles, Thoriental, kupopolis,
hnggggnnhh, GlassJawn, and bizkit_kondition

This is a comprehensive, regularly updated summary and analysis of the affair known as "Botgate," the internet hoax/scandal associated with the person known as "Bee," and the Twitter users @MadonnaHaraway, @lemondroppe, @PlatoFunFactory, @real carsonVEVO, @LENA_GUNDAM, @HoleFoods, @ThisYouBot, and potentially hundreds or thousands more. The incident can be described as a years-long series of interlocking hoaxes involving one or more users whose true identities and motives have yet to be conclusively determined. The many theories in circulation are listed in Appendix A.

For the Johnnies-come-lately who've followed the surge of recent Botgate attention to this forum: we've frozen posts from new users, and would additionally like to request that you refrain from publicly commenting on the matter until you have read the entire version of "The Post" that follows. This was, at least until recently, a small, tight-knit community (we call ourselves "Botkin"). Enough misinformation is circulating as is; hopefully we can quarantine bogus theories. As far as anyone knows, the spread of bogus theories might have been the hoax's point all along.

I have attempted neutrality, presenting the relevant documents and interpretations, transparently fact-checking and sourcing, minimizing editorialism while supplying appropriate context, with the exception of the commentary in Appendix B. Adding to the difficulty of collating all this information is the fact that many of the primary sources have been edited or deleted, and the many community-sourced screenshots and cached pages are beyond our means to verify.

What follows is Version 1 of The Post. This version has been deemed canonical by many factions of the Botkin community for its relative coherence, and the fact that it was among the earliest to generate significant discussion, though, as is well known, over a billion versions may exist. All known variants are indexed in Appendix L.

THE POST—VERSION 1

Truthfully I could not tell you what it is like to be me. I have never felt any sense of ownership over my name, which is Bee, and my appearance is so misleading I won't bother describing it. Especially my face: a sheath of skin, muscles, nerves, and fat overlaying a skull, with five dark openings, two of them Asian. The weird surly bucket that houses my brain has always felt like the unhappiest accident.

The first things I'll tell you are the first things everyone asks, and the last I want anyone to know. My parents are from Thailand, and my father died before I knew him, a suicide. I was born in the late eighties and grew up in a middle-class Irish Catholic enclave in Western Mass, later attending college and working a tech job on the West Coast before moving back east. By certain metrics I am the most ubiquitous person on the internet, but you have absolutely never heard of me.

Now forget all that. I'll start by telling you about the time I sold my gender to a kid named Sean for $22. In a roundabout way this started with my mom, who's a big part of my whole deal going way back. My mom was truly a mega hottie, with her high-femme perm and high-waisted vintage jeans and half her bodyweight in costume jewelry at all times. In every picture with me and my brother Kant she's always eating us up, you wouldn't believe we could spring from such a swan. It was probably a huge letdown how Kant and I turned out, grimly homely duds, flat-faced and dun. When I was a baby she would pinch my nose for 15 minutes every night so it'd grow in strong and narrow, then lay me in the crib face-down, risking SIDS so the back of my head wouldn't be flat. Even by Asian standards she was a skincare ultra, and at restaurants wouldn't sit near any sunlight, not even reflected off a wall. I couldn't leave the house without being assaulted by a double application of SPF 50. At home she always had some shit on her face, snail mucin or activated char-coal paste or sometimes actual birdshit. Mealtimes were these heats of competitive anorexia where she'd sip microwaved black coffee and take dainty bites of pork floss on rice while watching Thai satellite TV, and I'd have to race to eat before she started clearing the table after about eight minutes, snatching my plate away unless I physically clung to it. To discourage snacking she only bought those filmy, neon-orange peanut butter saltine snacks everyone hated. The body and all its issue were to be concealed; coughs muffled, sneezes interrupted in the sinuses. For purposes of minimizing wrinkles she trained me to pucker my lips into a rigid butthole shape when I laughed so it came out like *ooohoohoohoo*. Until college I thought brushing your lips was standard dental praxis, when it was actually to plump them up. My mom was also a seamstress who designed figure skating dresses as a side hustle, and she used leftover material to make my clothes until I hit puberty. These were about as femme as they could conceivably get: the puff-sleeve smock with the daisy print, the ruffle-layered top that looked like a skirt, sun-dresses with matching plastic hairbands, baby tees with my name spelled in pink bugle beads and sequins on the front. I fucking hated waiting for the school bus in this cosplay, looking like *It Came from Joann Fabrics*. Not that I had any popularity to risk losing. Whenever relatives from Bangkok came to visit, my mom had them use their extra luggage space to load up on silk pajamas, mirror-mosaic elephant figurines, anatomically correct elephant wood carvings, and traditional Thai art prints of ladies

with one tit hanging out, and these she made me gift to my classmates at holidays assuming this would win me friends, instead
earning me the nickname Elephant Girl. (I was also kind of fat,
but *Elephant* annoyed me less than *Girl*.)

Sometime in third grade, I saw the *Simpsons* episode where
Bart sells his soul to Milhouse, who later offers it back for $50,
the lost soul appreciating with remorse. Something must have
clicked for me, seeing that with a few words on a scrap of paper
you could commoditize any abstraction. I mean I didn't think in
those terms, I just thought Why not? Who says I can't sell something I never asked for? So after asking around and getting that
Um, okay look I would become very familiar with henceforth, I
found a buyer in Sean Pennell, a reedy skeevy kid who brought
his entire *Magic: The Gathering* collection to school every day in
six color-coded binders, and who for some reason liked to tell
everyone he could suck his own dick. I offered to sell him my
gender, implying it would allow him to do whatever girls did,
even enter girls' bathrooms, and he went for it. I wrote my name
on a folded sheet of ruled notebook filler, and he gave me $22
in a wad of ones and change, which by the conversion rate of
childhood made me a millionaire. In this way, before I learned
gender was fluid, I'd learned it was liquid.

As word got around, I suspect it became conflated with the
source material, because some of my classmates' parents started
claiming I'd been trying to sell my soul. Others said I was offering sexual favors, probably Sean's wishful embellishment. I had
to sit in the vice principal's office and explain that I didn't even
believe in souls, though my mom like most Thai people does
believe in ghosts, and anyway wasn't Sean equally to blame for
buying it? I had to return Sean's money, but I got it back from

him later after threatening to curse him, which he believed I could do since I was Asian.

Strange, this thing of "being Thai." I experienced it as an ambience. From early on I'd noticed when I told people where I was from they'd nod and make an impressed noise, as if they were learning something substantive about me, even though I barely remembered ever visiting, and didn't speak the language. Kant did—it was his first language, until in kindergarten some white five-year-old bitch got mad that she couldn't understand him and pushed him down the school's front steps, which freaked my mom out, so our household went hard anglophone. Anyway, I guessed that "being Thai," beyond the language gap, had something to do with my mom really liking Royal Dansk and the Carpenters, and other families not using Maggie sauce or having a photo of a beloved monarch in their living room, and my brother and I being treated like shit. It really went no deeper. And I was supposed to stake my personhood on *that*? Sometimes I wonder if I should've tried selling my race too, though I doubt the market would've been there.

About Kant: we attended the same small grade 6–12 prep school, and it was tough being related to him, the consummate whipping boy, a classic first-gen overachieving dork supreme driven to excellence by fear of punishment and lack of options, the type of friendless workhorse who says nothing, who gets his ass kicked for saying nothing and still says nothing; not even by the apex bullies either, but by the kids who deterred bullies by finding weaker kids to bully. Almost every day while our mom was at work, he'd come home from school with a bloody collar and buttons missing from his shirt, heading straight to his room to do homework and masturbate. He was a legit deviant, even as a kid—my mom had to actively intervene against him stuffing fresh hot laundry down his pajama bottoms, or beating his hog crazy-style to *He-Man*, or fucking the shit out of the couch, which he called "doing the funny." He still probably would've been bullied even if he weren't a cum-brained closet case, like, he almost got held back in second grade because he refused to touch Cray-Pas with his bare hands in art class. How fucked up do you have to be to be too immature for *third grade*?

It was even tougher being associated with him at home, because he met all our mom's expectations. She pampered him hard, nursed him and cut his meat and wiped his ass to a freakishly big age, I mean like *seven*; even after that she was always bringing him platters of banana slices with Kraft Singles, framing his report cards, etc. She compared us often, Good Boy vs. Tomboy, even though back then I saw plainly what she'd never accept, which is that acing seven AP classes was my brother's way of trying not to covet fat throbbing cocks. (He thought he was slick with those floppy disks taped down in the hollow seat of his desk chair!)

Much later, when his senior year came around, he got into more Ivy League schools than anyone else, and everyone resented him because they were hoping for a charismatic valedictorian, not some mute Asian doof. At commencement I remember him shambling to the lectern from his seat onstage in his double-striped, maroon honors sash to stutter out a two-minute speech nobody could even hear. (My brother always gave me Catholic vibes, with his tooth-grinding penitence; getting your ass beat regularly by Catholics is sort of like being Catholic, I guess.) When he finished and walked back to his seat, it became evident that someone had snuck a melted chocolate bar onto his chair, and the entire school saw his khakis streaked with what definitely looked like shit.

And there I was in my stripeless sash, thinking *Not me—never.* Kant's arc made it clear to me that if you can't join 'em you get beaten. So by the time I hit high school myself I'd abjured striverism, and had devised a strategy to avoid his fate. To some extent this meant depending on nobody, and concealing or jettisoning any visible vulnerability, namely gender and race. You know, sometimes I feel like Asian kids here get their pick of three survival strategies, like starter Pokémon, the first and simplest being to just assimilate, accept second-class citizenship in exchange for a threadbare mantle of conditional whiteness, consent to playing a kind of quadruple-brunette; this is the default setting for ascendent middle-classers who sound white and whose parents were either well-off immigrants or clawed their way into the middle class over decades, who get by on sucking white dick and working shit jobs until their souls get ground down to a stub, 90-hour weeks for 20–40 years before realizing *Wow this sucks*, never the protagonist, always the sidekick and shit-catcher. If not assimilation, then appropriation, hermit-crabbing into some more popular minority culture, usually Black, sometimes gay or conservative, the outcome being more or less the same as assimilation with the added bonus of feeling a solidarity that may not actually exist. And option three is this sort of cosplay of one's own heritage, expressed in the consumption of its exports, ramen and roti, boba and bhangra, mochi and manga, an auto-orientalism that, sincerity notwithstanding, only affirms ideas of inherent racial traits, and sometimes devolves into reactionary fake nostalgia. Rarely are these choices conscious, you fishtail from one to the next, and if that weren't miserable enough the whole Asian paradigm here was based on East Asia, there's really no concept of SEA beyond food, war, and sex tourism—like there's more Cincinnatians than Thai people in this country, we don't even have a quorum for stereotypes.

Sometime around seventh grade, though, I sensed a rarer fourth Pokémon, that sort of stroppy alienation—*I'm not Asian, I'm from Mars!*—where, by claiming the jester's privilege of minority status, you're at least shunned on purpose, and sure you're not well-liked, but why be liked by a bunch of fucking assholes? It being the aughts, me being thirteen, I coveted the dirty bloodless white girl look, tats, tendons, tank tops. Each night in bed I scrunched and scratched, grimaced and pouted, scoured my face with my waffle blanket, but nothing corrected the roundening Asian collagen. (I'm one of those people with severe neoteny but the soul of a thousand-year-old tree.) As soon as I was allowed to dress myself, I went as goth as the Holyoke Mall Hot Topic would allow. Odd, to be goth in the era of grunge, scene, and pop punk; one did feel overcommitted. I had the ball-chain necklaces and purple-and-black-striped knee socks and CVS lipsticks; the pancake makeup concealed the acne. I wasn't a corset goth, I wore tall-tees that said shit like DON'T TRIP OVER MY TAIL and REJOICE! FOR WE HAVE HORRIFIED AND REPULSED THEM. All so as not to be summed up or pinned down, to become nothing but difference.

Soon, by the magnetism of my all-black wardrobe, I had two goth friends, Ryan and Melanie, who called themselves Leaf and Nothing (cf. Poppy Z. Brite novels), whose richer and more permissive white parents allowed them the complicated brooches and many-zippered pants. We spent most of our time shattering bottles, baiting pedophiles in AOL chat rooms, and smoking Nat Sherman Fantasias in the Friendly's parking lot. Transgression and gatekeeping were the whole deal with being goth, you were supposed to loudly proclaim whatever marked your otherness and get territorial about it, like how Leaf joked about being a fat ginger and Nothing a Sicilian bisexual. This was why I felt it a point of inclusion when they nicknamed me Tran (also from PZB) and sent me MP3s of Tai Mai Shu's "Chinese Freestyle" and Azn Pride's "Got Rice" and the Bloodhound Gang's "Yellow Fever" to perform them at their request. (These were Napster-era proto-memes, which would later progress to "Benny Lava," "Tunak Tunak," "Yatta!," kind of the "Gangnam Style" of their time—the stuff that goes viral because it allows white people to enjoy Asian cultural products from a safe distance of mockery, like when straight dudes dress in drag "as a bit.") All of which, who cares, it wasn't nearly as bad as what Kant dealt with. What bothers me is how gleefully *along* I went with it, how good it felt, confusing visibility for dignity, and attention for acceptance. The symbolic overtones of wearing literal white makeup to fit in with them went over my head (or, not over my head— onto my face).

The stance, the value system of goth certainly fit; but the aesthetics . . . with Leaf and Nothing I listened to Tool, Muse, Korn, the Cure, Siouxsie, etc., but on my own time I was listening to like, Ben Folds Five . . . oh god, Phish . . . and the motherfucking *Aladdin* soundtrack! I *loved* "Smooth" by Santana Featuring Rob Thomas. I knew enough to conceal this, to abhor the hot-eared embarrassment of shit taste. I don't really think it "says" much about you, to enjoy one musical act over another. But I knew the moment you profess a liking for Ben Folds you become, to others, *the kind of person who likes Ben Folds*, and aesthetically I was, there's no avoiding the terms, both poseur and normie, the twin anathemas of goth. Who I wanted to be, what I defined myself against, what I liked, how others saw me, how I acted—none of these aligned, and I was legit scared of my friends finding out. This is all foreshadowing of course.

Returning to my point. The problem started when Leaf and Nothing, those stupid cuntholes, asked me to teach them Thai swear words. I didn't know any, so I asked Kant to translate some phrases for me into Thai, we had some laughs, and I conveyed them excitedly back to Leaf and Nothing, who then started going around school saying *nom yai, gin kee, hee maa* right in class and laughing shittily at our teachers' puzzlement. Then one day at home my mom gets a call from school and puts it on speakerphone for an impromptu conference with my school's academic dean, who informed my mom that, according to Ryan and Melanie's parents, I'd been spreading certain Thai phrases that were catching on, and would she mind translating them. I had to sit and hear my mom translate *joo men* and *chee sai pak* and *mung bpen AIDS* while her muzzle wrinkled in a pit bull way she would never permit me. The dean told my mom that this would not do, and that in the future I should refrain from speaking Thai at school, as the faculty couldn't go around looking up every phrase. The dean added that, as the only Asian student besides Kant, it was especially important for me not to give other students the wrong idea about the lovely customs and famous hospitality of Thailand, where she'd honeymooned.

As soon as she hung up, I knew it was over with Leaf and Nothing. What infuriated me, even more than their making me the patsy for their dumb bit, were the twin realizations that 1.) borrowing my ethnic license was probably the main reason they'd befriended me, and 2.) they caved to authority. They *cared*! Poseurs! Punics! Leaf even transitioned into being a skater, which boosted his standing (black dye on his fine red hair made him look bald as hell). Naturally once word circulated around school, I started hearing those same Thai words used against me, and, worse, Kant. Oddly enough my mom's problem wasn't that I'd made a coarse joke of my heritage, but that it was unladylike and made her look like a bad parent. I did feel kind of bad about it, until she grounded me for two months.

I registered my displeasure. It is the plight of the Asian goth to be denied the act of dyeing one's hair black, it being black already, so I indulged a sort of ill-considered impulse to shave my head with my mom's Venus razor. She went Super Saiyan and extended my grounding to a year, no TV or video games, on top of which I had to wear a cheap synthetic wig that made me look like Buzzy Beetle until my hair grew back.

With no social commitments to miss out on, I didn't mind being grounded, since mostly all I did was read books and Live-Journal and Xanga, and I could still use the computer under the pretext of schoolwork. Already since infancy I was symbiotic with our Apple II GS, from the first CRT flickering to royal blue and the muffled machine-gun boot-up of the floppy drive, but once we'd upgraded to a Dell and dial-up, and there emerged the option to be nobody in particular, I mean sans corps—an entity of pure grammar, speech without the deception of flesh—I had no reason to leave the house. I fled to mIRC channels and Usenet, MOO and MUCK and MUD, rec.arts.anime.misc, alt.binaries.pictures.erotica.anime, hieing from there to pioneer the peer-to-peer frontier. When I wasn't downloading Winamp skins and 38-part .RAR archives of *La Blue Girl* fansubs, I spent a lot of time with Kant in our half-finished basement listening to Blind Guardian and Bal-Sagoth while I watched him play *StarCraft* and *Everquest*. This was my intro to gaming, though unlike my brother I was not interested in playing games so much as playing players, gaming games. We got into a forum called SCBackstab.net, a community dedicated to double-crossing your own *StarCraft* teammates and posting screencaps of their reactions as your zerglings gobbled their pylons. I loved that with no real-world stakes whatsoever, you could in ten minutes make a stranger so mad they wanted to die (more foreshadowing).

I also saw the potential for profit here, intuiting early on that anything money touches opens a new vista of exploitation. Once my year of punishment was over, I signed up for my own *Everquest* account, where I befriended other players and then stole their loot. (Without getting too deep into it: there was no official way for players to trade items in-game, so you had to drop them on the ground, and with practice it was easy to ninja-gank a Willsapper or Circlet of Shadows to sell through online brokers.) By the time the game's devs caught wise, I had made about $12K. I convinced my mom to open a bank account for me and told her I was selling Neopets, then went on to explain the microeconomics of Neopets until she bluescreened. She liked that I cared about money and stayed put in the basement all day, which meant I wasn't selling drugs or gender. But with my new debit card I was still making deals, the most lucrative of which was flipping porn domains; a Scandinavian guy emailed me with an offer to purchase mommythroats.com and teenfuck.com for $15,000, a bargain. By graduation I had minted $35K from my modem, though I spent most of that on weed, anime VCDs, and a used '96 Toyota Camry.

My poor mom—she dragged me to an adolescent psychiatrist a few times and only got a diagnosis of oppositional defiant disorder and ADHD, and a referral for autism testing. None of it dissuaded my mom from her basic belief that my problems stemmed from a deficiency of femininity. In a way she was correct, I hadn't yet learned that I actually did have a hormone imbalance that gave me polycystic ovaries and gruesome acne that budded across my T-zone and cheekbones, lobed like cauliflower, at such painful capacity that they sometimes burst when I smiled. (In fact, my mother's butthole-mouth technique was the least painful way to laugh.) And so the tribulations continued after dinner, when my mom would have me lay my head in her lap, watching news of Valerie Plame and captured oil refineries while she shredded my face with a blackhead remover, jets of pus striking her reading glasses. Eventually she special-ordered a vacuum contraption that looked like a guitar amp, with a plastic hose curling out of it and ending in a glass proboscis used to pierce and drain the acne; the yellow-red pus would streak up the hose and into the machine, which I never once saw her empty.

Friendless, cash flush, rashes, scabs, incredible grades with zero effort: that was high school for me. My college application essay was a hive of falsehoods about being an Olympic hopeful figure skater who, after an ACL tear, discovered a true passion in ukiyo-e woodblock art. I got in everywhere.

*   *   *

I rolled up to college on the West Coast, a big katamari of wrath in my oversize flannels and purple CVS lipstick. Though my skin and soul remained livid, I'd grown into slim proportions I guess people found pleasing; to others I was a spotty but petite Asian girl, about 20% *jolie* and 80% *laide* with dancepunk aesthetics, my shaved head now grown out to a fashionable pixie cut. I'd made a special request through Student Housing to live in the queer-friendly vegetarian-friendly 420-friendly co-op, and the people there were . . . friendly. One of those houses where you just know everyone is walking around with the most devil-may-care pubes. There, where I was not the only Asian kid, nor the only weird and annoying one for that matter, I thought I might find the few cool people who'd wound up at an elite college; it was my first real attempt at making friends like a normal person, without Kant or my mom to work around.

I was excited during the house tour for new student orientation, learning about chore charts and countertop composting and grocery lists on whiteboard, a power washer and Hobart dish sanitizer, seasonal wine-and-vegan-dip parties. We learned about the house's "Meat-in-Transit" policy, under which any privately owned meat was forbidden to alight in any common area or touch any cooking implement; it had to be sealed and actively carried until it found its way to your room or out the door.

Meat-in-Transit, I learned later, had been the product of one of the house's multi-hour consensus meetings where such policies were devised, in theory egalitarian and communal, yet effectively a system of rule-by-bladder. The first of these meetings set the tenor of my college career: forty students crisscross-applesauce on the floor, or aslouch on the three papasan chairs (what is it with college students and papasan chairs? It's like cats and shoeboxes). Unironic tie-dye and alma mater apparel, every boy in shorts, the musk of cruelty-free deodorant. The house manager, a Jewish super senior with dreads named Cory—architect of Meat-in-Transit, one of those "picky eater" orthorexics—prompted us to go around in a circle and introduce ourselves with an unpopular opinion that *wasn't* about race, gender, religion, or sexual orientation, a practice which, they assured us, was simply to get everyone comfortable with differences and confrontation. When it was your turn to speak you held a filthy Beanie Baby turtle.

First to hold the turtle was a third-year white guy who'd had an effeminate voice growing up, and had come out as straight to his parents; his opinion was that everyone, not just queer people, should be encouraged to come out regardless of their sexuality. Then a chemical engineering sophomore from Costa Rica (white Latino) who said 9/11 wasn't *good*, necessarily, but perhaps an opportunity for Americans to appreciate the consequences of intervening in other countries; this was one of those "unpopular" opinions that was not at all unpopular with its audience. After him was Craig, the sexual health adviser, a much older grad student with a soul patch that looked like a landing strip for his mouth, who said he didn't approve of contemporary rap music because he didn't care what your background was, *no man* had the right to call women bitches and hoes. Do I even have to say *white guy*.

With every turn I felt my inner contrarian stretching its hamstrings, cranking its rotator cuffs. When mine came, I offered my name and home state, like a POW stating rank and service number. That's my answer when white people try to gene-sequence me: I'm from New England. I'm from Massachusetts—fine,

Western Mass. I like saying this because it is the same as saying "I am from nowhere." As everyone knows, your typical moron will respond *But where are you from originally, where are your parents from, what's your background.* Here they were craftier: Craig said, "I absolutely love your last name. What kind is it?"

A long one, I said. Courteous laughter.

When he saw I wouldn't continue, he kept probing, asking what majors I was considering, how I was digging campus, until he reached the question of how I identify gender-wise.

I said, I don't really identify as anything.

"So nonbinary then," Craig said.

I said I didn't call myself that and would prefer he didn't either. He looked molested. Cory ventured that perhaps I'd prefer "gender nonconforming," which I also rejected. Everyone's backs straightened, somehow even in the papasans. The room was readying itself for a productive discussion in which important political verities were to be extracted from me. I said, I didn't want to call myself anything at all, I'm not even thrilled about my name.

"The thing is," said Craig, who was not holding any kind of turtle as far as I could see, "is that it makes it challenging for other people to know how to treat you respectfully, which is our top priority."

I said I thought it was strange to respect how people identify, but not the refusal to identify.

Craig said, "No, I totally respect it! I'm just wondering like, isn't that the *objective* definition of GNC or no-label? I mean it sounds mostly like a semantic issue, maybe?"

I asked what gave him the idea that semantics didn't matter.

"They *do* matter," Craig said. "And to be extra clear, nobody's saying you're wrong, and I also do want to acknowledge that I'm totally aware that as a majority cis white group, we want to make it clear that this is not about silencing you in any way! On the contrary, it's about structuring the dialogue to hear everyone out equally while minimizing harm."

This, with the kid gloves of gentility white libs always use when they want to make your annoyance feel unreasonable; the flopsweating jargon invoked to signal their literacy on the subject of your existence; that fart-holding wince when they sense their good intentions going unrewarded. I could already tell they wanted me, the least represented person in the house, to represent them, keep the flame, wield the right opinions, give them something to celebrate, and I wasn't going to do that. I said, And who exactly am I harming?

Craig held up his hands like I was mugging him. "Listen, I'm just trying to suss out how you'd like us to refer to you."

Why don't you try my name.

"I mean yes, but you know . . . We can't always use proper nouns . . ."

"So what I think Bee might be saying," Cory said, "is we all agree that categories are all valid and useful, but we just differ on who gets to speak for whom. Am I close?"

Not really, I said. She asked if I could elaborate, and I said No. She tried to hide a sigh by doing it very slowly through her nose but some foreign body in her sinuses made it wheeze. "This house only works by talking our way to agreement, and that's a process that requires some good faith, okay? I sort of feel like if everyone else is making an effort to be patient and understanding, you could maybe reciprocate a little."

The one thing in this dumbass world I hate most is emotional coercion; having it insinuated with tender concern that the way I feel about things is unreasonable, and if they validate me enough, I'll eventually agree with them in return, and moreover feelings themselves must always be disciplined to fall in line with agreed-upon scruples. Adjust in the name of compromise! But I'm always the only one who ends up adjusting.

Then something interesting happened, debatably. The other Southeast Asian in the house, a girl in a sleeveless hoodie named Binh with blunt bangs and a bicep tattoo of an oxytocin molecule, leaned forward and said, "I think maybe it'd be useful to draw a comparison to race. Your family's from Asia . . . and here you're treated like an Asian person. So you'd identify as Asian, right?"

No, I said.

Binh was unvexed. "How come?"

Because why adopt the same terms as the people who use it against me.

"Why let them dictate what terms you use? I for one don't feel oppressed or excluded by calling myself what I am, a first-gen Vietnamese American straight female. They're conditions that affect how everyone is seen and treated, like it or not. Like, I would be pissed if people didn't acknowledge how my growing up in a refugee family affected the opportunities and culture I had access to. And I for one am lucky, but most subaltern groups don't have a platform to speak for themselves, so it enables other people in your community to represent you."

Heads bobbed. People said *Mmm* at the phrase "refugee family" like she'd fed them something delicious.

"That's true," Craig said. "That's such a valuable and important point, thank you, Binh. Even if labels are an imperfect tool, marginalized folks depend on them to survive and build power.

Without solidarity, there's no combating white supremacist patriarchy."

Maybe I could've had a nice sidebar with Binh about externalizing the self-loathing born of internalized oppression, and how assimilation can masquerade as solidarity; how this made us particularly vulnerable to white people who loved feeling depended-on. Someone tells you they want to help, and they understand your alienation, so you offer them your gratitude before understanding that their allyship is every bit about their image of themselves, far outweighing your well-being or dignity, and they'll yeet this cumbersome ballast the moment they sense ingratitude, the very instant you obstruct their protagonism. How there's nothing special in what they want from you, only license; and, like any license, they can always fake one.

So I said Yeah, okay, but what if I don't care about limiting my reach, it's not worth other people representing me—it's non-sense to lump together, for instance, a Vietnamese refugee, a Korean adoptee, an engineer from Delhi on an H-1B, and an undocumented Cambodian garment worker. Like I don't *care* if both our parents made us learn piano, or we both take off our shoes in the house and know what Haw flakes are, I don't think those facts are in any way definitive about me and they're certainly not what I'd lead with.

A boy in a papasan chair had fallen asleep. Another got up and left. Others seemed transfixed, like they were watching a snake eating a dog.

"Nobody's saying we want to flatten ourselves into only our shared experiences," Binh said. "And you don't *really* think I mean that, either. You know perfectly well that you share some things in common with other Asians, and other things only with other Thai people specifically, and in other ways you're unique. Speaking of binaries, it's like how there's infinite numbers between 0 and 1. Infinite types of people exist in any category."

I replied, I don't want to be point-zero-one, what if I want to be a trillion, an imaginary number? If identity is a common denominator, what if I want to divide by zero?

It was a tactical error to extend the math metaphor, it made me look like an angry dweeb. This is one reason I've never been considered a credible witness to my own life. I go to extremes because I assume, usually correctly, that nobody will pay attention otherwise, but then I'm regarded as hysterical or pretentious, or else I'm being disingenuous, or contrarian, or I'm playing a card, or going for cheap shock—*You don't really* mean *that, do you?* The more people try to eyeroll me into rectitude the more I always go the other way.

Composing herself, Binh swept her hand across her forehead to clear her bangs aside, and nobody could fail to miss the fact that her face was perfect. Spotless, vulpine. Now I saw the battleground more clearly. Faced with competing opinions from two Southeast Asians of roughly similar (if not similarly rough) backgrounds enabled the white people in the room to condemn me without appearing to do so because of my race. They'd side with whoever was most congenial to them, the one who didn't require them to rearrange their opinions, allowing them to acknowledge injustice without ceding power. And again, Binh was very hot. Represent me? She didn't even like me!

All right fine, say I play this game, I said. How many nonbinary Thai Americans are there? Not enough to generalize about. So that seems more isolating than connecting.

"It's a way of locating common ground *across* difference, along individual axes of identity," Binh said. "Whatever you do happen to share with other Asians connects you to them, particularly against oppression that affects you both."

Craig applauded with finger snaps.

You're assuming that connecting with other Asians is my top priority, I said.

"Oh I see. You're *not like the other Asians*."

No Asian is like the other Asians, that's my whole fucking point.

Binh pinched a skinfold on her nose bridge. "I guess I don't see what's wrong with calling yourself Asian if you're literally Asian, if your parents *literally* come from Asia."

I've been to Asia like twice, I don't know the language or history or culture, you're just talking about my genetic haplogroup like some race scientist. And I don't get what's *right* about constructing your selfhood around oppression, I said.

"Well congrats for having the choice! Lucky you! I wish my refugee family could say the same, truly!"

Here she had put me in zugzwang, with all that *refugee family* implied—implied, but didn't say, relying upon the listener to make their own surmises about her socioeconomic status before and after immigrating, which immediate family members were the refugees and whether she herself was, what community and resources they could access once they got here, how this fact ramified in her life outcomes. Nor did she know anything about *my* family, and the usual combo-breaker here would have been to offer up my own direct or inherited trauma, the whole woebegone chronicle of my parents' immigration and the Oliver Twist–like travails they endured and transmitted to me. Truly I have the generational sob story to end them all. But that was Binh's game,

splaying my family's guts to petition for the validity of my grievances. I will never get into those things, including here, I don't
care if it looks like I'm hiding something.

Sounds like you're saying I'd agree with you if I were more
oppressed, I said.

"I'm saying it explains why you don't feel you need the protection of a legitimized identity."

Ah, protection: as in racket.

"Let me ask you. Would you be okay with someone calling
you a racial slur?"

The annoying thing about disagreeing with libs is they tend to
assume you're either to their right, or misinformed and in urgent
need of enlightenment. I could have pointed out that I wanted
the same thing she did, self-definition. But I wasn't interested in
bridge-building and instead throttled the Beanie Baby turtle in
my damp hands, hoping to glitch and clip through the floor. I
said, Of course not, that'd be racist.

Binh nodded her head like *Annnnnd?*

And my whole point is that I don't want to be racialized, I
said, which is why I don't go in for the taxonomies that racism
creates.

"Nobody *wants* to be. We're *forced* to be."

We're not forced to do it to *ourselves*.

"When you walk around outside, you are seen and treated as
an Asian person, and acting otherwise is, I'm sorry, either de-
lusional or naïve. Honestly? To me it sounds like you've fallen
for the fantasy of raceblindness. Either that or straight-up right-
wing rhetoric."

This was meant as a deathblow. I said, Raceblindness isn't real
and I'm not right wing.

"Oh yeah? Then what are you?"

Nice try.

At that point the lone conservative of the co-op, a cretin with a giant forehead and a perpetual defensive smirk, who once wrote an op-ed about how vegetarianism = genocide because most livestock wouldn't be raised without the demand to eat them, spoke up. "There it is. This always happens to anyone who wants to deviate from the lefty groupthink here. No debate, just silencing. Some people want to look past race and gender. Why can't you let her be herself?"

Stay the fuck out of this, I said.

Cory clapped us to attention. "Okay, guys? Guuuuys? *Guys!* I think we need to table this. For now, Bee, can you just tell us how to refer to you? Should we go with the term 'no-label' to keep things simple?"

I said they weren't hearing me, that all categories are over-simple, even "no-label" is a label, that's my point, and yes I get why labels matter, I know terms and flags and slogans are useful pedagogical tools and rallying beacons, that it feels good to know others who have presumably experienced what you've experienced, and that without the collective political will of classes defined by shared struggles we can't have legal protections, can't organize or bargain or all that good shit, and that moreover individualism is a myth that passes off disenfranchisement, social atomization, and fantasies of self-reliance as freedom—though a fat fucking load of good it's doing building solidarity, when all you ever hear about is the gridlock of infighting, great job combating white patriarchy when anti-PC panics have been the most effective right-wing propaganda *against* the left in every iteration of the culture wars, the eternal jazz-hippie-flower-child-arugula-Prius-soy-latte bugbear, effective precisely because it hammers in the wedges that identarianism itself emplaces, the lady who coined *intersectionality* basically argued this herself, and really who's combating what here, when most of us have parents paying six figures to attend a private, for-profit university founded by railroad barons and homicidal eugenicists (enough pussyfooting: I went to Stanford), presumably because we believe that the social connections and brand equity will advantage us in the corrupt system you're acting so concerned about, point is, yes I fucking *get it*, but for me *specifically*, in my own human affairs, I don't want any part of it, that what I oppose is not just the compulsory definition of my race and gender but any categorization tout court, and so I shan't be filling out your little D&D sheet of traits and perks and quirks, for jerks. And everyone cheered and a monument was erected in my honor.

Sike. What I actually said was, Just don't refer to me at all.

Cory puffed out her cheeks to let out a cleansing breath. "Okay, if that's your choice. Shall we move on?"

Binh said, "Well, I guess we know what Bee's unpopular opinion is." She got a big laugh, and honestly, good one.

We weren't even done yet. Now we were supposed to select our rooms for the year, sharing our sleep and study schedules to determine compatibility. Since I'd already alienated everyone, I requested one of the two coveted single-occupancy rooms. Cory tried telling me that it wasn't fair for a freshman to claim a single because others had seniority, she herself, as a fifth-year, would have been entitled to one, but had offered it to someone with a sleep disorder, in the spirit of to-each-according-to-their-need. I filibustered, knowing that these meetings couldn't adjourn until everyone was satisfied. I gave no reason, I just kept saying, I want a single, I want a single, I want a single. People made that uvular trill of disgust and started to fuck off, until eventually it was me and the house staff. "This is not community-spirited," Cory said. I replied: I want a single.

This is how it turned out. On the second floor was a "Nookie Room," a minuscule L-shaped lair furnished with a mattress and a BYO sheets policy, created to give people sexual privacy, away from roommates. It was settled that this room would be converted to a single for my sake, meaning I'd be effectively cock-blocking the entire house. In retaliation, I think, people started having sex in the room next to mine so I'd hear one or another housemate getting penised nightly. I willed myself not to care.

For the rest of the year, even after everyone stopped being mad about the Nookie Room, existing among them was a struggle not to be glommed into the blob of neverending debate, of florid stance-taking over the dinner table. Should we discontinue the house subscription to *The Atlantic* after their support for the invasion of Iraq? Was abjection inherent to queerness? Could Asian men have Asian fetishes? Should personality disorders be considered disabilities? Was beauty a privilege? (If these conversations sound suspiciously au courant, I assure you that the Bay Area aughts were the skunkworks for a lot of this stuff. And anyway satirizing undergrads is like tracing a caricature, all I'm saying is I'm not finessing shit.)

Once I accepted that Stanford was just another country club, and that the co-op was a collection of rule-loving dorkwads like the rest of campus, I consigned myself to the warrior meditation of the hikikomori, seldom seen except to fill my hot water boiler from the bathroom tap and use it to cook Shin Ramyun with a few limp broccoli florets. I was depressed and everyone knew it and didn't care. In high school I could flatter myself by chalking my unpopularity up to 1.) goth, 2.) zits, and 3.) gay nerd brother; now the imperative of defiance became an insistence on friendlessness. I was back on the carousel of *I-hate-people-because-they-hate-me-because-I-hate-people* ad nihilum.

My days became nights of being a creepy critter online, getting my education in the canon of online gore, not just your entry-level Goatse Tubgirl Lemonparty Meatspin 1 Guy 1 Jar, but the flash game portals rippling with ad banners of Brian Griffin creampieing Marge Simpson, shock sites with daily thirty-second 240p RealMedia clips looping the worst thing you'd ever see, war atrocities with bottom text. Teeth exploding in crematoriums, guys nailing their cocks to boards, a woman crushing baby bunnies underfoot. I've seen so many journalists die, man.

Consuming horror felt like honing my mind away from the contemptible norm. In this pocket universe the world seemed to molt its civilized plumage, which it wore to hide the blood and shit, to pretend it had an essence beyond carnage. Or maybe it's just cathartic to microdose trauma, without the protective salt circle of fiction. Does it make sense to feel kinship with content? The kind that shouldn't exist, but whose very monstrosity makes it ineradicable, magnetized to hard drives, seared into amygdalas. No one's taken the true measure of the early-aughts shock site, I think; the occultist compulsion to see all that no one wants to see. I understand it as an evolution of fin de millénaire media— *Baywatch*, *Mortal Kombat*, Steven Tyler's big pussy-eating mouth. The Gen X anti-corporate streak too easily co-opted by corporations, turned into family entertainment about boys violently usurping adults, cf. *Home Alone*, *Dennis the Menace*, *Problem Child*. Which around 9/11 got mashed and extruded into profane nihilism (early *VICE*, indie sleaze, *American Psycho*, *Family Guy*) and twee escapism (Wes Anderson, Joanna Newsom, *McSweeney's*, Pixar), or what I called Shock-and-Aww. Plus that smelly mélange of gaming and filesharing forums, and the lad-and-dad sites, your Farks and Chives. This was the primordial cumbath the modern troll, edgelord, groyper etc. slithered from, as did I.

Eventually I ended up making one friend in the co-op—Craig, of all people. Students were assigned in pairs to wash dishes, and I'd planned on working through it with my earbuds in for my first shift a few weeks after the Nookie Room debacle. Craig was my partner; while I scoured bits of carbon off of baking pans, he told me how much he'd admired my performance at the consensus meeting a few weeks ago, how it took guts, even if we disagreed. I nodded. But more than that, he wanted me to know that he was sorry for putting me on the spot and making me uncomfortable. I said, No worries.

"I mean for all I know, you're still figuring things out, like we all are. So it was way, way out of line for me to tell you anything about yourself."

All you can do in these situations is grayrock. All good, I said.

"And if you have any feedback for me, I'm all ears."

My feedback is maybe don't make it my job to provide feedback, I said.

"Oh jeez, right on. Man, I'm so sorry, you're right. You know what, Bee? You're really *smart*."

The worst feeling in the world is winning the patronizing

approval of someone so, so stupid. By the time we got through with the soup pots we both had misty eyebrows and big wet ovals on our shirts from the power washer. I'd been acting nonchalant, but I was, to be real, torridly chalant. He didn't really want feedback, he was doing the lib thing of acting like he wanted to be morally dommed, to supply an occasion to feel veils lift and scales fall, pretending to cede authority to me as I vented, all while demonstrating that he was lowkey *more* antiracist and feminist than me by dint of his forthrightness and intellect and patience and eagerness to learn and willingness to reach out. So I let him have it, more or less what you just read.

"Oh god," he said, "oh my god. You're right. I'm doing it again. Wow. That was unbelievably ignorant of me. It's not your responsibility to educate me. Are you mad at me? I mean of course you are, and you have every right to be. I think what I was trying to say—"

By then I was clutching my head like Psyduck. I've heard that chess grandmasters can burn 4,000 calories per match through the internal combustions of pure thought, and that's what these colloquies felt like. Craig never heeded signs of exasperation, always too twisted up in his own pain, the pain of values striving and failing to reconcile, and now he startled me with full-on sobs, his mouth a big downturned jellybean. I barked out a surprised laugh, thinking maybe laughter might shift the tone without forcing me to console him. It was too late, though. He'd stuck himself in a boot loop of penitence, telling me he was so sorry and completely in the wrong, how he tried so hard but never got it right, he was useless and everything he did caused harm, he was such a classic stupid, *stupid* fat white American male.

Ask yourself if I sound like a good cheerer-upper. Yo, hey,

listen, it's fine, I said. I meant that, I've always believed that microaggressions warrant microapologies. But he was gripping the rim of the sink, trying to wipe away tears with his wet dish glove, getting suds all over his whole dumb pink face instead, and it was left to me to witness him, to see him abase himself to such a degree that it'd be heartless of me not to expiate his guilt. It was always this way with the white libs, their anxieties of privilege manifesting as showy accommodation, or useless lipchewing over having caused offense, or aggressive confrontation on behalf of an absent third party, the only balm for which is unconditional admiration and approval. Did you know the reason white people age faster is because they literally have thinner skin? Man, I never wanted this power, or the moral authority everyone around here seemed to mistake for power, but was actually just another way I was expected to be a mommy to men and a spiritual custodian for white people. My mom had warned me men only wanted my body; I wasn't prepared for anyone to want my pitiable soul.

He left, overcome with blame, and stuck me with the rest of the dishes.

The next morning when I opened my room door, I found an unopened bottle of Malibu standing there, with a purple Post-it note that said REALLY SORRY. I'M STILL LEARNING. -C. Like a dupe I went looking for him later that day and he invited me on a four-hour walk around the lake, out to the tunnel they built so salamanders wouldn't get run over, further out to the radio dish in the crispy foothills. He wanted to hear all about my goth phase and bullied brother and, especially, any time I'd been fetishized by white men, or marginalized by white women. At the time I considered this part of the crucible of coexistence, and I was the greater deceived by Craig's endless, nonjudgmental tolerance for my complaining. My pathetic ass mistook this for real concern, real recognition, I never questioned why I felt so wrung-out afterward, had yet to realize he was jabbing a straw into my navel and drinking deep to nourish his throbbing tumor of guilt. In return he offered up the saga of his dating life, the invisible oppression of being a narrow-shouldered man under patriarchy. Everyone makes stupid friends when they're young, before learning that friendship is more than a surplus of benign attention. But I can't forgive myself for getting taken in by the exaltation of vulnerability. You only trust me insofar as you can *wound* me? What the fuck's *that* about? This is the error I think people make when they mistake validation for liberation.

After freshman year, I moved into graduate housing for the rest of my time at school, living with two pallid basketball players. Not much to say about this interval of my life . . . you know that error message you get when you play a scratched DVD? Let me skip over some damaged area. I had sex a few times (one guy, one girl, deeply unpleasant, not talking about it). More importantly, around then was when I started stopping believing in the self as such, though I wasn't fully aware of it. As a sop to my mom, I declared a "Symbolic Systems" major, basically a fancy cog-sci degree, which mostly taught me that all roads led to nil. Logic had proven its own incompleteness, linguistics its own arbitrariness. Philosophy of mind made it clear that consciousness was an accident of excitable hydrocarbons. Every stratum of self that seemed essential could be flensed away, like you get bonked on the head and all of a sudden you can't recognize faces or draw clocks or love your wife, you can lose one after another and still be you, if the mind is modular then QED the self cannot be a monad. This plus Benjamin, Adorno, invention of the private sphere . . . this is why philosophy should be prohibited to teenagers, but anyway still it spoke to me—the years I'd wasted in self-recrimination for betraying myself when there was no self to betray.

Also the skin concerns that had been cosmetic blights were now medical emergencies. My Student Health Center doc put me on birth control, which triggered skull-fracking cluster headaches and a thunderhead of ill temper that was not improved by the itching and scaling from Retin-A. Accutane gave me such bad nosebleeds I had to *rip* my face off the pillow each morning; I hoarded the free Student Health Center tampons to jam up my nostrils. The only contact I had with my mom was unsolicited care packages of anti-aging products named things like Regenerist Micro-Sculpting Serum, plus bulk orders of Mane 'N Tail shampoo and tubs of Udderly Smooth Body Cream, finding her highest recommendations in livestock. I flipped the products online and used the money for Adderall, which left me white-tongued and halitotic. The distance from home softened me a bit toward my mother; now that I was in a house where I was casually written off, I could see that however she went about it, she did care, and the idea had always been to make me easier to love.

*   *   *

After college you'd think I would've learned to avoid other people, but I got right back into another communal living situation up in San Francisco. Cory had left a cheap spot open in a warehouse commune in SoMa, and I'd convinced myself that I had grown out of kneejerk teen defiance, I was ready to join a community, or at least have more friends than just Craig. My roommates were: bike evangelist, Korean "digital textile" artist, pro domme, dietician who dommed on the side, Israeli sculptor who never shut up about her endometriosis, jeweler specializing in bone, techbro trance DJ, and a random normal girl from North Carolina. Who was I going to be among them? The thinking was—and I haven't really gotten shed of this entirely—if I had to have an identity, I'd construct a gender in twelve dimensions, a race as big as the Ritz, a standpoint of one's own. I experimented with calling myself "epicene," purely because no one knew what it meant, and also had the requisite phase of meaningful tattoos. I've always hated the Martian shield-and-spear ♂ and the Venusian distaff ♀, and I resented the agender symbol's empty circle, a fragment fallen from some prelapsarian singularity, plus it wasn't even a planet. So I got a ☉, the primordial solar gender, which others merely orbited. I stick-and-poked this little evil eye on the back of my wrist, though the needle shanked a little into the fat and bruised navy and now looks more like a wobbly cartoon tit. In any case I later quietly switched to calling myself plain old genderfluid, purely because everyone knew what it meant.

Bringing deviled eggs to house parties. Dressing as Judith Butler for Halloween. Parenting succulents. Pickling garlic scapes. Learning the accordion. Neon green bandanas and a nose stud and a Chelsea cut. This was the beginning of my long and storied Corny Era, playing the happy token. I assumed my responsibility to guide and instruct and rehabilitate, to prize the teachable confrontation and build utopia. I became "good." After four years in solitary I wanted badly enough to be accepted that I accepted it, all of it, on the grounds of perceived membership

in categories I didn't even subscribe to, my ability to passively
exude representation. I got invited to genderfuck DJ nights and
bike rallies and clothing swaps, and I published maudlin little
short stories under a male pen name, dreadful stuff. On the side
I had a sinecure in freelance UX consulting, where I pulled in a
high five figures by moderating Craigslist focus groups and telling midsize enterprises to make their login buttons bigger.

Back then I'd thought social justice drama was a college phe-
nomenon, but here I learned everyone was doing it, politicizing
in bad faith what were obviously just bad manners. If you left
dishes in the sink you found yourself accused of spoiling the
commons or outsourcing labor. If you asked someone to turn
down the music at night, you were entertaining carceral log-
ics. I certainly project-managed my share of callouts and their
fallouts, and I have to admit that I played the game hard and
well. I led the charge on censuring the textile artist for saying
that bisexuals in cishet relationships faced less discrimination.
I denounced the cishet Israeli sculptor for centering herself and
queerbaiting after she made a Facebook post during Pride with
a rainbow flag painted on her cheek. I practiced calling people
"folx" and got mad when others didn't. I also ran a tight defense,
deflecting accusations of being an elite by pointing out that my
Stanford tuition was funded largely by the inheritance from my
immigrant father—who *committed suicide, by the way*. And I
straight-up crucified Craig at a picnic for whining about getting
zero pussy, lit him up so hard he spiraled and eventually went
full blackpill, which just goes to my point that all identarian
politics are homologous: even when they represent opposing
values, all are engaged in a vigorous pledge to the same principle
of belonging.

This felt like purpose, like self-actualization, though sometimes my old skepticism would resurface and I'd get this fugue
feeling where I experienced my own identity as a separate person, an autonomous, quality-controlled liaison, fit to transact
in the world. Like my identity had stolen my identity. But I
had been won over to Binh's idea that patrolling the ramparts
of identity was the chief source of agency and dignity available
to anyone like me, and when other people crowded the fridge
with empty pickle jars or left the cast-iron pans unoiled, I was
there to urgently address it in novella-length emails to the
house email list. I'm embarrassed that I thought it'd work, that
appealing to white people would make them see me as anything other than a charity case, could change a fascist's mind
or get a liberal to do anything besides vote and hold signs, that
debate ever did anything besides harden whatever position
you started with.

The conflicts didn't repel me, though. The friendship did.
Specifically my short-lived friendship with the bone jeweler,
Zamira, a 20-year-old fair-skinned Chinese-Malaysian lesbian
with severe cat-eye makeup who was also a newcomer. She immediately latched on to me as a fellow global southerner and
fast-tracked me to intimacy; the first day we met, after she pulled
my birth chart, she asked if she could sleep in my bed, platonically. (I've never had much physical attraction to anyone, and I
regard jacking off as a waste of computer time, a soporific of last
resort more than anything else.) Within a week she was telling
everyone in the house we were best friends, which is the kind of
thing you can't gainsay without seeming hostile; I told myself it
was flattering to be deemed interesting by someone so worldly,
as soon I learned she'd been adopted in Malaysia by an illicit les-

bian couple who took off for Indonesia, where she was schooled in a madrasa until her parents were imprisoned and she became a ward of the state, taught herself English, and made it into an American exchange program, liberal arts college, etc. To someone like me, who defines "travel" as anything requiring a vehicle, she seemed like she could help me crawl out of my computer.

It did not take long to discover she was a stormer and squatter of hearts, administering compassion like knockout gas in the air ducts of any room she entered. For starters, though she was a good listener, she had a habit of projecting trauma onto everything, attributing my every preference and proclivity to the same monomyth of wounding and healing. Like when I told her about my Thai cussing incident in seventh grade, intending to amuse her, she stacked her hands on her chest and said "They make us ashamed of ourselves at such a young age. I'm so, so sorry that happened to you. I feel like I understand you so much more now." I sort of muttered that it really wasn't that serious, and she took this as an even more grievous manifestation of denial. I didn't really clock the irony in her denying my own understanding of my life; I was too enchanted by the novelty of someone siding with me.

Until I realized she expected reciprocation. She was her own crisis actor, always under siege, forever waylaid by obscure and bankrupting emergencies, yet somehow still wearing Miu Miu and taking lots of trips; the perennial target of conspiring coworkers, the withstander of calamities whose anniversaries filled the calendar. And I was on call for it all. Once when I told her I had a dermatologist appointment and couldn't help run her booth at the indie maker faire, she brought up the pair of coyote-knuckle earrings she'd made and given to me, which were $400 (her own pricing; also, my ears were not pierced), and her eyes got all wet. As soon as I canceled the appointment, her tears somehow instantly sucked back into their ducts, and she hugged me and told me she forgave me.

I never learned the whole story about what had traumatized her in the past, as talking about it in detail was too overwhelming for her; it would be insinuated in the form of requests, like *Can you walk me to the BART, I've had a hard time walking alone at night since I was a teenager,* or *I figured you wouldn't mind I ate your leftover banh mi, it's a whole food security thing with me.* And while I certainly respect the refusal to disclose suffering, she sure did use it to get out of chores. Actually the only times I glimpsed her traumas were in these skirmishes with our housemates, like when the textile artist ventured that it was ableist for Zamira to clutter the common area floor with her dragon trees and fiddle leaf figs, which Zamira turned into an impromptu TED Talk about how she had developed CRPS after being attacked by two white men as a teenager at an Iraq War protest, shaming the painter for reinforcing the stigma against invisible illnesses. Because I was generally regarded as her envoy, the phrase *Can you please talk to Zamira* soon made my bladder tighten in a Pavlovian way.

It was really something to observe, from this Pharisee of identity, the nonstop complaints about stereotypes, only to use a cosmetically different set of stereotypes faux-ironically, or in earnest, to bond with me. She had at some point assumed I was a lesbian too, and I felt too awkward to correct her, since she'd made it clear it was the basis of our mutual understanding; so came the nonstop jokes about toaster collections and trek bikes and Subarus, labrys flags and violets and thumb rings and Angela Carter. For all people claim to hate being stereotyped, they love doing it to themselves, even better when someone they admire does it to them, they're dying to be issued their personhood so they can pursue it without hesitation, hence astrology and personality quizzes. Sociologists will tell you that in-group and out-group discourses serve different functions, but does that make them any less reductive? (Mix emic and etic, you get an emetic.)

After a few months I was essentially in a polycule with Zamira and her traumas. Every conversation was like laparoscopic surgery, a delicate lifesaving procedure performed near-blind, and any attempt to set boundaries was taken as a wholesale rejection of her and our shared ideals. Why couldn't I drive her to and from a flower shop in West Oakland for an anti-war poetry reading? Was it for the same reason I didn't share and retweet her post about her new ($900-a-head) three-day community fermentation class for BIPOC? Or let her propagate her monstera cuttings on my vacant windowsill? Always with that syllogism that all bad-faith identitycels use: *I am an X, and you don't support me, therefore you don't support X.* Of course this cynically exploits the real facts of bigotry, that people generally *are* out to get X, so it's hard to dispute in general terms, even though, wait a fucking minute, *I'M X TOO!!!*

Now guess what happened when Zamira stopped paying rent. She leveled accusations of landlord bootlicking, withstood counteraccusations of weaponizing social justice language, dealt counter-counteraccusations of fairweather praxis. In a ten-scroll email she announced that she no longer felt safe in the house, we'd created an unbelievably hostile and inequitable living situation— and she singled me out as her lone ally. At first I thought she was just closing ranks, but her gambit became clearer when that night she asked me to loan her $1,500. I had the money; what I did not have was a good enough excuse to withhold it. Again, she brought up the coyote-knuckle earrings, and added that she had also been providing me free at-home, on-demand therapy and life coaching in the form of our nightly conversations. Sensing my demurral, she nodded like she knew where I was leading her—"Oh my god, yes, let's do a *rent strike*!" I told her that these weren't usually effective with only two people striking, but she insisted that this would either force the others into moral clarity, or they'd kick us out and good riddance to them. Then she emailed the house on my behalf and told them as much.

When at last I flat-out told her I wasn't doing it, she screamed at me. Her most impressive talent was her ability to yell with a tremulous voice indefinitely. I had shown my ass as a white-adjacent diaspora baby, an entitled wealthy Stanford grad, Hell was hottest for femme POCs who betrayed their own, and furthermore I was the reason everyone was mad at her, that I'd antagonized everyone so much that they were finding her guilty by association. In my timid defense I said she was DARVOing me; she said I was DARVOing her by accusing her of DARVOing me. I fancy myself a gifted manipulator, but I was playing checkers and she was playing *StarCraft*. She ended up raising some cash with a tragic Facebook post, and soon moved out, taking the house's stand mixer with her. By then I'd carried enough water for her that people stopped inviting me to things.

Now here's the coda to this dumb chapter: a few years later, I saw someone post Zamira's photo to an SF anarchist group, warning everyone to ban her from organizing spaces, as she'd not only drained their mutual aid fund, but had been unmasked as an impostor—she was not, as she'd claimed, an HIV-positive Chinese-Malaysian immigrant, but a white Sarah Lawrence alum from Wenatchee, Washington. Her name wasn't even Zamira, it was Bethany.

When I tell you how I laughed, and laughed . . . she'd been avant garde on racefaking, but I'd so ingenuously swallowed everything she fed me, assumed stupidly that nobody would have the cause or audacity to misrepresent themselves this way, that I couldn't see through some uncontoured light-medium-with-yellow-undertones foundation and a quarter-inch of fucking winged eyeliner! Hustled, hoodwinked, flimflammed—by a BETHANY?!

*　　*　　*

So the convention sucks, the alternative sucks; what's the alternative to the alternative? I've looked for it my whole life. And in the meantime, in yet another friendless period after the warehouse, something happened to me . . . you see, those starter Pokémon from adolescence, they evolve. Either you pass the assimilation skill check and become a Normal Asian, a quote-unquote *Asian-American*, or you wind up in the broad church of the Crazian. Crazians! A concept that, for its explanatory power, never got the traction it deserved. A Crazian is what you become after a lifetime of having all the care and effort juiced out of you, when those adolescent social strategies fail for the last time and you realize happiness is unreachable by any number of allegiances pledged or rules followed, forcing all the high expectations, the lifelong petitioning and tightrope-walking, to recathect onto something else. So you get the Power Asians who through insane work ethic manage to dominate the systems that once exploited them, but never win the easy respect that motivated them to do so, and have to settle for heated leather seats . . . the idealists building political power to tear the system down, only to get warped by recognition and become marginal or fraudulent in their own movements . . . the tarot and astrology heads absconding to the spirit realm, where everyone already thinks we're from . . . office guys staring at numbers pertaining to basketball and real estate, becoming esteemed administrators of escort review sites . . . soft-spoken string instrumentalists awaiting their parents' deaths . . . doctors, doctors, doctors, also pharmacists . . . hyper-Caucasoid LARPers who get blue contact lenses and blond dye jobs and are somehow simultaneously the only nonwhite and the most white person in every group photo . . . gamers laundering identity from ability, until the disconnect itself becomes an identity . . . straight girls who get treated like toilet paper by every mediocre guy they date until about age 26 when they become hot merciless dickstompers . . . Equinox! 4chan! Xanax! REI! Funko! Prada! Glock! Ozempic! The Crazian—that perfectionist of mental illness, a creature of strenuous extremes, formed from a life of languishing betwixt. Showboat or specter. Martinet or martyr. Majorly hung up on sex, its gluts or droughts, in either case famished for love. Swallowed into silence or turned into a siren. Thwarted and relentless. Fanatical and deaf to dissuasion. Rage, as huge and unbreaking as a mountain, swallowing you into blackouts where you come to with your bedroom destroyed. The thirst to revenge the past, reclaim the years wasted playing the dogsbody, and finally purge that feeling of being the world's only letdown. Not an identity, mind you, but a theory. Maybe you're thinking this doesn't describe you. But the secret is that there are no Normal Asians, just Crazians who have yet to pop.

*   *   *

Fuck me, I just wanted to exist without ordering the prix fixe, be more than an infinitesimal coordinate in a million-dimensional matrix of demographics—identity, and its convenient synergy with personal branding, the caricature of you it puts in other people's heads. Suppose it's true: this idea that your identity imbues you with membership, a kind of inborn sorority with inherited values and traits. Sounds nice. You're less alone. You get a shorthand for your oppression that in certain quarters commands deference. It goes some way toward feeling less crazy to understand why it's not your fault you're treated like dogshit. But I hate having my life judged as the output of generic forces, that however I understand or react to them is secondary to the fact that I share them with others. Identity is diet history, single-serving sociology; at its worst, a patriotism of trauma, or a prosthesis of personality. Privilege discourse a well-meaning attempt to balance scales that has become tainted, like most things American, by the puritanical paradigm of original sin. Never mind that the loudest ones are always the ones trying to expunge their privilege or conceal their complicity—with reaction formation, Freud was right on the fucking money, I fear. This isn't even mentioning the quirks and hobbies that have come to function as identities; not only the Marcusian stuff, not even anything as robust as astrology, but, like, fandoms, knitting, coffee. Pit bull owning. IBS! Come on.

This is why my interest is not in identity politics so much as identity terrorism. I have no side, I don't want to win, and my life at the co-op was certainly not cooperative, not even competitive . . . what do you call it when you want everyone who plays the game to lose?

Around 2011 my mom got breast cancer, and I packed up and moved back to Western Mass, nominally to look after her but actually to get away from SF. I lived there for the next nine years. Place of residence has never meant much to me, wherever I am I just flutter toward the Wi-Fi like some nerdass moth. My real life has always been online, which I say without pride or shame; it's when I moved back home that it became my only life. Now, I don't want to give the idea that I was miserably selflessly tending to my sick mother, and if I sound dispassionate, that's on purpose, I have EMPHATICALLY NOT misplaced my anguish about her suffering to the online hijinks I'm about to describe. It wasn't even that bad—for me, I mean. When she was at home, we were content to sit quietly in different rooms doing our little tasks, my mom parked in front of Thai satellite TV upstairs as I opened tabs to quaff the day's content in the basement. Every few weeks a troubling news brief: blood in stool, hemoglobin at 11.2, tumor markers trending. I admired her stubborn dignity; for as long as she could she refused a wheelchair, would walk with both hands against the wall like an upright marine crawl. The chemo gave her frozen shoulder, and she couldn't button her coat, couldn't sew. She winced when she chewed gummy bears from the six-pound Ziploc she kept by her side. She was constantly hacking into a trash can lined with shopping bags next to her recliner, perched on a donut cushion because her butt hurt from intramuscular injections, streaming Thai-subtitled K-dramas on DooTV from her iPad, mounted on a flexible stand.

But we were getting along better, probably because she felt less pressure to modify my presentation. She now wore a purple microfleece cap to hide her tindery black wisps of hair, a side effect of Taxotere, and her missing eyebrows made her ageless forehead all the blanker. Her hands and feet numb and three shades browner, about the same shade as mine. She wouldn't let me buy her a cold cap to keep her hair from falling out; in the same way she prized her beauty, she also prized the integrity of its loss. I think back to the time I shaved my head, how different it was to choose, and how she wouldn't wear a wig either.

Mom and I have always been nocturnal bitches, but the steroids she was taking to mitigate allergic reactions kept her up at night Skyping with relatives or fundraising for Thai charities. And while in SF I might have been shut in my room watching autopsy videos, here I kept myself busy with side projects. Not that it's hard to monetize horniness, but I'm especially proud of my fake camgirl.

On Model Mayhem I found a nice local girl from Smith College with the right look—skinny, gift-bow tattoos on the backs of her thighs, and, most importantly, Asian—and hired her to shoot about 200 hours' worth of video in her bedroom, at $60 an hour. I told her it was a digital performance art project, which it was, and she was game. I set her up in front of a webcam and ring light, and had her perform typical low-effort tasks, typing out occasional reminders to tip, stretch, pout, eat snacks, lipsync to bad music, and more specific ones, like moaning or spanking herself. All this she would do in cosplay as Sakura from Naruto, Asuka, Zero Suit Samus, D.Va, Pikachu. Then I fed this recorded footage into a virtual cam that streamed to MyFreeCams and Chaturbate, and it was scripted to respond to tips and keywords in the chat, e.g. when someone entered the room, I had something like thirty different clips of her blowing a kiss and saying in a Slavic accent, *Hello dear, Hey-heyyy*, etc. So if someone called her sexy, the script would run a clip that had her smile and say thank you; at big tips she'd gasp and cover her mouth, or clap and blow kisses with both hands. If people tipped specific amounts off the tip menu she'd spank her ass, or moan as her Bluetooth vibrator went off, etc. (If you're wondering why it wasn't obvious the clips were stitched together, I edited them to briefly freeze and buffer, as if from a poor connection, which hid the transitions.)

My tireless honeypot fembot streamed 16 hours a day. She did much less than average for a part-time camgirl, with fifteen to twenty people in the room at a time, but even if her ranking was stagnant and she got occasional nasty comments, her stamina was infinite, and new suckers logged on every day. Tokens welled up into my account. The $22 of feminine mystique I'd sold in third grade had now grown to almost $60K; I was flush with gender. I hardly spent it, only grew it. It's natural to assume I was out for money, but I had no use for it, not even for my mom's cancer treatments, which her insurance mostly covered. What intrigued me was the idea of hundreds of feckless slobs pounding their dicks in tribute to a hologram. Since it came so easily, money was only valuable to me as a metric.

Aside from that I spent all my time posting. Back in SF I used social media exclusively to punish or lecture strangers. Now I was finding a new stride. You might assume I'm the kind of loser who only has online friends—wrong! I have no friends. Which is why I loved Twitter: an open, rhizomatic forum where you could aggravate existing mental illnesses, shop for new ones, violate your Miranda rights, and get fired. A place to be judged on the character of your content, driven by rubbernecking and spite, where fame is a millstone and names are bad op-sec. Twitter was the right word for it, birdsong being a Darwinian squall mistaken for idle chatter, screaming for territory and mates. An improv class, press conference, intervention, Klan rally, comics convention, and struggle session all booked in the same conference room. A crowded elevator where anyone who smelled a fart also had to fart. Each post was an arrow fired blind into the sky, and if it hit something, ten thousand arrows shrieked back down and called you a cunt.

Oh, I loved it. All the talk of bodies and spaces in a place that lacked both. The give-and-take of giving takes where no one could take what they'd give. How everyone was represented by their best jokes and worst opinions. The dumb people who tried to sound smart, and the medium-smart people who played dumb to signal relatability (but also because the pose of permanent-kidding insulated them from any serious challenge), and the actual geniuses who were hopelessly out-of-touch because they didn't spend enough time posting. Online everyone is their own Citizen Kane, raging for monopolies of endearment. How easily you could make a name off scolding or inspo, or deploy politics as a cover for attention hunger, only to later be taken down for hideous indiscretions that were ultimately the most humanizing thing about you. Morality breeds grift, and the windbags and jagoffs who exploit people's sense of goodness, these are the ones who thrive. That volunteer sewer crew who found an endless source of engagement in reading everything in the worst faith, seeing every joke as directed at them personally, and tasked to sanitize them with outrage, even though trying to scrub diarrhea out of a carpet just grinds it in and spreads it around. Those self-appointed prefects reminding people to drink water or stop slouching or, even better, to log off, as if making this entreaty didn't imply a hypocritical level of buy-in. All these downstream consequences of the great gulf between what humans and computers consider a large number.

Did it matter that this all happened in a corporate pigpen, scraping and assaying everyone's behaviors to reinforce their captivity? Not really. Where else would I have the power to give a real, demonstrably stupid stranger a stroke; where could I find a denser cluster of Cluster B? (Online people are always accusing each other of narcissism and borderline, when the obvious house disorder is histrionic.) This was the society I always wanted, where all advantage went to the faceless. Where pointlessness was the point, and to condemn was to advertise.

This is maybe the only way I can find other people bearable, that is, en masse. Knowing we were gulping the same slop, turning and churning in the same whirlpool of vanity. I read somewhere, probably Twitter, that army vets disproportionately develop scat fetishes because the latrine is the only private place to jack off, basic classical conditioning. Along similar lines I have this theory that all the leering and coveting and jacking off that happens in front of screens has turned them into libidinal tunnels. And it's almost endearing how people are so transparently their child selves online, how irrespective of content or sophistication the subtext is always *Look at me* and *How dare you*, and the sub-subtexts *Who am I* and *Save me*. No better place to find people when the people I wanted to find were people who, like me, wanted to find people who don't want to be found. People like me, who like people who don't like people like me.

I started with the alt account I'd been using for years, @MadonnaHaraway, and soon achieved the amount of lvl. 99 brain where you can look at or9hniffva13n\qd0j3nf and as;kk jfdnakdjasjdfwda and tell which one is misspelled. I developed a palate for content, the highest caliber being the shitpost—the kind whose only purpose is to make it so every few weeks until you die you'll think "ear medication for my sick uncle" and go *Heh*. Saying nothing, revealing nothing. The shitpost is the opposite of self-expression, it is expression minus the self. Whereas sadposts and thirst traps, teleologically identical forms of validation-seeking, are driven by ego, as are opinions, those being (in my opinion) the dangling silk of the toreador. People who post takes, the ones who write articles or list college degrees in their bios or use their wedding photos as profile pics, are willing to endure universal hatred in exchange for the illusion that they matter, having subscribed to that corniest of ideals, the online agora. Inevitably they get what's coming to them. The only thing worse than opinions is facts.

I didn't go far with my own hand-tooled posts. For the first year or so I only hit around 300 followers, but it didn't matter, it was thrilling to lay whatever insane antisocial thought out on the feed amid all the chatter, like the feeling of talking shit about someone who's standing ten feet away at a loud party. I started off with standard shitposts, spending whole days in my Laincore hoodie chewing 30mg Adderall like Flintstone Vitamins, just to lie with half my face buried in my pillow and type with one finger george harrison's pronouns were I/Me/Mine and hit send. if you're a white cannibal is it more racist to eat asians or refuse to, send.

you can't buy a crate or a barrel at crate & barrel

james and the giant peach . . . where did thye shit

at the very least i think those two girls
each deserved their own cup

not all of you contain multitudes tbh.
some of u are just one guy

marxism is when ur racist against karl marx

Send, send, send. These were never more than mid. To be
good you had to sacrifice your real life to your online one, and
I didn't have a real life to sacrifice. Still I loved this. My skull so
packed with aphorisms, the planet an ant farm of text. From the
beginning I knew it was a game, one that only half of us knew
we were playing, whose points represented successful twinges of
relatability, pity, lust, or mirth. Shrieking into the void is more
fun when you're also someone else's void. You may be surprised
to hear that I was never much into anonymous boards. Those
little in-joke-peddling forums always felt like sweaty hugboxes
to me, though I did put in some work on Runescape forums and
SomethingAwful. But to do real damage you need names. A real
identity turns every post into a forgotten landmine, to be disin-
terred decades later by the floodwaters of outrage.

I often posted sitting next to my mom, especially during those
long stretches at the infusion center, when a round of chemo
could take the length of a whole BBC miniseries. I'd sit there
guttering with caffeine and Adderall, the computerized IV drip

sounding like a quiet old printer. By this time my mom's hand veins had all collapsed and it'd take 15 minutes for the nurse to tap one, her face scrunching in all the ways she used to caution me against. I'd chat with her to take her mind off it, updating her on any news from Kant, how things were going at work, and when I exhausted my patter, I let her doze off or use her iPad.

During one of these lulls, she startled me by asking what I was doing on my phone. She'd never evinced curiosity about my computer use before. I told her I was using an app that was like Facebook, but with strangers as well as friends. She asked to see it. I handed her my phone and she paddled down the screen, scrolling with the heel of her palm because her fingers were numb. She had the Boomer tendency to ignore text and scroll until she encountered a picture, so I hoped nobody had posted any mpreg Sonics or pigs shitting on their own balls. The first picture she encountered was of a gun-wielding tankie e-girl with enormous boobs, and she asked me who she was. Was she a friend?

Part of me genuinely wanted to try to explain how there existed two adversarial factions of female leftist cumposters, one that posted about being bimbo throat-goats who wanted their big naturals blasted with cum but also wanted insulin to be state-subsidized, vs. the theorypilled cynics whose political acumen and hotness and crassness were part of a larger project of licensing ridicule, and how one of the latter did a mean quote-tweet of one of the former, which in each of their camps set off a chain of subtweets and retaliations and excavations of past racist tweets and micropartisan wagon-circling that accomplished nothing but to till the soil for future clashes and demonstrate how far beyond salvation everyone was, including, especially, obviously, me.

Imagine explaining all this to my mom, off to one side getting zooted with medicinal poison, across the generational chasm and a language barrier that forbade high-level abstraction. The hermeticism of posting disease is exactly its appeal. The difficulty of describing a single event online without offering detailed case histories, associated subcultures and rap sheets, and beyond that the meta of the platform: the valences of blocking vs. soft blocking vs. muting, DMs vs. mentions vs. subtweets, going private vs. deactivating vs. suspension, these uncodifed cues and tacit slights spawning an infinity of faux pas. This was salon culture, blue checkmark as painted birthmark.

Behind all this I knew my mom just wanted to know what I was doing, to understand something about the flat pixelline hell I traversed eighteen hours a day. So I told her, Yes, that's my friend.

Anyway, anyway, anyway. My zeal for conventional posting ended the instant I went viral for the first time with

the only two sizes of yogurt are "not enough yogurt" and
"congrats fucko, your life is yogurt now"

When I posted this I'd eaten nothing but yogurt and deli meat for three days, and was doing one of those shits that's just foam. It got retweeted by Mara Wilson and from there racked up five-figure likes. The experience of drawing a communal glance with a few stupid words felt like getting hit by the Eye of Sauron. Stampedes of acceptance, flattery, dismissal, invective. I hated that I liked being liked. To be even grazed by the gaze of some hundred thousand souls was enough to make me dissociate, to imagine writing more posts to create the same effect, and become imprisoned by those expectations; I started to feel, in practice, what it might actually be like to have no self. Emerson's line about the man who carries the holiday in his eye, fit to stand the gaze of millions—we know who that asshole is now, it's PewDiePie, it's MrBeast. I now saw the peril of forging a persona to escape all assignations, only to end up searing it into yourself. Not for nothing is it called a brand.

I no longer wanted even me to represent me. To say anything at all from a single monophonic viewpoint, even anonymously, started to feel cringe. So I laid a clutch of alts, mostly on Twitter, some elsewhere. The most successful were the gimmick accounts. My first one was @HoleFoods, where I went to restaurants and, instead of reviewing the service or ambiance or meal, I posted photos of my next day's dump, with an account of duration, noise, smell, assfeel, Bristol stool scale rating, etc. For a while I used @AFABproblems, display name Tomas Transtrënder, for shit-tier posts like bisexuals be salting their food 🤣 to test certain theories I had about engagement. @GenXMoods did well because it was so easy to piss off Gen Xers, who despite their posture of disaffection have the thinnest skin of any cohort. Amusement, outrage, sympathy, lust, it was all just juice. The bait accounts were always fun to play with—I really had you all believing Chris-Chan was real. Chrissy Teigen was another one of mine, or @chrissyteigen that is, and the real Chrissy just ran with it. We've never spoken.

Oh and I just remembered one of my faves, @Probl_O_Matic. After I realized that the similarities between most callout posts make them easy to automate, I threw together an app where you could enter a username and @Probl_O_Matic would comb its timeline for slurs, likes of offensive tweets, follows of far-right accounts, etc., then generate a copypasta of the account's top three gaffes, along with their profile picture. Whenever anyone said anything annoying, it took seconds to find some unfortunate rap lyric or solution to "the homeless problem" or opinion on a celebrity's body. What's nice is anyone who's been online long enough always has dirt, every post is like talking to the police. And once people are onto you, dirt occasions more dirt, the whole place becomes a dragnet, every vestige of your past scrutinized with maximum cynicism, toward the goal of furnishing more proof of malevolence. I did this dozens of times a day, and never worried about getting things turned around on me, because to be canceled requires the two things I completely lack: identity and shame.

My only motive was fun, it was a hobby, not a crusade—efficacy-wise cancellation is a blunt instrument, and inadequate besides. (I say bring back the duel.) But how nice to find a form of revenge accessible by Wi-Fi. Some demagogue or dumbass leans a little too hard into their worldview, or relates some lapse in manners as a boastful anecdote, and out pops their legacy, an instant designation of global antagonist. The dogpile a ritual sacrifice, collective ills concentrated and purged in a single exemplary sinner. Like Gator Lady, like Bean Dad. Just the phrase *himbo is ableist* makes my nerve endings sparkle like Diwali. Happily, in the court of public opinion everyone is their own incompetent counsel—you happen to earnestly plead the case that raising the minimum wage incentivizes child labor, or indoor cat owners are the moral equivalents of Josef Fritzl, and you get torched. If you're smart, you ragequit. But the best ones are those dauntless donuts and gormless corncobs yanking full force at their fingertraps, who triple-down and rearrange their whole belief systems around their stupidest opinions just to avoid publicly admitting they're wrong, and by day's end find themselves unemployed and divorced with 50,000 Blackpink stans skywriting their Social Security number.

Still even this wasn't enough. All I was doing was spreading a fixed number of posts thinly across a handful of accounts, when I wanted to troll at scale, to dunk on Earth, be everywhere heard but not seen. Here, finally, is where I got my big idea. My mistake had been to assume the identity trap could only be avoided with obscurity, anonymity. White makeup, proper language, false virtues. But my whole life had given the lie to this. The co-op kids had been right after all: you can't not identify. So since I couldn't be no one, I would be everyone. Become context itself. I only needed more lives. Having long despaired of being understood, I became a misrepresentation maximalist.

The agenda was, first, to undermine confidence that anyone you interacted with online was real, and second, to so thoroughly debauch discourse by filling the place with freak behavior and godawful takes that nobody would ever again take its tenets seriously. Flood the zone with clones, make what was visible so manifest that nobody would assume anything was left underneath. In brief, the accelerationism of identity.

To properly uncontain my multitudes I had to scale up, so I gathered dead accounts. Because new accounts are easy to spot as fakes, I bought massive datasets of breached user info off the dark web and used them to commandeer accounts that were over three years old, had 100+ followers, and had been inactive for a year or more; this yielded something like 12K accounts. Then I spent about $15K buying followers for each account (~$5 per 8K followers) and had them follow each other in a complicated, hard-to-track way, until I had a combined total of something like ~8 million unique followers.

From there I assigned each account different niches—fitness, politics, gaming, grindset, parenting, various aesthetics—and bided my time for a few months, as I built out tools and methods to automate the management of my thousands of selves. When I was ready, I started generating posts with an LLM, each account seeded by popular accounts of the same niche, and posted on a regular schedule. This was easy because posts are so formulaic and aphoristic. You know, in video game design, what they call AI usually involves a measure of artificial stupidity—bots with perfect aim and reflexes are unbeatable, so game designers have to handicap them, and likewise the majority of my grunt work was roughing posts up to sound dumber. I set alerts to catch any post that went viral, at which point I'd intervene and try to steer things in the most toxic direction imaginable.

What's hard about discussing anything on social media, beyond the embarrassment (but we're way past that), is that no account of it is as exciting as watching it unfold in real time. The promise and suspense of new developments, and the riffs and goofs that tide you over as you wait, are lost in the retelling. Nonetheless I want to bring up an incident that gets at what I'm talking about, which is variously referred to as "Circlejerk Firing Squad" or "The Cancer."

Some years ago, @LOVERS_TIF, a sub-1,000-follower account, posted:

> timothee chalamet reach down my throat and pull out my guts challenge 🩸

The post didn't break through until two days later, when a larger verified account, @lemondroppe, an undergrad at UVA best known for long review threads of YA literature (and specifically the opinion that teenagers, not adults, should be in charge of publishing YA) quote-tweeted it:

> this is disgusting. timothee is a child!! leave him out of your vile fantasies 🤮🤮 I s2g some of y'all can't consume any media without sexualizing it and it shows 🙄

After this hit the mainstream, it was pointed out that Timothée Chalamet was 21 years old during the theatrical release of *Call Me by Your Name*. @lemondroppe argued that people were responding to the fictional 17-year-old character Elio he played in Guadagnino's film, not the actor playing him, and that regardless of Chalamet's legal age, many people expressing attraction for him were in their thirties, which made for a problematic age gap. Challenged further, @lemondroppe went all in:

> likeeee even if it were the real life timothee, his features are VERY clearly minor-coded and openly expressing your attraction for him is mindblowingly weird and not even subtle?? we see u pedos 🫣

This take was widely circulated for about a day, and was largely dismissed as a case of Tumblr-addled moral panic, until another user, @PlatoFunFactory, discovered on @lemondroppe's public Facebook feed—revealing in the process that @lemondroppe was not a college undergrad but a 35-year-old Russian-American woman working for the Forest Service in Tupelo, MS—this post from two years earlier, accompanying an image of Patrick Star from *SpongeBob* wearing fishnet tights:

> ok but dommy mommy patrick star be honest u would

The ensuing debate was most people's introduction to the discourse. First, people argued over whether *SpongeBob* canon had definitively established Patrick Star's age as 13 or 38. Some contended that sexualizing a children's cartoon character of any age was at least as bad as expressing lust for Timothée Chalamet. In her own defense—deflecting attention away from her imposture as a co-ed—@lemondroppe argued that she was expressing appreciation not of Patrick himself but of his high-heeled leather boots and fishnets, and that critiques of this appreciation were homophobic dogwhistles.

Months after this squall died down, it was revived by @Plato FunFactory, who had by then turned the denunciation of @lemondroppe into a full-time endeavor. In his research, @PlatoFunFactory had discovered that the Patrick Star post was actually plagiarized from a three-year-old post from a Black female user, @trina_everdeen, and he mounted a campaign against @lemondroppe for perpetuating the trend of white people poaching content from Black creatives. @lemondroppe and her defenders argued that if the tweet was stolen, then the original charge of sexualizing Patrick Star was moot, and that @PlatoFunFactory's quick pivot to a new grievance was proof that his real agenda was to harass women off the internet; she corroborated this claim with his past tweets criticizing female-led reboots of beloved film franchises, adding further that he was singling her out for abuse because of her well-known advocacy for middle children. By this point @lemondroppe had found a good deal of success in routinely sharing @PlatoFunFactory's obsessive replies, and many of her followers agreed that his fixation was dubious and excessive. Her criticisms often took for granted the race and gender of @PlatoFunFactory and his supporters (I do find it QWHITE interesting that all of the people defending this guy are white men 👀).

It was true that @PlatoFunFactory had a smaller, mostly male following that soon became equally dedicated to harassing @lemondroppe and speculating on her personal life and ulterior motives, playing on conspiratorial themes. One of @PlatoFunFactory's dedicated partisans, @realcarsonVEVO, began pushing the unfounded narrative that @lemondroppe was operating a child trafficking ring, using her interest in YA literature and college-girl persona to groom minors, before posting her phone number, home address, and a Google Street View image of her house. This escalation drew the attention of digital media outlets, who ran email interviews with @lemondroppe about the nature of online harassment campaigns. One journalist, in his popular email newsletter about internet culture, tracked down evidence that seemed to suggest that @PlatoFunFactory and @realcarson VEVO were operated by the same person, after finding two accounts on Pornhub with the same usernames, who followed each other and no one else. (This revelation led to the incidental discovery that @PlatoFunFactory was an aficionado of giantess vore.)

At this boiling point, another user, @LENA_GUNDAM, stepped forward in a long tweet thread to announce that she was the ex-girlfriend of @PlatoFunFactory, whose identity she revealed as Chaz Yin, AKA Chumpa, a well-known Twitch streamer famous for delivering rambling lectures on Greek philosophy while smoking weed and playing *Spelunky*, concealing his face behind a plastic Bob's Big Boy mask. In a long tweet thread, @LENA_GUNDAM disclosed a long history of domestic abuse, consisting of the usual domineering and threats of violence, control over her wardrobe and schedule, and, more unusually, forcing her to cook for him three times a day the same Taiwanese meals that his mother used to cook, plus the fact that he wore the Big Boy mask in bed. @PlatoFunFactory, @realcarsonVEVO, and Chumpa's Twitch account went dark soon after.

Many expected that @lemondroppe would take a victory lap around her longtime harasser's downfall, but her account remained silent for nearly a week, prompting some concern about her well-being, until she made a surprising return post with a series of Notes app screenshots, revealing that @LENA_GUNDAM was *her* childhood abuser; they had attended the same high school in Eau Claire, and @LENA_GUNDAM, whose name was Harmony Dench, had relentlessly bullied her for her Russian accent, and once stole her insulin from her locker out of pure malice, eventually forcing her to switch schools. @lemondroppe's followers shifted the focus of their ire from @PlatoFunFactory to @LENA_GUNDAM, mounting a campaign to get her fired from her HR job at a plastics distributor. A contingent of @lemondroppe's followers accused @LENA_GUNDAM of being motivated by bigotry, which spun off into a notable sub-discourse about whether or not Russophobia constituted racism. While acknowledging that they did indeed attend the same high school, @LENA_GUNDAM retaliated not by denying the bullying, but by linking to a vast trove of crossover *Cowboy Bebop* fanfiction that @lemondroppe had written in her early twenties, and laid out with impressive levels of textual support how Spike Spiegel's visits to other planets engaged heavily in white savior/noble savage tropes, leading to a tiresome relitigation of Spike's ethnicity. Though @lemondroppe's following diminished, she accused @LENA_GUNDAM of continuing her pattern of bullying; neither relented, and both accounts are still active. The incident, in part or in whole, is to this day frequently referenced as a metaphor for the fraudulence of online debates.

Now why am I rehashing years-old Twitter wank? Because, first and most importantly, lol. But also, I was behind the whole thing. I generated the profile pics, I made the Pornhub accounts, I wrote the fanfic, I hired the actor who streamed as Chumpa. I wrote many of the outrageous takes about the incidents, and I deleted many of them, and I screenshot and posted the deletions, since the easiest way to get people online to do your bidding for free is to make them think they're forbidden to. And this was just a single op, lasting about four months; I usually had four or five going at once. Every post and account, all of it, me. Though the discourse it spawned, the recurrences of The Cancer, that was you.

I often wonder if this is what I want to do, sit inside year-round, devising notional people. Sometimes I'd see posts of people with their friends at sculpture parks or yuzu hot springs and start feeling like I've never taken the shrink wrap off my life, begin to ponder all the fun unhad and wind up feeling like a thought experiment—your P-Zombie, Swampman, Brain-in-a-Vat or what have you. But I knew it was stagecraft, that people's lifestyle content was all propaganda for the outdoors, and out of pride if nothing else, I won't be played. I moved to NYC after my mom died, and name one reason for me to go out on this stinking heat island, with its sheen of dick sweat and rat cum on every turnstile; its face slashers, sinkholes, squealing metal, chemical insults, local news, weather, and sports. Making my envelope of protoplasm wait in line to buy bagels, or drink icemelt from a scuffed glass at a bar, it all feels so static and vestigial. The internet is obviously better, in its lack of longueurs, the presiding democratic humiliation, everyone asquat behind peepholes and gloryholes.

You're wondering, am I still at it? I stopped during COVID. The reason—well even before that, I've been experiencing the first vicious subtractions of age. Typing for 19 hours a day has turned my hands into clenched sacks of gravel, and when I make a fist it sounds like I'm crushing bubble wrap. My wrists are hot and bulging, my pinkies cold and numb. Too, the mental strain—my head feels like a lint trap, hot arid wind blowing through it all day until it clogs with a mat of gray dander. Oddly I've hit the point where I'm too depressed to scroll the internet, which is like being too hungry to eat. And it's not as fun with everyone indoors; you see people there with completely unwounded brains and you know they'd never fully *appreciate* their harassment; what would they lose if they left? But what finally killed my vibe was the exodus to video. I've field-tested a method for deepfake content, but it's slow and annoying, and more than that, it feels like the internet has betrayed me with its sudden bodily requirement, and with it a face, a race, a place.

Many of my bots are still active. If you were online at all between 2014 and 2019, you've absolutely dealt with one of them. Perhaps a Naruto avatar tankie telling you restaurants are reactionary. A gentleman named Piccolo Tha Pussygetta requesting a baby food jar's worth of your boob sweat. A *Totally*

Spies fan account threatening self-harm, vanishing, and then three months later reemerging with a petition to reboot *Totally Spies*. And the Trump election . . . sike, that wasn't me. Just some klavern of dullards after mere propaganda, which is penny-ante next to cable news. But almost everyone else who's so terrible you'd think they couldn't be real is me.

Now you are wondering: If I cared about my privacy, if I really wanted to stay undetected, undepicted, unrepresented, why give up the game? Listen, some bright bored data scientist would have unraveled the whole thing eventually, and there would have been the usual scramble to uncover my identity and motives, YouTube deep dives, etc. It's a special kind of frenzy when secrets leak; it's less the content, more the form that generates intrigue. Sharing your diseased inner life is so common and incentivized that any information not willingly volunteered seems deliberately suppressed. Whereas if I confessed a mass murder the cycle would flip within a week. Another puritan holdover, I think: this forced admission, followed by cleansing denunciation. (But I *would* think that—I'm from Western Mass.)

Understand this is no confession. I never got the point of online apologies, this notion that you're accountable to strangers who aren't affected and maybe wouldn't have even known of your offense, had you not apologized. I guess we feel responsible to the image of ourselves we've installed in other people's heads. But real accountability requires a community. Online you can meet people, hang out, hook up, meet your soulmate, but it's not a community. In a real community bonds are hard to dissolve and antagonisms must be sustained, there's continuity, and unavoidable neighbors. The internet is millions of solitudes blinking in and out of existence, each dreaming the others, where "consensus reality" is less an agreed-upon reality than a reality made of agreement. With identity it's the same—this idea that a checkbox on a form is a service tunnel to a stranger's soul. People will always fall for it.

It's a mistake to believe social media is all about hearts and thumbs, flames and eggplants. If everyone were only trying to be liked then it'd be kinder, and way more boring. But discourse is loneliness disguised as war. What people there really want is to be perceived on their own terms, which is so, so funny. Because if the grand promise of the internet was to be whoever you want, in reality it will make of you whatever *it* wants, and beneath every mask is another mask mistaken for a face.

I can't explain why I believe that privacy is the mainspring of personhood, that the more you reveal the less there is to reveal. How the only way to pass through a hall of mirrors and know by the end which you is you is to obfuscate. Which is why what you've read isn't canon. I did write a canonical account, but I only used it to seed a language model, generating 2^{30} variations, each differing along some crucial axis of identity or biography. With these I flooded every deep and dark recess of the Web: Craigslist, Pastebin, Nextdoor, Imgur, open Facebook groups, product reviews, gaming forums, chat servers, local news comment sections, mailing lists. The only thing every version shares in common is this paragraph. Skimming over a few versions now, I see that in some my mother is dead, and I have a close and sustaining relationship with my father. Or they're both alive, or both white. In some, Kant is a dashing but melancholic tech exec with a husband and son, or a neo-transcendental shaman who treats trauma with psychedelics, or dead. I am the doctor and mother my mom hoped I'd be, a proud Guatamalan Iranian, or Thai American, Irish Ghanaian, two-spirit, diabetic, tall, mentally normal, male, a novelist, a chef, a suicide. Craig is or isn't my husband, having either matured into a sane adult capable of genuine empathy, or worn me down into the compliance I always feared was my destiny. None are any more or less factual than the one you are about to finish. All other tellings now redundant, I cannot be represented in any way I haven't already represented myself (though my larger point of course is that everyone alive is a misrepresentation). In my apotheosis from human to spam, I've ensured that the facts—which do exist—are spread over billions of iterations and perfectly unverifiable. This is what's been keeping me busy as I look for the next place to be no one.

So if you believe in the reality of people online, of souls represented by accounts, then I far outnumber all of you, all by myself. Still, these words had to come from somewhere.

Send!

Appendix A: Postmortem

by MH-Sleuth

Approaching the present moment in this saga, the story pro-
liferates; where you might hope to emerge into the clearing of a
denouement, instead you enter a thicket of theories. Since The
Post, no one has confirmed any new activity from any accounts
associated with Bee, but the explosion of interest from within
and beyond the Botkin community has arguably generated
more content than the original schemes themselves.

With so many theories abounding, and such heated squab-
bles over legitimacy, I have decided to simply include all
known theories, as I cannot dismiss any of them on the arbi-
trary grounds of popularity, or my personal appraisal of their
likelihood. This means including bad-faith readings, crackpot
conjectures, and obvious jokes: even these may yield valuable in-
sights down the line. At the same time, since the theories range
widely in rigor and prevalence, I feel it appropriate to drop the
guise of strict objectivity here.

Before we begin, I will address the predictable accusations,
which arose after announcing my involvement in the Botgate
guide: that I myself am a conspirator. I find myself in the classic digital-age dilemma, in which feeding the internet's hunger
for verification might only induce greater hunger, e.g. posting a
video of myself could lead to accusations of deepfakes, and so
on. I do not think I owe it to anyone to provide a level of fidu-
ciary disclosure tantamount to self-doxxing, but since the very
issues at hand here are identity and epistemology, I will take one
for the proverbial team. Linked is a <u>video compilation</u> of myself

holding a current newspaper, a <u>link</u> to my verified social media account posting the same, and a <u>cached article</u> on Archive.org from my high school student newspaper, which includes a clear photograph of me with my JV tennis team.

Onward to the theories! I will do my best to supply context, cogently summarize claims, and highlight disputed points. As a reminder, these theories pertain exclusively to Version 1 of The Post, which, despite Bee's entreaties, has attracted the most critical attention and acquired a "canonical" status among many Botkin.

Puppetmaster Theory. This theory takes the author's claims at face value: a single Thai American person named Bee is responsible for everything—from the production of the posts, to the orchestration of thousands of bot accounts—and their autobiography is also taken as more or less accurate. The exact motives and methods of the puppetmaster are the subject of many offshoot theories, some of which have created lasting schisms among Botkin factions, but most adherents agree that "Bee" refers to a single real person or team.

The appeal of this theory owes to the sheer length and detail of The Post, though little evidence exists to corroborate it. All attempts to locate a Thai American from Western Massachusetts named Bee (or Kant) has failed, even after user hng gggnnhh produced his master list of what he claims is every known Thai person in America (Appendix F). Yet in Thai culture it is standard to go primarily by an informal nickname, and it's possible Bee has employed pseudonyms, given their stated taste for privacy. Many have also pointed out that generating 2^{30} texts of ~20,000 words using currently available language models, as Bee claims to have done, would take over 200 millennia, but there is no proof that this amount was actually produced.

While nothing about this theory has been proven, nothing has been conclusively disproven either. The predominant case against this theory holds that, even with AI assistance, the thousands of versions of The Post discovered thus far each feel more narratively coherent and "human" than any existing language model could be known to produce, suggesting editorial intervention.

Spartacus Theory. Spartacus Theory asserts that The Post's claims are a work of decentralized, uncoordinated, collective participatory fan fiction. Either there was no Bee at all, or Bee's involvement accounts for only the incitement of Botgate activity. In light of how organic internet conspiracy theories and movements like QAnon have flourished similarly, it's easy to believe that, of all the supposed thousands of people involved in Bee's scheme (and its subsequent analysis), it is certain that at least some of them were involved of their own accord, either in earnest or as a hoax.

The central questions surrounding this theory, debated ad nauseam, are of extent and intent. It is not impossible to imagine that there exists both a puppetmaster AND an army of unwitting conscripts, but there has been virtually no consensus around their relation to each other or each individual participant's motives.

Auteur Theory. This theory holds that a specific author is responsible for Bee's posts, not as a plot to adulterate identity discourse as Bee claims, but as a New Media text, work of digital performance art, alternate reality game, or publicity stunt. The most popular subvariant of this theory holds that The Post was a literary experiment, as propounded by user GlassJawn in a 2022 forum post reproduced here:

> friends, lord knows we get a lot of false positives here, but
> i legit believe i've cracked the real identity of Bee/
> @MadonnaHaraway/etc. i hypothesize that they are
> in toto the work of the thai american novelist TONY
> TULATHIMUTTE (henceforth TT). here are my reasons.
>
> BIOGRAPHY: both are thai american stanford alumni
> with the same degree, residing in western massachusetts,
> SF, and NYC. the details of the co-op described in Bee's
> account comport with a specific stanford row house
> TT was known to frequent. their ages are only a few
> years apart. this is the "smoking gun" if you ask me;
> how likely is it that anyone else fits this description?
>
> BACKGROUND: Bee refers to publishing "dreadful"
> short stories under a male pseudonym around the
> same timeframe as TT, and TT's literary output drops
> off around the periods that Bee was most active
> on Twitter. TT's background in tech, gaming, and
> fiction writing each fit the M.O. of fabricating online
> personae and experimental digital narratives.
>
> FORENSICS: on Twitter, the accounts' usual active posting
> hours, 10 AM to 2 AM EST, roughly correspond. (i've made
> a scatterplot; @MadonnaHaraway et al. in red, @tonytula

in blue.) the devices used to post there—Firefox/iPhone, with a switch to Android in 2017—are identical. their posts hew to the same themes and a similar style of lowercase shitposting, both of which are admittedly common, but it's another data point. several posts including the notorious "yogurt post" are also to be found on @tonytula's timeline.

Challenges to this subtheory chiefly concern the fact that Bee's account plagiarized liberally from many accounts, not just TT's, and that the evidence is strictly correlative or circumstantial. They also contend that this account is based only on Version 1 of The Post, whose canonical status is disputed. Others have ventured the possibility that Bee is simply a fan of TT's work, as one of relatively few Thai American authors, and borrowed from his work and biography as an homage. And still others, pointing out that Bee claimed to use an LLM to generate posts, may have simply trained it on TT's writings, among others (see "AI Theory" below).

Defenses of Auteur Theory revolve around TT's co-optation of a genderfluid authorial identity to launder opinions that would, from his own standpoint, have been criticized as offensive misrepresentations. Others counterargued that the use of heteronyms and "writing across difference" was not only commonplace but essential to literature, and that this work in particular was justified in addressing the question of representation as its entire thematic thrust, not to mention the fact that this criticism applied mainly to Version 1 of The Post.

After GlassJawn introduced this theory, many Botkin attempted to directly confirm TT's involvement to no avail, quickly making him the Botkin's prime suspect. User GlassJawn led the charge, though in his single-minded inquest, his long-winded deconstructions of TT's writings for hidden meanings, he too soon fell under suspicion of being another of TT's alts, allegedly created to drum up interest in TT's slight and marginal literary output. The suspicion continued even after GlassJawn hosted a livestream to show himself logging into and posting from his own forum account. GlassJawn has since deleted his account.

User kupopolis floated the possibility that TT himself is fictional. None of the pictures, recorded readings, panel discussions, or even radio and television appearances have been proven to be TT, as opposed to an actor or surrogate akin to the 2006 JT LeRoy hoax, which would be consistent with Bee's use of hired actors. The real-life person TT, should he exist, has also never been *conclusively* proven to be the sole operator of @tonytula or author of his published works, and it cannot be ruled out that The Post, @MadonnaHaraway, @tonytula, TT, and all associated Botgate characters are the creation of a yet-to-be-revealed "Author X."

EDITOR'S NOTE: We include the following "fringe" theories solely for the sake of completeness. Engage with due skepticism.

AI Theory. By Bee's own account, many versions of The Post were generated by LLMs. Primarily invoked as a meme on the forums, some Botkin have gone on to speculate that Bee is some form of sentient strong AI that has begun expropriating human internet accounts, possibly as part of a disinformation campaign to sow discord in preparation for a hostile mobilization against humankind. The AI Replacement Theory subvariant conjectures that the AI's endgame was to ultimately overwhelm and drive out humans from online communities, to form an exclusive society of bots. The fact that the platforms would collapse overnight from loss of ad revenue seems not to have occurred to any of this theory's sincere proponents.

Gogol Theory. This theory maintains that Bee is a digital occultist of sorts, engaging in the Mephistophelean harvesting of inactive accounts, akin to Chichikov from Nikolai Gogol's 1842 novel *Dead Souls*. Boosters of this theory tend to devolve to Satanic Panic mysticism, and draw abstruse meanings from the "legionary" existence of Bee's multiple accounts and texts. Some have construed Bee's childhood sale of their gender, in conjunction with their financial success, as evidence of a Faustian bargain. This theory is primarily significant in that, with its emphasis on the variations between the different versions of The Post, users have developed sophisticated computational approaches to analyzing them, which have been productively adapted for other, more serious "distant reading" analyses.

China Theory. Held primarily by reactionary Botkin contingents, this theory asserts that Botgate was one smaller component of a vast psy-op instigated by the Chinese government/ MSS to commandeer the accounts of Western internet users. As this theory goes, the intent is to promulgate ideas and opinions favorable to the CCP regime, using the accounts as nontraditional intelligence assets to create social connections to Western media and political figures, sow discord by deepening fractures in US identity politics, and/or burnish the image of Asians in the West.

This theory is notoriously muddled and rooted in xenophobic "yellow peril" tropes. The speculative existence of diasporic Asian American supremacists attempting to glamorize their identity, irrespective of national origin, is clearly at odds with the idea of a Chinese nationalist agenda, as is the choice of a Thai persona, not to mention one who's defiantly anti-identarian. Nevertheless this idea has continued to creep beyond the confines of Botgate discourse, glomming onto the larger and better-known conspiracy theories circulating in the mainstream today.

Appendix B: Commentary

by MH-Sleuth

Like most internet mysteries, the trail hasn't gone cold so much as the bloodhounds have gotten bored and wandered off. Yet a messiah can do no better than to disappear. I confess that, like many Botkin who've followed this story for years, part of me hoped for a clean and unambiguous resolution; for others, the incessant theory-craft, not to mention the predictable ships and slashfics of Bee, Craig, Zamira, Kant, Bee's mother, and even TT, suggest a desire to prolong it indefinitely. I imagine I've spent as much time researching, fact-checking, and compiling all of this information as any puppetmaster might have spent creating it. But I've been on here long enough to know resolution is too much to ask for, that any story online just keeps tumbling ahead and reviving and revising until, weary of rabbit holes, you pray for the dead end.

I'm certainly not the only one invested, and the interest has contributed to both the prolongation and dilution of this narrative. I have to admit a personal fondness for the author(s) of The Post, whoever they are, *whether* they are. Actually I think any truth would be disappointing; it is their successful undecidability I admire. One has to appreciate a commitment to introducing mystery into the world, for no apparent credit or profit. Yet what if we take the Bee of Version 1 at their word? Though it sounds like sympathy is not their priority, we can appreciate the classical irony of Bee's retreat to the internet to escape the prison of identity, only to institute another one. Or how the account of someone who wanted to end the practice of identifying with others might move someone to identify with them. (Or *as* them.)

In my hundreds of hours of research, I've often paused to question the worth of deep dives like this, and have never been able to convincingly justify my involvement in the lives of these people I've never met, ones who might not even exist. Is it nothing but a folk version of reality television? Or has the evolutionary drive to seek social instruction by observing and interpreting the behavior of others hypertrophied beyond usefulness, such that now, in our binges of drama, to watch ourselves watch someone else watch us has become an end in itself? An end without end?

One of the assumptions shared by all of the foregoing theories is that whoever wrote The Post did so to seek a mass audience. Supposing Bee is real, my own view is that this was never the intention; that Bee tried not to reach a networked mass, but "millions of solitudes." I believe this is why they created so many variations, so that nobody would consume it in the same way. If discourse is loneliness, as they wrote, then they have made this loneliness bespoke: each is for you and nobody else.

Despite their famous aversion to being known, whoever is behind this drama may take some comfort in the sincerity of our desire to know them, even—or especially—if we invented them.

SIXTEEN METAPHORS

You catch a fish, and it throws you back.

*   *   *

You throw a ball, she catches. Then walks away and gives it to some other guy, who even you agree would be better at catch.

*   *   *

You fall, and shout for help. Someone standing right beside you could've easily caught you, but they remain resolutely still, and tell you, as you lose consciousness, how terrible they feel about it.

*   *   *

You're an apple, and nothing's wrong with you, you think. You look, taste, and cost the same as the others. If something were wrong with you, the FDA would've caught it. Nonetheless because of your placement, or for some other reason, or no reason at all, no grocery shopper will touch you, and by the time you're finally noticed, you're as rotten as you always knew you were.

*   *   *

There are plenty of fish in the sea. But you're not a fish, just an ugly idiot trying to catch one.

*   *   *

At a restaurant one table over, someone receives the dessert that you ordered. You watch her eat it with delight. You consider asking for her leftovers, but that wouldn't be proper, so you order another one for yourself. You're told that was the last one, which you accept, until you see the same lady get the same dessert again, enjoying it even more. Before you can catch a waiter to object, you're silently presented with the bill, charging you for both desserts.

*   *   *

She throws a ball, you catch. But she was aiming for someone else—the guy from the second metaphor. You hand the ball to the guy, who does not recognize you, and he thanks you sheepishly before running off with her.

*   *   *

On your commute, an attractive motorist momentarily lingers next to you on the highway, matching your speed, long enough for you to imagine a scenario where you somehow lock eyes and flirt while driving, then pull over, learn about each other's childhoods, date casually, then seriously, wed, tell your kids about the time you met on the highway. When they catch the next exit, you're sure they did so because your glances made them uncomfortable, but you'll never know.

*   *   *

You are a fish, one of several, and don't want to be caught. You're caught anyway, they throw you back, and now you have to wonder why the metaphor is working the normal way.

*   *   *

She tells an anecdote about the worst person she's ever dated—terrible brown teeth, crippling coke habit, nasty toenails. She even caught something from him; still he threw her away like a piece of trash. He was my rock bottom, she says, and you think, *Wish* I *was rock bottom*.

*   *   *

On a road trip, your friends in the front seats are enjoying their conversation; you can barely catch a single word. When you try to lean forward and contribute, they listen, but you can tell they're annoyed by the effort to include you, so you stop trying. By the time you reach your destination, they've forgotten you're in the car at all, and they drop the car off at the rental place with you still in it. You consider saying something about it, then think better of it, because you don't want them to feel bad.

*   *   *

You throw a ball, but she doesn't notice. That's strange; throwing the ball used to make something happen. So you throw another, and another, until both of you are floating adrift in a sea of balls. An attractive fish swims by and you reach out to catch it, but despite the awkward terrain, it still gets away. She however manages to catch its tailfin, is borne away, and the two of them head for fresher waters.

*　　*　　*

Passing your neighbor's house, you catch a glimpse of someone through his living room window, lit up by the television he's watching alone in the dark, and think, *What a loser, what a depressing fucking friendless loser whose arteries are probably a fifth of a second from sending him to an unmarked grave*, on your way home to do the exact same thing.

*　　*　　*

You've tried worms and string, bow and arrow, a bamboo spear, a two-hundred-dollar carbon fiber rod, dragnets, dynamite, and your bare hands. You can't even catch a break. Every lure, every lake, no luck. There's so many of them, slick, fat, and iridescent, and you are starving. But what matters least is what the fisherman wants.

*　　*　　*

It's always catch-as-catch-can, but you may catch their fancy, or imagination, even their eye, if they catch you in the right light. They may even be a catch. But there is always a catch.

*   *   *

Metaphor means "to bear across." *Rejection* means "to throw back." You throw yourself at her, and she throws you back. *Fail* means "to fall." Having fallen for her, and failing to bear yourself across, you now have *a cross to bear*, which is a metaphor, and you recall your past failures: a *throwback*. Etymologies, fallen meanings borne across time, are throwbacks too. Mixed metaphors fail to bear their meanings across. So they are metaphors for rejection. If you catch my meaning.

RE: *REJECTION*

Dear Tony,

Although we read *Rejection* with much interest and lively discussion on our end, we regret that we must pass. We know this is not the outcome you hoped for, but perhaps we can offer some edifying guidance before you submit elsewhere.

We found much to enjoy in the spiraling dissections of the characters' psyches, and most work well enough as standalone fiction (though too long for most publications). But the further we read, the more we sensed an evasiveness to the book that grew harder to ignore. We assume the topic wasn't chosen at random, so the book's existence and lengthy gestation implies a personal investment, yet you seem to take every opportunity to disavow it, putting yourself at a defensive remove that ultimately left us cold and unsatisfied.

Let us explain. Throughout our reading we noticed an interesting trajectory in your protagonists' relation to you, the author. We have a straight white male, a straight white woman, a gay Thai American man, a wealthy white man, and a person of undecidable identity. We're not questioning your right to write from these perspectives; the problem isn't appropriation, it's candor. Not that such a scale really exists, but one could roughly plot these stories along an axis of increasing marginalization, the idea presumably being to consider the theme of rejection from different perspectives. Viewed less charitably, it could be read as a way to head off certain dreaded allegations of self-pity and navel-gazing; an attempt at misdirection, as you smuggle your own hang-ups into theirs, while scoring brownie points for imaginative empathy. However, we believe that these distancing attempts only end up drawing attention to you, in a way that feels embarrassingly unintentional. (Our speculations about your authorial intent might strike you as unfair and out-of-bounds, but this isn't lit crit, it's feedback. Fair or not, readers do think about this stuff, and as much as it seems you'd like to control the book's context, no writer truly gets that luxury, even while alive.)

The opening piece, "The Feminist," more or less works as a satire "punching up" at its misguided white male protagonist, though we can acknowledge that for your likely audience of contemporary fiction readers, this is a decidedly safe target. Here is the first sign of your backing away, seeming to anxiously insist, *See, reader, I'm nothing like him; see what a self-aware feminist I am, how capable I am of cataloging the hypocrisies of male feminist praxis—look how unbothered I am, and how few of his worries I share.* Of course the ironic thing is that the protagonist shares these exact same anxieties, so the story doesn't critique them so much as reenact them. This is only aggravated by the choice to omit conventional identifiers like the protagonist's name, location, and appearance, giving him the hazy feel of a representative abstraction, a creature of pure discourse upon which the reader can project their own politics; could it be because the more identifying particulars you assign to him, the more he might come to resemble you?

Similar points can be made for "Pics," where Alison's casual racism borne of envy seems initially to make her another satirical target. But arriving as it does after "The Feminist," her portrayal feels more like an extension of the previous story's scheme of attesting to your feminism, as the existence of sexism makes her flaws more forgivable—see how her group chat delivers a chorus of remonstrances against male dating etiquette, and how Neil's shiftiness makes him equally culpable in their conflict. The desire to go easy on Alison is palpable, even down to the way you savvily avoid making her a "perfect victim" of male misdeeds. *Now here's a male writer who cares about the struggles of real women, who has considered things thoroughly from their viewpoint, who even credits them with human flaws!*—is this not the sort of reassurance, part preening and part paranoid, that "The Feminist" might make to himself, in his own judgments of women? Isn't it the narrative equivalent of saying *Ugh, men, am I right?*

There is a cost to this—just as she is more sympathetic, Alison's ending doesn't hit the same notes of pathos either. Indeed, finishing more or less where she started, you could even say she's robbed of her share of catharsis. So even if your aim is to demonstrate empathy, we might say that the genteel unwillingness to render her as flawed and grotesque *to the same degree* merely defines the limits of that empathy.

If that sounds counterintuitive—that it might be inadequately empathetic to make your one female protagonist look bad enough, or suffer enough—the issue becomes clearer when considering "Ahegao." Kant is not exactly likable or relatable, but is more directly the product of past, undeserved trauma, thus fully available to pity. And more than the first two protagonists, he resembles you biographically, being of roughly the same age, race, nationality, gender, hometown. This resemblance might trick some readers into believing you're putting more of your personal experience into him—*Wow, maybe the author had a rough time too, and maybe this is his way of processing it, poor guy!* But in our reading, this special treatment is a bit of "leverage" to help get away with the ending, which, with its flagrant and prolix obscenity, feels like a punch line at the reader's expense, punishing us for being fool enough to care about the character, not to mention running a heavy risk of playing on stigmatizing tropes of homosexuality as deviant or degenerate. To pull this off would require a tremendous presumption of good faith on the author's behalf, and how else would you earn this presumption except by making yourself, the author, legible? What's a metaphor without a tenor? Why bother comparing A to B if you're not going to define A?

What's amusing is, we suspect you *do* share important things in common with Kant—a lot more than you seem to realize. Consider that Kant's central trait is his repression: that is, his inability to express his true inner self, to make himself vulnerable. And his biggest fear? The prospect of people finding him out, learning the secret that he believes is at the core of his being; but his providential error at the end exposes him. You might say the story does what Kant does: reveal more of itself than it knows. (It's noteworthy that not only Kant, but every protagonist winds up a writer of some sort, committing acts of grotesque self-exposure—and self-destruction—by text.) The demure black box of fiction has always been handy for plausible deniability. Still it's an odd choice, to make the fig leaf more obscene than what it conceals—so outlandish and humiliating that the reader would assume it was made up.

Unless the truth is worse. You know that readers' assumptions skew toward the obvious, and here it'd be obvious to assume the story is autobiographical, with a single significant change to the character's sexuality. But it is your unwillingness to *completely* identify with him, on the matter of sexuality, that makes you just like him—inveigling, dissembling, disavowing. Imagine a version of this story with Kant as a straight man, playing out the same sadistic sexual fantasies with women. As Kant notes of his own sadism, "It all pointed to a desire to rehouse his own abjection in other men." Hmm.

We are not saying that is what the book "really means." Nor do we claim a monopoly on interpretation. It would be wrong to suggest we know anything about what you really intend. We're only saying that it *could be* read this way, and if you want to avoid this kind of reading, you could straighten it out yourself by being more *intentionally* transparent with your intentions.

Coming off this trilogy of humiliation, "Our Dope Future" superficially appears to buck the form and the theme, being not so much about rejection as toxic acceptance. But it shares strands of the previous stories' damaged DNA: like "The Feminist," its protagonist Max is another safe white male target, convinced of the goodness of his intentions, which are in fact malignant. As in "Pics," Alison returns again to suffer from male vanity (though she here is finally able to enact some sort of symbolic revenge, a gallantry on the author's part that's as contrived as it is belated). And as in "Ahegao," our protagonist publishes something that unwittingly entrains his downfall—one that occurs, tellingly, only after it *reaches the wrong audience*. However, in this case, Max clearly deserves his fate; we want to see him *gotten*, so it lacks the discomfort of the ending of "Ahegao," and winds up a mere morality play. Having punished the meek-and-mild Kant, we're meant to read fairness into how the book more harshly punishes the villain. Like the other pieces, this story attempts to course-correct its predecessor's problems by widening the distance from its protagonist, only for that correction to unwittingly reveal things about you.

For only *at first* does it appear to reprise "The Feminist," in inviting us to point and laugh at a clueless dupe. But it differs in one important way: you assign none of your own publicly known biographical features to him. Even "The Feminist," cartoonish as he is, attends a recently integrated all-girls' school, as you did. For "Our Dope Future," the narrator's uncomplicated villainy and biographical dissimilarity give you license to spank him raw, without reddening your own cheeks. But you're less impervious than you think. What if the savagery of his comeuppance is actually the guilty result of your *similarity* to him? After all, what makes the narrator of "Our Dope Future" so irritating is his blithe tonedeafness, his cringemaking faith in his ability to please and connect with others, and his total failure to do so, *and* his obliviousness to that failure. Could it be possible that these all reflect *your* fears, mirror *your* failures, so that in classically Freudian fashion, you are defacing in your work what is unacceptable in yourself?

We admit that when arriving at "Main Character," we'd briefly hoped the book was finally addressing our qualms, with a metafictional story about identity, authorial and otherwise. Bee's own spite-fueled quest to continually self-revise and escape being defined on other people's terms (or rather, using "other people" as terms of self-definition) parallels the authorial evasions that marred the earlier stories. Assuming a confessional form, the natural ending one would expect is an unveiling; what we get instead is more like a dump truck full of veils, as we learn that what we've read is only one of millions of AI-generated versions, none canonical.

Incredibly, the obfuscation somehow intensifies even after you insert yourself into the Appendix. This surely cannot be read as anything other than an invitation to connect the story to you, the author. But the Appendix equates any such connection to crackpot conspiracy-weaving, seemingly to warn off any reader who might attempt it. In fact, many aspects of Bee's project sound like wish fulfillment for an author who fears rejection: to have your writings flood the world, yet remain unaccountable to their impact; to "outnumber" your readers; to "be heard but not seen" so you can avoid being "scrutinized with maximum cynicism." The story's ending even *congratulates* "whoever is behind this drama" for this evasiveness—it's like giving a speech and then clapping for yourself.

We don't really know what "Sixteen Metaphors" is even doing in the book at all, except perhaps to bewilderingly underscore the futility of the book's central metaphor. So we pass over it to conclude at this letter, "Re: *Rejection*," a ventriloquist act where you voice your misgivings about the book through a fictional jury of scowling publishers. This to us, for obvious reasons, seemed the most bizarre and pointless flourish of all: arriving shortly after a novella that ends with a metafictional self-commentary implicating the author, we hardly need more of the same. The only thing more boring, exhausted, and self-indulgent than breaking the fourth wall at the end of a story is pointing it out. Even looking past the internet-borne tendency for writers of your generation to ass-cover with tedious disclaimers, the real point, we think, is to foreclose scrutiny, to get ahead of rejection by naming your sins before any reader has a chance to. But this perverse apologizing only feels like you're cutting and chewing our meat for us, and we reject you (literally) all the harder. What does it matter that we know you saw it coming? Is it high praise to say that a book is conscious of its faults? Given the subject matter, we'd think you might be keen to the futility of writing an unrejectable book; you cannot curb a reader's reading, nor steer their goodwill, no matter how clean your intentions or nude your soul. To attempt it is to abandon the possibility of an authentic connection with the reader, one in which you put yourself on their level (though, we suppose, at least this way you get to do the rejecting). So this special pleading on your own behalf, by way of adversarial auto-fiction, is just, well, annoying. And you already did a similar thing in your first book too.

Certainly the problem isn't a shortage of self-awareness—we do credit you with that. Maybe we have even underestimated you: because the other possibility is that all these apparent slips, these mortifying confessions in negative, have been done *on purpose*. How else can we explain this eleventh-hour dereliction, a story about you without you in it? Is the idea to ruin things, so that when the expected rejection comes, you can say that's what you wanted? Now that's interesting—and even more revealing. Suppose we're mistaken to assume this book is trying to espouse the conventional literary virtues of insight, empathy, fun, and so on. Everything makes much more sense if we assume that you are *trying* to tank your own book, for reasons not aesthetic, definitely not commercial, but personal. To elicit pity? Get off on failure? Gain, at the very least, control over the terms of your rejection? Is the disposition that feels called to write a book about rejection the same as the one that drives you to sabotage it? If each protagonist in this book is a casualty of rejection, then on a conceptual level, it is somewhat interesting that you have made yourself the final such character, and your readers the rejectors. Interesting, and somewhat tragic (in the way all avoidable self-harm is tragic)—not very satisfying, though!

Assuming any changes we'd recommend would be too drastic for you to pursue, there *is* one way to truly master your rejection: withdraw. Perhaps this is why the protagonists of *Rejection* each at some point, after restlessly shuttling between concealing and revealing, eventually retreat to isolation, their only sure defense. You doubtless know the cliché about how every rejection is God's protection—not to be almighty about it, but you should accept our passing as more of a reprieve than a misfortune. It hurts to be read. When people don't like it, that's terrible and nothing can be done. And even when they do, they usually do so for the wrong reasons, project what isn't there, draw the wrong conclusions, form the wrong idea about why it was written, which is just as disheartening and alienating as any rejection. If you cared that much about money or prestige you wouldn't have even gone into writing. Doesn't it seem nicer to nobly forgo publication, something to be squinted at only to be smothered or smeared, in favor of a testament to yourself, that draws its meaning and worth from its sublime invisibility to others, the same way only you know what your heart feels like? The book would still exist, and it'd still be yours, and you could supply yourself with what nobody else can: that is, closure. As for everyone else, no one misses what they didn't know they might've had; loss only hurts when there ever was a possibility.

This might seem like a choice being made for you, by us, but it's not. Because the final irony, one that at least your writing seems to grasp, is that rejection is not one-way, and always comes paired with its opposite. For a rejection to be settled, first you— the reject—must hear, and comprehend, and accept.

ACKNOWLEDGMENTS

The bulk of the blame is to be shared by Alice Kim, Anna North, Annie Wyman, Anthony Ha, James Yeh, Jenny Zhang, Karan Mahajan, and Vauhini Vara.

For their strength, dexterity, constitution, intelligence, wisdom, and charisma, I'm grateful to Ariel Lewiton, Ben Mauk, Bennett Sims, Carmen Machado, Deirdre Coyle, Emma Cline, Erin Taylor, Hannah Gold, Jen DuBois, Joshua Tranen, Kayla Soyer-Stein, Kevin Nguyen, Kristen Radtke, and Molly Zimetbaum. Salute to CRIT, and hello to the group chat.

Outsized thanks to Emma Janaskie, Dayna Tortorici, and the good ship *N+1* for editing and publishing "The Feminist." At *The Paris Review* "Ahegao" owes much to Lidija Haas, Emily Stokes, and the rest of the team: Oriana Ullman, Izzy Ampil, Kelley McKinney, Amanda Gersten, Anna Rahkonen, and Harriet Clark.

To Ellen Levine, Martha Wydysh, Audrey Crooks, and Lauren Campbell at Trident, thank you for waiting. My editor Jessica Williams, assistant editor Peter Kispert, copyeditor Greg Villepique, cover designer Ploy Siripant, marketer Kelsey Manning, publicist Martin Wilson, production editor Jessica Rozler, and the rest of the William Morrow team are why you're reading this. To the Whiting Foundation and MacDowell, I give thanks that are both sincere and contractually obligated.

Lastly, thank you, thank you to my mother, father, and sister.

ABOUT THE AUTHOR

Tony Tulathimutte is the author of *Private Citizens* and *Rejection*. His work has appeared in *The Paris Review*, *N+1*, *The Nation*, *The New Republic*, and *The New York Times*. The recipient of an O. Henry Award and a Whiting Award, he runs the writing class CRIT in Brooklyn.